DEVILS RIDGE

SHADOWS

OF THE

OLD WEST

JOSEPH SACKETT

RAVAGED REALMS

EST. 2023

Contents

Prologue

L ife had changed little for me after the war. Despite all the external differences, the new job, so-called friends, and those pests known as neighbors, every monotonous day was a humming drone, only ever interrupted by my brother Bill's disfigured, ghostly presence lurking over my shoulder. As I sat on the train, heading toward the small desert town of Devil's Ridge, storms of dust made me hopeful that my memories could finally be laid to rest. And if they couldn't, I thought maybe the ghosts that surrounded that fateful day could keep my brother company, and perhaps he would give me a break.

From what I'd read about the place—and I'll be the first to admit I'm not much of a reader—Devil's Ridge had been a highly contested settlement during the tailend of the Colorado Gold Rush. While it eventually became a miner town, the good times didn't last for much more than a year. Records have little to say about it, although some speculative historians have debated whether a drought or a pest wiped out most of its inhabitants. Yep, as far as I can tell, the great desolation of Devil's Ridge seems to be a thing of mystery. It gets only the briefest of mentions in the history books, because once the railway tracks were laid just south of the town, it slowly morphed into one of those quaint stop-overs you often hear about—complete with artisanal jams, dancehalls, and bustling theaters.

Shortly after Pearl Harbor, however, the draft sucked the spirit out of Devil's Ridge. Very few residents stayed, and many expected it to become yet another ghost town, the fossilized remnants of a once-vibrant community left adrift until finally eroding beyond recognition. However, shortly before Bill and I left for Iraq—a moment in my life that will forever be indelibly etched into my psyche—he showed me reports that suggested it was still alive. In fact, it was booming!

"The true jewel in the navel of Colorado, Jay. It's honestly the dream place to head off to. You could come with me, and we could disappear from all this fucked up mess and really *live,* you know? "

That's the way he spoke about it, as if he'd grown up there, which of course he hadn't. He was my brother and we'd both lived with our parents in the suburbs of Chicago; but for two whole years in the desert, it was all he talked about, as if yammering about it for hours on end was cathartic in some way. It never struck me as anything to write home about, but by the time I came back from Iraq, a shell of the man who had left American soil all those years ago, I would have done anything to quiet the voices in my head. I thought if I could find some way to settle down in the very place that Bill had bent my ear about for such a long time, then maybe it would make the voices stop—or quiet them down a little at least.

I knew it couldn't be worse than the fray, after all. A tiny city, brought back from the brink of death by the few survivors who had learned to tolerate each other and make a go of it.

How wrong could I have been? Jesus, looking back on it now, how could I have been so stupid?

CHAPTER ONE

Boomer

M y train rolled into Devil's Ridge at a little after two in the afternoon. I yawned, stood up and grabbed what little possessions I'd brought with me. I was dog-tired and hungry. I'd boarded the California Zephyr almost 12 hours earlier in Chicago, hungover and with barely $300 to my name.

The trip from Chicago to Denver had taken more than 18 back-breaking hours and my seat had been less than comfortable. The train pulled into Denver just after 7 am, and I then had to wait three long hours for my connecting train to show up—which it did, but almost an hour late. I'd spent the past two hours sitting on an empty train with nobody but my dead brother for company. I needed somewhere to hang my head, and what's more, I needed a drink.

"This is it, Jay," Bill whispered in my ear. I could feel his ice cold breath on the nape of my neck. "This is the place I was telling you about. Isn't she a beaut?"

"Yeah, a real peach," I said, stepping off the train and peering at what could only be described as a timber shack. "Is this what they call a station down here in Colorado?"

Bill grinned, but I could see he was offended. "She's a little basic I know, but she's fully functional and efficient as hell. Trains come in and out of here almost three times a day, and it's all run by that guy over there. Old Boomer, we call him."

I turned my head and spied the old man in the beige slacks and tight waistcoat. Old Boomer had a hunch in his back, and his right leg bent outward at an acute angle. His hair was white and wispy, and his face was scrunched up into a tight ball, as if he was chewing on something particularly bitter.

"Welcome to Devil's Ridge," he said, approaching me. He held out his hand, and I handed him my ticket stub. "Name's Hank, but people call me Boomer."

"Why's that?" I asked, trying to look interested.

"I was a miner, back when people in this town still prospected. Explosives expert. I could blow a hole the size of this train in a mountain at sunbreak, and a team of men could be down there mining for gold by lunchtime. Ain't no rock I couldn't split open."

"So, nobody mines down here anymore?"

He shook his head. "Not for a very long time, and more's the pity."

I couldn't help but think the old guy had a long story he was in no mood to tell. "Do you happen to know where the nearest hotel is?"

"Well, that's an easy one. There's only one establishment worth a lick in Devil's Ridge, and that's Penny's."

"Penny?"

"Penny White," Old Boomer replied. "A saint of a woman, I can tell you that. Hotel's called The Regal. It's maybe a 15-minute walk north. Take a right at Governor's Boulevard, and then head east for six blocks. You'll see Penny's place right across the road from the police station. You can't miss it."

I cocked my thumb and forefinger. "Thanks, Boomer. You're a gent." I slipped the old guy a five-dollar bill for his troubles and hauled my suitcase down the staircase that led to the street below.

"Say hi to the sheriff if you see him!" Boomer yelled after me. "Tell him I haven't forgotten about that incident with the Indian. He owes me."

His words washed over me as I took in my surroundings. I'd hoped to catch a cab to take me to the hotel, but the street was almost completely deserted. A garage lay dormant to my right and a vacant diner, the windows boarded over and the carpark riddled with overgrown weeds, sat like a bitter memory of a bygone era to my left.

"Well, that's not how I remember Pat Moynahan's place," Bill whispered, standing beside me on the street. "I used to eat there all the time. He made the best meatball sub, and his coffee was just as good as back home. Woah, just thinking about it is making me drool."

"You can't drool, Bill," I retorted. "You're dead, remember?"

"Oh yeah. I forgot about that," he replied, sticking out a lip. "Like I didn't know that already, wise ass."

I carried my bag half a mile along the road to what I took to be the main drag. I couldn't have seen more than three cars the whole way, and I swear, each of those vehicles had only one occupant—their eyes never leaving the road, their faces seemingly drained of all emotion. I started to wonder whether I'd made the right choice to leave Chicago, but then I'd never really had a choice at all. I had to get away. I knew if I'd stayed, Hogan would have found me; and if he found me, he'd have had me killed in an instant. Maybe that was what I deserved after what had happened with

Bill—maybe it was even what I wanted—but before I let the end come, I knew I had to try to find some sort of resolution, some closure at least. I just couldn't shake it, what happened. It was forever with me, like a deep, painful scar that simply refused to heal.

I shook myself from my thoughts, turned left onto Governor's Boulevard, and almost walked headlong into a woman who was racing hastily in my direction.

"Oh, oh!" she cried as the folders she was carrying spilled onto the pavement. "I'm so sorry."

"No, no," I replied, bending down to help her collect her paperwork. "It wasn't paying attention. I just arrived from out of town on an overnight train last night. Sorry, I'm a little tired."

The woman brushed herself off and smiled. "No, honestly, it was totally my fault. I'm late for class and I wasn't looking where I was going. I'm Linda," she thrust out a hand. "Linda Thornton."

I glanced down at her hand and then back up at her. She was short in stature, around five-foot-five, with shoulder length blond hair, and glasses that highlighted her brilliant blue eyes.

"Aren't you going to take it?" she asked.

"Sorry, yes." I grabbed her hand and shook it. "See, told you. I'm all over the place. I'm Jason Carter, but people call me J.C."

Linda grinned, but I couldn't stop looking at her eyes. They sparkled like finely polished topaz.

"Well, J.C," she said, "Are you in town for long?"

"I don't know. Maybe. My plans are a little indefinite."

"Ah, you're a seat-of-your-pants kind of guy," she offered, stifling a laugh. "I like that. Anyway, as I said, I'm late for class, and those kids won't hang around for long if I'm not there. They'll be out on the streets and up to no good before you can say *misdemeanor*."

"Copy that," I said laughing. "You'd better get going."

"Maybe I'll see you around. Where are you staying?"

"I was hoping to stay at The Regal. That's if Penny has any rooms left."

Linda's composure shifted just a little. "Oh, she'll fit you in alright. Penny never says no to a tall, handsome man."

"I take it you're not a fan."

She shook her head but I could see that she was hiding something. "Hey, stay where you want. It's a free country. People seem to like The Regal, and who am I to argue with them?"

I had the feeling I'd offended her. "I didn't mean to—"

"See you around, J.C," she said as she hitched her bag over her shoulder and headed off into the distance. "It was nice to meet you."

Before I knew it, she was gone and I was standing alone on the sidewalk once more, taking in the sights and sounds of Governor's Boulevard.

I'd never seen anything like it. It was as though somebody had thrown a glass bubble over the 1950s and dropped it in the middle of Colorado. The storefronts displayed the fading remnants of brightly colored paint that peeled from the timber like scabs. The few cars that trundled along the road could have been straight out of a Jimmy Stewart movie, except these automobiles were rust-addled and noisy, as if they barely had any life left in them. And the shop signs overhead hung like crooked limbs, the lettering so badly faded it was barely legible.

"Cool, isn't it?" Bill said, his arm around my shoulders.

"It's a little outdated," I replied, shaking my head. "Could use a lick of paint here and there."

Bill folded his arms. "I think it's charming. The problem with you, J.C., is that you like your creature comforts. You've been spoiled by the 21st century. Here in Devil's Ridge, life has moved at a much slower pace for the past 80 years or so. And, it's much better for it."

"If you say so," I replied, turning to face the bright red facade of the Regal Hotel. "But if this place doesn't have a hot shower, you and I are going to have a little talk."

I opened the door and walked inside. The foyer smelled of moth-balls and peppermint and I fought the urge to pinch my nose. The walls were decorated in a floral-patterned paper, and the easy chairs were red velvet, worn and with more than a dozen cigarette burns. An elevator sprung into my life to my right, its motor whirring like a World War II fighter engine as it strained with every sinew to deliver its beleaguered occupants to one of the many floors overhead. To my left sat a dark oak counter, behind which stood a woman with a broad, red smile, long, hazel hair that hung over her broad shoulders in silky strands, and hands that were clutched tightly together at her slim waist, her long, red fingernails expertly manicured.

"Well, hello there," the woman said, her voice loud and forceful. "Welcome to the Regal Hotel. You look like you're from out of town, if you don't mind my supposition."

"You'd be right," I said as she rounded the counter, her high heels clacking on the hardwood floor. "I'm from Chicago, actually."

"Ah, the big smoke," she replied, taking my hand in hers and pumping it firmly. "I've never been. Is it as dangerous as they say it is?"

"Well, I guess that depends on your perspective," I said, thinking about the whole world of trouble I'd left behind. "I've gotten pretty used to it."

"I don't think I could ever get used to a big city. That's why we love it here in Devil's Ridge. Everybody knows everybody. If you so much as sneeze, the whole town knows about it. Sometimes even before you do."

"I'm guessing you're Penny," I said, cutting through the chit-chat. "I'm looking for a room. Something with a comfortable bed, hot water, and a coffee machine if that's something you offer here. I've had quite the journey."

Penny looked me up and down, the quiet interrupted only by the painful grinding of the elevator gears as the empty car returned to the first floor. I instantly felt like I was being inspected by her dark eyes. "We have everything you could ever need at The Regal," she said, her tone flat and somewhat deprecating. "Everything you could ever want. How does that sound to you?"

"Sounds pretty good to me."

Penny reached behind the desk for a set of heavy keys. "I believe you will find room 301 to your liking. It has all our very best amenities."

"That's perfect," I said, holding out my hand and expecting her to slip the keys into my palm, but Penny snatched them away at the last second.

"Ah-ah," she said, smirking. "Don't you think you owe me something first?"

I reached for my wallet, realizing that I hadn't even asked her the cost of the room. "Right, yeah. Sorry. I'm guessing you want to swipe my card."

She reached out and grabbed my hand in hers. I could smell her perfume. It was like lavender mixed with a scent I couldn't place.

"Put that away," she said, plucking my wallet from my fingers and returning it to my jacket pocket. "I just need to know your name, honey."

"It's J.C," I said, my voice faltering. "Jason Carter."

Penny walked me to the elevator and pushed the button for the third floor, ushering me inside.

"Well, Jason," she said, shooting me a wink as the doors slid closed between us. "I believe you'll enjoy your stay here with us so much, you might never be inclined to leave."

CHAPTER TWO

Little Bear

That night, I slept like I'd walked all the way from Chicago. In my dreams, Hogan was with me in my hotel room, looming over me, leering with a long line of spittle hanging from his grotesque lips. Boomer was sitting in the chair by the window, reading a book and stuffing tobacco into a wooden pipe, and Penny stood in the open doorway, a pistol tucked into her waistband.

When I tried to sit up, Linda pushed me back down, but her folders slipped from her hands and landed on my face. When I pushed them away, I found myself back in Fallujah, the desert sun hanging high in the sky overhead. The blazing heat scorched my eyes and burned my bloodied skin. My lips turned painfully dry and my tongue became sandpaper in my mouth. After a moment of panic, I realized the morning sunlight was streaming through a gap in the drapes and I was back in my room at the Regal Hotel. My brother, Bill, laying beside me.

"Morning, sleepy head," he said. "I thought you'd died or something."

"No, that was you, remember?"

"Haha. This gallow's humor of yours is starting to get a little annoying, little brother."

"Tough luck," I replied, sitting up. "Get used to it. And, anyway, you're not really here. You're just a figment of my fucked up imagination."

"Oh, you say the nicest things."

I took a shower, which was lukewarm at best, made myself a cup of coffee, which was tepid, and got dressed. I planned to have a look around the place. Bill had told me a few stories about his time here, and I wanted to check them out for myself. After all, if everything he'd said was true—and I didn't, for one second, believe that it was—then my little problem with Hogan and his goons could be solved in a matter of days. And, I'd be a very wealthy man, too.

Penny wasn't in the foyer when I exited the elevator. Instead, another much older woman was seated behind the desk and sticking coupons in a book.

"Morning," I said after standing and waiting for the lady to look up from her handiwork. "Name's J.C. I need to book a cab."

"The cab company's down the hill," she replied without looking up. "Turn right out of here. Two blocks that way."

"You can't book it from—"

Her head snapped up, her thick spectacles perched on the edge of her long nose. "Do I look like a cab dispatcher to you?" she asked, her eyes wide.

"Well, I guess not."

"No, I didn't think so." Her eyes returned to her book. "As I said, the cab company's two blocks that way."

I was too taken aback to argue, so I exited the hotel and did exactly as she said. It was 11 in the morning and the temperature was already pushing 90°F.

"She's a bitch, isn't she?" Bill said as he kept pace alongside me. "She was always rude to me too. I thought she'd be dead by now. She must be a 100 and change. What do you think?"

"I think you've sent me to the boonies on a wild-goose chase. That's what I think."

"Well, you're the one who needs the money, Mister Grumps."

"And you're the one who told me I'd find peace in Devil's Ridge."

I stormed into the office of Big City Cab's (what a joke) and tapped on the perspex window. A man in a yellow cotton shirt and suspenders looked up from his paperwork.

"I need a cab to Kiowa Rock," I said. "Right away if you can."

The man glared at me through the plastic screen. He was chewing gum like it was going out of style. "Kiowa Rock, you say?"

"I sure did."

"It's going to be pretty hot up there in the mountains this time of day. You sure that's where you want to go, mister?"

"I'm sure."

He tapped on one of those calculators with the big buttons and sat back in his chair, letting out a long breath. "That kind of trip's gonna set you back 50 bucks. You got that kind of money?"

I grabbed my wallet from my jacket, withdrew two 20s and a 10, and threw it on the counter.

"Right away," I said, feeling hot and frustrated. "That's the deal."

The journey took a little over 30 minutes on a trail that snaked up through the Sawatch Range. The cab dispatcher was right about one thing: the heat was fierce. It became almost unbearable by the lack of air conditioning in a cab that could only be described as antiquated. I peered out the window at the snow covered peaks in the distance. As much as I was growing to dislike the relative discomfort of the little town called Devil's Ridge, the views across the Rockies were truly astonishing.

The cab pulled off the road and parked alongside a section of dense woodland.

"Kiowa Rock is just through those trees," the cab driver said. "Ten minute walk. I haven't brought anybody up here myself, but from what I've heard, you can't miss it."

I stepped onto the dusty path and leaned into the window. "You'll wait for me?" I asked, withdrawing a 10 from my wallet.

"Sorry, no-can-do," he replied, firing the engine. "Got another job to go to. I can be back in an hour or so, if that suits you."

"I guess I don't have much of a choice, do I?"

He smirked and plucked the 10 from my fingers. "I guess not."

As the cab pulled away, I turned toward the thick section of pines and spruces and sighed. "You have a lot to answer for, Brother."

The undergrowth and densely-packed thicket made the walk more difficult than it should have been, and I found myself stumbling and staggering on a number of occasions. The cab driver had told me to walk north in a straight line for 10 minutes, but the way in front of me was so overgrown, tangled, and wiry, that my route was anything but straight. The sunlight overhead barely penetrated the canopy, and the darkness began to draw in on me like a heavy drape.

I started to wonder if the whole thing had been a trick on the cab company's part to rob me of $60. Bill was nowhere to be seen, but I did catch glimpses of a shadowy form lurking among the cottonwoods. However, whenever I spun my head toward it, the shadow immediately disappeared, only to reappear moments later in my peripheral vision. There were voices too, like the cold, lifeless whispers of the undead, calling to me and beckoning me toward them. Their breathless sighs turned my blood cold. I thought of Fallujah, of my brother's blood on my hands, of the ghostly remains of what would have once been a noisy schoolyard, and I started to shake. I became so unsettled and confused that I lost my bearings entirely.

"Bill?" I called out. "Are you there?"

There was nothing. No voices. No people. Just a forest welcoming me into its cool embrace as I floundered in the darkness like a fool.

"You lost, friend?" a man said. "Looks like you need someone to show you the way."

I turned to face a tall, thick-chested Native American man. He wore a khaki shirt, blue jeans, and a New York Yankees baseball cap.

"I really do," I said. "Somehow I've managed to get myself pretty lost."

"Happens to us all at some point in our lives," he said, holding out a huge hand. "Name's Little Bear."

"You're not so little, if you don't mind me saying." I said.

"Not at all. I get that a lot."

"My name's J.C." I said, shaking his hand and trying to hold my own against his firm grip.

"Like the good book?"

"Something like that."

He smiled. "Well, where you looking to get to, J.C.?"

"Kiowa Rock."

His eyes narrowed. "And what do you hope to find at Kiowa Rock, friend?"

I grinned as Bill appeared from the gloom. "I was kinda hoping you would tell me."

I stood at the base of Kiowa Rock, my hands on my hips. Sweat was pouring from my brow and running into my eyes. I reached into my pants and pulled out a handkerchief, which I used to dab most of the slick sheen away.

"That's quite something," I said.

"That she is," Little Bear replied. "That she is."

Kiowa Rock, as it turned out, was just that—an enormous slug of granite and limestone that stretched 10 feet or more straight upward. Its huge bulk sat between two mountain peaks in what appeared to be an unnaturally large indentation in the Earth.

"Looks like it just fell out of the sky," I said.

"Legend has it that that's exactly what happened," Little Bear replied, taking a seat on a rocky ledge. "The way the story goes, the spirits decided to place it here to separate the valley of Devil's Ridge from the demons that dwelled in the mountains?"

"What kind of demons?" I asked, eyeing something sparkly embedded in the rock.

"The Wendigo," he replied. "A spirit that can inhabit another human's body and make them do all sorts of things."

I ran my hand along the glimmering slither and followed its path deeper into the crevice separating Kiowa Rock from the mountain face. "What kind of things?"

"Evil things, mostly."

"Sounds like superstition to me."

Little Bear stood. "Maybe," he said. "But, it's what my people believe, just like your people believe in a man who can rise from the dead and float into the sky. We all have stories we like to hold close to our hearts."

"I guess you're right," I said, but I was barely listening to him. All I could think of was the streak of glistening yellow that wormed between the jagged rocks, and then trailed down through the mouth of an abandoned mine that opened up between Kiowa Rock and Dead Man's Peak. "Have you seen this?" I asked.

"I have," he replied.

"Do you know what it is?"

"I'm guessing it's exactly what you think it is."

I wiped saliva from my lips. "I think it's gold."

Little Bear's eyes fell to the ground. "Some people call it that. Other people call it trouble you can't afford."

I sort of heard him, but I was too busy grinning from ear to ear and attempting to slow my racing heart to acknowledge his warning. My brother hadn't been spitballing after all. He'd been telling me the truth—I'd just been too stubborn to listen to him. There was gold in Devil's Ridge, after all. There was lots and lots of gold.

CHAPTER THREE

The Curse

That night, I sat in a bar, aptly named The Prospector, and sipped a Jack and Coke. It was my third. I was celebrating after all.

"I told you it was there, didn't I?" Bill said, jabbing me in the ribs, although I didn't feel a thing.

"You sure did," I replied, crunching a cube of ice between my teeth. "I'm sorry for not believing you."

"Hey, no problem. You always did have trust issues."

I held my hand up to the bartender and ordered a pizza with all the extras—I was ravenous.

As I downed my fourth drink and devoured my fifth slice, the door to the bar opened and a stout guy with a thick, brown beard and a sheriff's uniform walked in. To

my surprise, he approached and took a seat opposite me in
the booth.

"What you eating there, cowboy?" he asked.

"I believe they call it the chili-chicken barbecue," I
replied, trying hard not to slur my words. "It's pretty
good." I eyed the sheriff's name badge, which revealed my
new dinner date to be Sheriff Elijah Harris.

"Would you mind if I tried a piece?"

I was feeling pretty full so I shook my head. "Not at all.
Be my guest."

He pulled a cheesy slice from what remained of the pizza
and took a large bite from one end. He sat there in silence,
chewing the food and peering across the table at me. After
a moment, he spoke. "Penny tells me you're from out of
town."

I nodded. "That I am."

"Chicago, she says."

"Right on both counts."

"You're a long way from home, aren't you?" He dabbed
at his mouth with a napkin. "Would you mind if I ask
you what type of business you have down here in Devil's
Ridge?"

I shook my head. "I wouldn't. You see, I don't have any
business down here. No business at all. My brother always

spoke fondly about the place, so I decided to come and see what all the fuss was about."

"And, what do you make of it so far?"

I peered at my drink and decided my best approach was to try to sober up quickly. I had the distinct impression I was being interrogated. "I think it's pretty nice. In fact, I'm thinking of staying down here for a while."

The sheriff nodded in silence, his gaze unwavering. "Hey, what you drinking there? Jack and Coke? You want another?"

I shook my head. "No, I'm fine. Thanks."

"Sure you do." The sheriff raised a hand. "Cody? Would you get my friend here another JD and coke. In fact, make it two." He turned to me. "You mind if I join you?"

I held out my hands. "Looks like you already have."

As the drinks arrived, I finished the last of the pizza and glared longingly at the door. I was no longer hungry or thirsty. My bed at The Regal—as hard and unwelcoming as it was—was calling to me, and my body craved sleep.

The sheriff sipped his drink, set it down, and leaned across the table. "Ray at the cab company says you've been up to Kiowa Rock."

I guessed Ray was the guy with the yellow shirt and suspenders. "So, what if I have?"

"A lot of bad things happened up there."

"Such as?"

"It's not really the kind of thing folks 'round here like to talk about."

"Well, maybe you can educate me."

The sheriff took another sip of his drink and eyed the bartender. "Let's just say, you'd do well to stay as far away from that place as possible. Folks who spend a lot of time up there in the hills seem to earn themselves a whole lot of bad luck."

The sheriff was talking in riddles and it was beginning to annoy me. "I think I can look after myself, but thanks for the advice, sheriff. I really appreciate it." I necked my drink and stood to leave, but he reached over and grabbed my hand.

"What you looking for up there, Carter? The old mine? You think there's gold in Kiowa don't you? Is that what you want? Treasure?"

"I know there's gold up there," I hissed, wrenching my arm free. "I've seen it."

"What you've seen is a hole in the ground where over a 100 men disappeared almost 80 years ago. There's been no gold in those mines since. It's just an empty pit, haunted by the many lost souls searching for a way home. You want to disturb the graves of the people many of us call family?"

I sat back down. "I know what I saw."

The sheriff shook his head. "Kiowa does that to people, Carter. It shows you what you want to see. You went there looking for riches, and that's what it gave you. It's just an illusion." He stood and collected his hat. "Look, just stay away from those hills. That's the only advice I can give you. If you ignore me, that's on you, but don't say I didn't warn you."

With the food in my belly and the fog of alcohol in my brain, I decided that having the sheriff on my side was a much better strategy than letting the conversation end badly. "Little Bear will tell you," I said as the sheriff opened the door. "Little Bear will tell you everything."

The next day, I awoke with a pounding head and a foggy memory of my encounter with the sheriff. We'd agreed to meet at 10 that morning and head up to Little Bear's trailer, which was situated just outside of town.

"You sure you want to bring this guy in on what we found?" Bill asked, standing behind me as I brushed my teeth. "I mean, won't we be giving up a share of the gold?"

"And you think I can just go up there with an explosives guy and collect the gold all by myself?"

"Well, yeah. That's what I would have done."

"Well, you're not here, Bill, are you?" I regretted the words as soon as they left my lips. The memory of my brother's body being zipped up in a bag and loaded onto the Chinook still haunted me. "Sorry, I didn't mean that."

"It's okay," Bill replied. "You're right. I'm sorry too. I'm dead and you're the one having to go through with my little plan. I wish I could help you."

I dressed myself in a pair of blue jeans and a loose shirt and headed to the foyer. Penny was on duty and she shot me a leering glare as I headed for the door.

"Don't do anything I wouldn't do," she hollered. I didn't think there was much that Penny wouldn't do, but I raised a hand in acknowledgement as I stepped out onto the street. The sun was high and bright, but thankfully there was a cool breeze that felt refreshing on my skin. The sheriff was waiting for me out front in his squad car.

"Hop in," he yelled. "I called the Indian and he said he'd put a pot of coffee on the stove for us."

The ride into the hills took a little over 20 minutes, and the sheriff used the time to grill me on my life growing up in Chicago. I gave him the diluted version: My parents had been hard-working Americans. My mother had been a schoolteacher and my father a banker. Both were now deceased; my father from a heart attack when I was 10, my mother from cancer when I was 13. My brother, Bill, who was five years older than me, looked after me until I'd left school. Then, at 18, I'd signed up for the army, and my brother—who'd sworn to my mother as she lay dying in her hospital bed that he'd look after me—had signed up too.

We were enrolled into the same unit, and were sent to Iraq to fight a war that neither of us really understood. Two tours in, our unit had been ambushed after we'd been given intel that a gang of insurgents were holed up in an abandoned school. The whole thing had been a trap, of course. These things always were. As we entered the property, some bastard detonated an IED, killing over half of my unit. It was the bloodiest, most horrific scene I hope I'll ever have to witness.

The whole area was carnage: limbs torn from mutilated bodies, blood covering the ground and walls, men screaming out in terrible pain. It was only after the ringing in my ears died down and I'd gained some semblance of my senses that I realized my brother was no longer standing alongside me. I scoured the debris, my hands sore from hauling stone and iron girders away from the remains of my friends, and dragging bloodied survivors—each of them desperately gasping for breath—from the wreckage. That was when I saw him.

He had been almost cut in half from the blast. There was blood everywhere. His guts had spilled out and were lying beside him on the concrete, his eyes lifeless. I'll never forget that image. I fell to the floor, my body shuddering from the shock, my hands trying to collect his spilled intestines to push them back into his body.

When I came back to Chicago after another four tours, I was 25-years-old and angry. I wasn't who I used to be. I was bitter, pissed off at the world, and hellbent on getting back at society. Everything had been taken from me. My parents, my brother, and, finally, my innocence. I was also penniless. There had been very little inheritance and I'd gambled away most of my earnings from my military career. I didn't tell the sheriff this part of my history, of course, or the part shortly afterward where I fell in with a gang of crooks and thugs. It wasn't a chapter in my life I was proud of, and not one I shared publicly.

"So, that's me," I said, winding up my tale. "What about you? How long have you lived in Devil's Ridge? Does all your family come from here?"

The sheriff swung the car off the road and down a dirt track. He then angled it round a sharp bend where a large, 40-foot trailer lay, steam drifting lazily skyward from the vent at the front. There was a flatbed truck outside and an overweight bloodhound asleep in the yard. "That story's going to have to wait for another time," he said. "Depending on how this conversation with the Indian goes, later on you can buy me that drink you owe me, and I'll fill you in on my life so far."

I smirked. "That's a deal."

As we exited the vehicle, Little Bear opened the door to his trailer and beckoned us in. We crossed the yard, and the bloodhound opened its eyes and peered up at us. "Don't mind Axle," he said. "He's about as lazy as they come. He won't cause you no trouble."

"Axle?" I asked. "That's an odd name. I assume you're a Guns and Roses fan?"

Little Bear held the door for us as we stepped inside and looked at me with a confused expression on his face. "Nah. The poor guy was a rescue dog. He'd been hit by a truck out on Route 24 and got trapped beneath the front axle and the asphalt. They'd had to call the fire department to rescue him. The owner couldn't afford the medical bills, so I took him in and nursed him back to health. I thought the name Axle was a good fit."

The trailer was neat, tidy, and quite spacious. The kitchen was at the front where a pot of coffee brewed slowly on the stove. The living area was in the middle section, which consisted of a dining table, two long sofas, and a bookshelf jammed full of mystery novels. To our right was the bathroom and two bedrooms.

"Nice place," I offered. "It's—"

"Not what you expected?" Little Bear said, smirking.

"I guess not."

"We're not all generic cliches you know," he said. "I like to read and I like to work. That's it."

"What is it you do again?" Sheriff Harris asked, accepting a cup of coffee.

"I'm a carpenter," Little Bear replied. "My workshop's out back if you want to take a look, Sheriff. I've just finished a pretty cool eagle. It would look nice on your desk back at the station, I reckon."

"Maybe," the sheriff answered. "As long as you're open to a barter."

Little Bear smiled and handed me my drink. He winked knowingly. "That's always the way with law enforcement, eh? Won't take anything at face value."

We each took a seat at the table. I decided to kick off. "The sheriff's interested in what we found," I said. "Yesterday, up at Kiowa Rock."

"Okay," Little Bear replied, guarded. "What do you want to know, Sheriff?"

The police chief eyed each of us in turn. "Carter here is under the illusion that there's gold up there in the mine. As far as I know, that mine's been barren for decades—since everything happened."

Little Bear nodded. "That it has."

"So, there's no gold?" the sheriff pressed. "Carter here's mistaken?"

Our host's eyes narrowed. "I never said that."

"Then, what exactly are you saying?"

"That sometimes nature will reveal things to us. Often-times, it will be something that we truly desire, but that doesn't necessarily mean that it's ours for the taking."

"You mean the gold?" I asked. "Because we both know it's there, right? I saw it and you saw it, too. There was no mistaking it."

"You're putting words in his mouth," the sheriff inter-jected. "I want to hear it from him."

"I know," I replied, envisioning Hogan's face as I hand-ed over the cash that I owed him. At least I could put that part of my life behind me; the part where I hurt people for a living, where I did bad things. I needed that gold. "But, all this is wasting time. If we don't lay claim to it, somebody else will, and I know the town needs the cash, Sheriff. Don't try to tell me it doesn't. It's obvious from the state of the place. Devil's Ridge is about as rundown as they come."

"That's my hometown!" the sheriff hollered. "And you'll do well to remember that."

As the discussion paused, I glared out the window. The forest leading to Kiowa's Rock was visible in the distance, high up in the hills. I recalled the shadows among the trees, the hiss of voices whispering in my ear, beckoning me toward them.

"There's gold up there, alright," Little Bear said eventually. "But, that gold is cursed. You should leave it be."

"How much?" the sheriff replied. "Are we talking a lot?"

I nodded. "It's a hell of a lot."

He stood and paced the room. "There aren't many in the town who'd know how to mine it," he said. "But there's a few old timers who could help."

"Boomer," I said without thinking.

"Yeah, Boomer's one, but there's a few others, too."

Little Bear grabbed the sheriff's arm. "You know what happened up there, Elijah," he said. "You know the stories as well as I do."

"I know this town desperately needs funds," he said. "This could be a lifeline."

"I need a stake, too," I said, sensing where the conversation was going. "I found it, so did Little Bear. We deserve a share."

"I don't want any part of it," Little Bear said. "Those spirits have lain dormant for a long time now. They haven't caused us any trouble. Waking them would be a bad idea."

"Oh, come on," I said. "Do you really believe in all that superstitious nonsense?"

Little Bear glared at me. "Listen to me, J.C. I'm not joking around. This could turn out really badly for the people of Devil's Ridge. You're putting everybody's lives at risk for the sake of a few dollars."

I felt something crawl across my arm and I subconsciously brushed it off. The hairs on the back of my neck were standing on end, too. I knew then that Little Bear wasn't kidding. He truly believed what he was saying.

"This isn't for us to decide. I'll call a town meeting tomorrow evening," the sheriff said, opening the door. "We'll put it to the vote."

I rose from the table, Little Bear's eyes still on me. I knew I'd cornered him into revealing what he knew, but I'd had no choice. I was in a desperate situation, and time was running out.

I've thought about that moment ever since and I'd take everything back in a heartbeat if I could. I wish with every ounce of my being that I'd listened, that I'd done everything in my power to put a stop to what I'd unwittingly started.

From that point onward, things in Devil's Ridge would never be the same again.

CHAPTER FOUR

There's Gold in Those Hills

The night was drawing in and there was a chill in the air. I pulled the collar up on my jacket and stood outside the town hall, watching as scores of residents arrived, hoping that they would all see sense and vote for the mining to get approved. Sure, I'd got out of Chicago and was no longer looking over my shoulder every minute of every day, half expecting a muscle bound goon to be lurking in the shadows and preparing to kick the living crap out of me, but I knew I couldn't stay hidden for long. Hogan would find me. He always did.

"You know, you've given away most of our gold making that little deal with the sheriff," Bill said, sitting on a bench and smoking a hand-rolled cigarette. "Good going, Brother. We're now significantly less rich than we could have been."

"Yeah, whatever," I replied. "But there's no guarantee that the town will vote this through."

"Oh, they'll vote it through, alright," he said, blowing smoke. "They're not stupid. They all see what you see, they just don't talk about it publicly."

"Hey there!" Somebody from behind me grabbed me by the shoulder and I whirled around, fighting every instinct I had to throw a right-cross.

"Oh, hi," I replied to the pretty lady with bright blue eyes, Linda Thornton. "It's good to see you."

"You too. I thought I'd come along and find out what this is all about. People are saying they've found gold up in the old mine."

I nodded. "It's true. Lots of it, too."

"Interesting," she said. "You think they're going to vote to start mining again?"

"Maybe." I had a thought. I knew I could use an ally. "You want to come inside with me and hear it for yourself?"

She took my arm as Bill shot me a wink. "Sure. Plus, I hear there's free donuts."

The sheriff had already appraised the mayor—an elderly guy called Arthur Pumpkin who's hair was red, streaked with white, and who's waist belied his love of pie and cold cuts. He was the one who gave the speech. Despite his age and size, he gave a good account of the situation and was clearly on board with mining for the gold. I wasn't a fool. I knew that everybody on the town council stood to gain mightily from my find in the hills, but I also knew that it played to my advantage. All I needed was for the rest of the town to buy into it, too.

"We all know the stories of what happened to our kin back in the day," the mayor continued, "and we've all heard about the curse of Kiowa Rock. That is why we've gathered you here today. We won't do anything without a democratic vote. If you all say it's too dangerous, then the gold will stay where it is and we'll all get on with our lives."

"And let someone else get to it first?" a young man behind me yelled. "Not likely!"

The mayor held out his hands. "Well, yes, there is that risk," he said. "Now that the word is out, I can't guarantee that some private company, or even some reckless individual, won't head up there and take the gold for themselves."

"That's our gold!" an elderly lady shouted. "They have no right to it!"

"That's true, too," he replied, agreeing. "But, we all know that when people get wind of a fortune beyond their wildest dreams, they're apt to do some very silly things. Illegal things."

"I'd like to see them try!" a guy in a flannel shirt hollered. "Me and my guys will stand guard if we need to. I've got the guns and I've got the men."

"You'll do no such thing, Henry," the sheriff called out. "The last thing we need is some vigilante group causing trouble for us all. If anyone's going to put a guard up there, it'll be me."

"How you going to afford that, Sheriff?" another lady shouted. "There's only you and two deputies, and you've all got your hands full as it is."

"Well, I can't argue with that," he replied. "But, we'll do the best we can. We always do."

"Well, it won't be good enough!" a wiry man with a heavy beard yelled. "I say we take that gold for ourselves while we still can!"

The whole room erupted in loud roars of approval and I glanced at Linda. Her eyes were wide and her mouth was open, as if she couldn't believe the chaos that was unfolding around her.

"You know?" she said, raising her voice so that I could hear her above the racket. "I've lived here all my life, I've grown up with these people, I've taught most of their kids, and yet I still don't understand them. They all know what went on up at the mine. They've all heard the same stories. Most of them have relatives they weren't able to bury because they were never found; and yet, here they are threatening to blow the head off of anyone who dares to pay an interest in Kiowa Rock. I say, let them have it. They can have all of it. I wouldn't set foot in that mine for all the gold in the world."

I sat back in my chair. *So much for gaining myself an ally*, I thought. It was obvious to me that Linda would be anything but. I decided not to tell her it was me who found the gold.

When all the commotion died down and the mayor called the meeting to order, the committee got down to the business of voting. When all was said and done, the mining activity was voted through with only a few residents voting against. By the look on Linda's face when the mayor announced the verdict, she was one of them.

"Crazy fools," she said as she stood up and stormed out. I went after her.

"Wait up," I yelled, heading down the steps that led to the park. "Linda, wait!"

"They don't know what they've done," she hissed, striding out in front of me. "What they'll bring down on all of us."

"Come on. This could be good for the town, couldn't it?"

"What do you know, J.C.? You're not even from 'round here."

"I know enough to see when a town is in urgent need of a revival. Another 10 years down the line, this place could be all but deserted."

"Well, maybe that's a good thing," she said, turning to me, her hands on her hips. "If everyone here is as money crazy as that lot in there, then maybe they deserve everything that's headed their way."

We were standing in a secluded part of the town park, a bandstand off to our right and a small pond to our left. I could hear the distant cry of a coyote and the rustling of birds in the branches overhead. Behind us, there were the faint strains of people talking animatedly as they hurried home for supper.

"I'm just saying, maybe the stories of what went on at the mine all those years ago have been exaggerated a little," I held her gaze, but I could see she was still angry. "People have a habit of elaborating, and over the years, I'm sure details have been added that perhaps never really happened. I'm not saying you're wrong, just that you should, perhaps, consider the possibility that this is a good thing."

"I lost my great-grandfather in that mine, J.C." she said, her expression hard and unforgiving. "Try telling my grandmother that her father was a detail that never really happened."

I watched as she turned and walked away, and I realized too late that I'd overstepped the mark. I really didn't understand the town of Devil's Ridge and perhaps I never would. I did, however, need that money; and if it meant making a few enemies along the way, then perhaps that was a price I had to be willing to pay.

Something moved in the bushes behind me and I whirled toward it. The lamplight in that part of the park was minimal and it was hard to make out anything more than a few feet in front of me. I started to walk forward, but I heard the rustling once more. I bent down, peered into the undergrowth, and waited for my eyes to adjust to the gloom. There was something there alright; something nestled among the trees. It was bent low to the ground, its arms wrapped around a slim tree trunk, its head cocked at an angle.

It peered up at me through the brambles, its eyes giving off a faded yellow hue, pupils like dark vertical slits. Its shapeless form moved and grew in stature, and suddenly I was confronted by something tall and sinewy, bear-like in height but slim and muscular in stature. I started to back away, to search for a weapon to defend myself, but suddenly the creature turned and moved. It was quick, like an alley cat, and before I had a chance to react, it had disappeared.

Standing alone in the darkness, my heart beating a frantic rhythm in my chest, I fought to regain my composure. I wondered what the hell was going on.

"Do you think Little Bear was telling the truth," I asked. "Do you think this town is cursed?"

"I think you've been listening too much to that girlfriend of yours," my brother replied, now standing in front of me and shooting me the kind of concerned older brother look he had been so fond of. "And, what you saw was a figment of your imagination. Get a grip on yourself, soldier. This isn't Iraq. This is Devil's Ridge, Colorado, and there are no assassins in the tall buildings, no IEDs in the streets, and no mythical demons waiting for you in the trees." He stepped toward me. I thought I could feel his breath on my face, which, of course, was impossible. "But, there's gold in those hills, J.C. There's gold in those hills."

CHAPTER FIVE

The Wendigo

The first detonation in Kiowa Rock occurred exactly one week to the day after I'd arrived in town. Things had happened so quickly after the residents had voted for the mine to be blasted that I'd barely had a chance to think about what I was going to do with my share. Little Bear was watching when the crew turned up, and he eyed me with a look of bitter disappointment as I helped a few of the others load the explosives onto the wagon that was being wheeled through the forest. I felt a pang of shame, but I was relieved things were moving so quickly.

The journey was heavy going at first, but the sheriff had a local landscaping company hack a path through the undergrowth and create a trail of sorts, which made our trek a little easier. I didn't spy any shadows lurking among the trees, or any bear-sized creatures crashing through the forest, but I did have the distinct and slightly unnerving sensation that we were being watched. I tried to shake it off as superstitious nonsense, but deep down, I knew what I felt. Whether the stories were true or not, there were spirits lingering in those mountains. I could feel them.

When we emerged from the trees, I spied Boomer hollering orders to a couple of younger men who were fooling around near the mine shaft. Boomer was too old and infirm to mine himself, but that didn't stop him from imparting his many years of experience onto the others with words of one syllable and in a tone that was as raw as gravel and as sharp as a razor.

They say the detonations were felt in town, and I didn't doubt it. I didn't hang around to watch, though. I can't be around explosives. Not since that day. It's just too much. In any case, I had some apologizing to do.

I found Little Bear back at his trailer. He was feeding Axle and carving what looked like a raccoon into a slug of hardwood. He glanced up at me as I strode toward him.

"Congratulations," he said. "You got what you came for."

Axle rolled onto his back and I stooped down to rub his belly. "I think the town will get most of the benefit from this, don't you?"

"I think you liked what you saw and manipulated the others into doing your dirty work."

The sharpness of his words stung. "Don't worry. I'll make sure you get your share." I made no attempt to hide my anger. "Every damn penny."

Little Bear turned to face me. He was a tall man, broad in the shoulders with a thick chest, but I'd taken down bigger. "I told you, I don't want any part of it," he hissed. "You've done a dangerous thing. Something that cannot be undone."

"And, what exactly is that?"

"You've woken the spirits."

"Oh, come on," I cried. "Give me a break."

"People will be killed, J.C! There's no going back from this."

"What? Because of some decades-old story about some miners disappearing?"

He grabbed me by the collar and I could feel his rough, calloused fingers against my skin. I tried to push him away but he was far stronger than I'd thought. "Because of those things out there, you damn fool!"

Suddenly, there was a deep rumbling sound, and the earth beneath our feet shook. My vision began to swim and I dropped to the floor. I was back in Fallujah again, my brother's body in my arms. In my mind's eye, I was grabbing my rifle and heading for what remained of the doorway. I spotted three men running in the direction of the highway. I yelled out but they kept going, so I aimed my M16A2 and fired. The first man took three bullets in the spine, but the other two were far quicker and ducked behind a wall before I could unload another barrage.

I could feel an intense, rage bubbling inside me that I was struggling to contain. I didn't wait for the others in my platoon. I raced across the street with no thought for my own safety. I wanted revenge. I wanted to kill the bastards who had murdered my brother. I wanted to strangle them with my bare hands, gouge out their eyes, and rip their innards from their still breathing bodies.

There was suddenly water on my face and I gasped for air. When I was able to catch my breath, Little Bear was standing over me, an empty jug in his hands, and Axle was licking my face.

"You okay, bro?" he asked. "You spun out on me there. You were thrashing around like a crazy person."

"I'm fine," I replied, sitting up and wiping the dog drool from my chin. "It happens sometimes."

He crouched beside me. "The war?" he asked.

I shot him a sideways glance. "How did you know?"

"You learn how to spot it in people. I knew you were a soldier as soon as I laid eyes on you. I knew you'd fallen on hard times, too. Don't make you a bad person."

I hung my head. "Maybe you don't know me as well as you think you do, Little Bear. Maybe I am bad. Maybe I'm about as bad as they come."

He laughed. "Well then, that makes two of us." He reached into his pocket and withdrew a silver hip flask. "You want?"

"I shouldn't."

"Don't mean you won't."

I took the flask, unscrewed the cap, and instantly the peaty smell of whiskey entered my lungs. It was like heroin to me. Like a first love. I took a long tug of liquor and swallowed. I wanted to be numb. I wanted Fallujah to evaporate from my memory like smoke. Above all, I wanted to be that 18 year old boy again, the innocent kid that had never worn a uniform, held a gun in his hands, or killed anybody.

The silence was broken by the screech of tires and a cloud of dust as a patrol call swung onto the track in front of us. Sheriff Harris leapt from the car, one of his deputies in tow.

"We've got a situation," he said. "I need the Indian to come with me."

I got to my feet. "What's going on?"

"It's one of the men," he replied. "He's talking crazy, like he's been spooked or something."

"So? One of the miners obviously has a touch of claustrophobia," I shoved the flask in my pocket. "Why do you need Little Bear for that?"

"He says he saw a ghost down there in the mine," the deputy said. "He says he saw The Wendigo."

CHAPTER SIX

Housemates

We stood over the man who was laying in the dirt with a rolled up jacket beneath his head; a thin guy in his mid-30s with a chin beard and spiked, blond hair named Zed. He looked like he'd literally seen a ghost.

"It came at me," he said. "Straight toward me, like it was going to swallow me whole or something."

Little Bear stooped on the ground next to him. "I see. What did it look like?"

Zed shook his head, his eyes wide. "Like a ghost! What do you think it damn well looked like?"

"I'm going to need a little more than that."

Zed looked up at the others and shrugged. "What do you want from me? I told you what I saw."

Sheriff Harris stepped forward. "He's just trying to help, Zed. Tell us what you were doing at the time of the...incident."

Zed's eyes narrowed. "I was putting in the timber supports, you know? That old mine was blocked up pretty bad, so we had to blow a great big hole in it. I've never seen that much explosive in one place before. It made a real big noise. *Real big.* After the dust had settled, Boomer said he didn't trust that the tunnel would hold out without something keeping the roof in place, so me and Caleb were sent down there to build a supporting structure so as the whole damn rock didn't come crashing down around us."

"How far did you go?" Little Bear asked. "Into the tunnel, I mean? Did you make it as far as the dorm?" I could tell his question was loaded; I just didn't know why.

"Not quite," Zed replied. "But pretty close."

Little Bear glanced up at the sheriff and they both exchanged knowing glances. "Was the spirit...the *ghost* dark, Zed? Like smoke?"

Zed pushed himself up. "I'm as dry as an old stogie, here," he said. "I can't think straight."

"Get him a drink, won't you?" Sheriff Harris yelled, sending Deputy Barns back to the squad car to fetch a bottle of water.

"Here," I said, retrieving Little Bear's hip flask from my pocket. "This could help."

Zed grabbed the canteen and took a big gulp, followed by an even bigger one, and then he turned to the sheriff. "It was as black as coal, Sheriff. Darker than night itself. I thought it was death visiting me. I fell back onto the rocks and it passed straight over me. I felt every inch of me turn cold, as if I was in a refrigerator or something. Then, it turned to look at me, and I saw hell in its eyes. I swear I did. Then, I saw my wife mourning beside my grave while my son threw soil onto the casket. I was dead and my wife and son were standing there, no older than they are now. I thought that thing was trying to tell me that it was going to kill me right there in that suffocating hellhole, so I screamed. I must have yelled so loud I blacked out, because when I came to, Caleb was dragging me from the tunnel and shouting for help."

Little Bear stood and walked over to us. The mayor was now standing alongside us, his ever-present beaming smile painted firmly on his gelatinous lips.

"This isn't good," Little Bear said. "Mayor, I suggest you shut this operation down right now."

"We can't do that," the mayor replied, glancing at the other men standing around us. They were watching our every move with a keen interest. "The town voted on it."

"I don't give a rat's ass what the town voted for, sir. You know what's down that tunnel as well as I do."

"We have no idea what Zed saw, or if he even saw anything at all. He has a history of marijuana abuse. Sheriff Harris here tells me he has arrested him more times than he cares to remember. He's only in this crew because the foreman said he needed a couple of guys who were small enough to go into the tunnel and secure it before mining could start. He's getting extra money for it, too. I wouldn't bet against this whole thing just being some sort of drug-induced hysteria."

Little Bear was incensed and I could see it. "If you really think that, why the hell did you drag me all the way up here to talk to him?"

"I didn't," the mayor said, glancing at the sheriff. "He did."

"I needed a second opinion," Sheriff Harris replied.

"And my opinion is you should shut this whole operation down, pronto."

The mayor raised an eyebrow, dabbed a napkin on his lips and grinned. "Opinion noted."

I took Little Bear to one side. "He's right, you know?" I said. "That guy could have seen anything. We can't shut down the operation just because one dopehead says he saw a ghost."

"My opinion hasn't changed," he replied. "This whole thing is a mistake."

"It's the Wendigo, isn't it?" Zed hollered. "I saw it. The thing that took those miners. We've woken it, haven't we? It's going to come for us, isn't it?" He turned to Little Bear. "That's what you're trying to tell them, isn't it, Indian? You're warning them!"

There was a commotion among the other miners, raised voices and yelling. I could see the sheriff starting to move.

"Okay, that's enough!" he shouted. "We don't need to hear any more about this so-called ghost. Zed here has had a shock and needs to be taken to the hospital. Everybody else, I suggest you go home for the night!"

Deputy Barns and the sheriff did their best to create a cordon and push the miners back toward the road that led away from Kiowa Rock, but I could see there was a lot of unrest. I knew the story would start moving through the town like wildfire as soon as the crew made it back to Devil's Ridge, and I could see the mayor knew it, too. Whatever diplomatic skills the man possessed, they were going to be put to the test, and then some.

The sheriff dropped Little Bear back at his trailer, and me back at The Regal, a little after 7 p.m. My stomach was growling, but I wanted to try to make amends with Linda. I felt guilty after our last conversation had ended badly, and I'd been meaning to catch up with her ever since. The sheriff told me she usually dined at the steakhouse six blocks from the hotel on a Wednesday with a couple of gal pals, so I decided to kill two birds with one stone. As I said, I was hungry.

Sure enough, as I entered the restaurant, I spotted Linda with two other women sitting in a booth in the back. I decided not to intrude, and asked the waiter to seat me at a little table some way from them. I didn't want her to see me just yet.

"She's not into you, you know?" Bill said, taking the chair opposite. "You're not her type."

"That's not why I'm here," I replied. "I just want to talk to her."

Bill exhaled loudly. "Yeah, right, and I'm Pope John Paul II."

I shook my head. "You've really got a nerve. You know that, right?"

Bill grinned. "But seriously, what you gonna do when they shut the mining operation down?"

"They won't."

"They might."

"The mayor won't let it come to that," I said, more in hope than with any semblance of belief.

"What do you think that thing was?"

I thought about my encounter at the park just after Linda stormed off. Zed's description of the spirit, or whatever the hell it was, was remarkably similar to what I'd encountered in the darkness—of that there was no doubt—but that didn't make it real. In fact, nothing in Devil's Ridge seemed real anymore. I was starting to wonder whether the whole thing was just some fucked up dream.

I ordered a steak and a beer and ate my dinner in silence while Bill sat across from me, his arms folded, glaring enviously at my food. After half an hour or so, I saw Linda's two companions depart, and I tried to hide my joy when she came and sat at my table.

"Hi there," she said. "I didn't know you dined here, too."

"Well, it's my first time."

"I've been meaning to talk to you."

"Me too," I replied, pushing my empty plate away. "Look, about the other night—"

"I'm sorry."

"I was about to say the same thing."

"Well then, we can both be sorry, can't we?" She tilted her head and smiled, revealing the dimples in her cheeks. "Can we start over?"

I nodded eagerly and held out a hand. "Hi, I'm J.C."

She took it and laughed. "Pleased to meet you, J.C. I'm Linda."

"Hi, Linda. Very nice to make your acquaintance."

We chatted for an hour or more, and I found myself growing more and more fond of the slightly flaky but well-grounded school teacher. She had grown up in the town—that much I already knew—and was single with no children. She did aerobics and yoga three times a week, disco music was her guilty pleasure, her favorite drink was rum and coke, and her parents still lived in town. I told her a little about my past, left out the bit about my brother dying in my arms, and avoided disclosing the reason I left Chicago. I could see she knew I was holding back, but it didn't seem to offend her.

"So, how long are you in town for?"

"I don't know," I replied. "Haven't made up my mind yet. But, I do know I need to find somewhere to stay pretty fast. I can't afford to stay in The Regal any longer than I have to."

Linda's expression hardened. "I can't imagine Penny's rates have gotten any cheaper over the years."

"Don't get me wrong," I chimed in. "It's not expensive as such, but I'm running out of funds and staying in a hotel is a luxury I can't afford."

She went quiet as if she was thinking about something. "You know, I have a spare room."

I was taken aback. "Oh no, that's not what I meant. I'm sorry. It's just—"

"No, it's okay. I didn't mean anything by it. It's just a practical thing. You need to get out of the hotel, and I'm swimming around in a three-bedroom house all by myself."

I had to admit, I did like the idea, but I knew that I'd be putting Linda in a difficult position. I was acutely aware of how rumors spread in a small town like Devil's Ridge.

"I don't know," I said. "I feel like I'd be imposing."

"You wouldn't be," she said, touching my hand. "I could use the company. Besides, I have a few jobs that need doing, and you look like the kind of man who knows he's away around a hammer and saw."

I felt myself blush, which was completely unlike me. There was something about Linda that affected me. Her eyes were so blue, I could barely get the sharp image of them out of my head. "If you're sure," I said eventually, barely believing that I was going to take her up on her offer.

"Great. Then, it's a deal."

All of a sudden the restaurant door burst open and a woman with wild eyes and a terrified expression on her young face ran in and grabbed hold of the waiter. She had blood in her hair and a ragged tear in her shirt.

"Help!" she cried. "Help me! He's going to kill me!"

CHAPTER SEVEN

Take a Raincheck

The crime scene had been cordoned off and a white tent had been erected over the victim. Red and blue flashing lights painted the scene with an eerie, disco strobe effect. The park was flooded with people, craning their necks to see what all the commotion was about. Linda and I stood at the back, watching as Deputy Barns interviewed the young woman who had called out for help back at the steakhouse.

Initially, when she'd come bursting through the door, I'd thought she'd been joking, stupidly believing that one of Linda's friends had spotted us together and was playing some sort of sick prank. Then, I saw the blood in her hair, like somebody had dyed red streaks through her blond curls. The terror in her eyes made me realize that something awful had happened.

Linda had been the first out of her seat, and she'd rushed to the poor woman's aid without a moment's hesitation. I was close behind, and then decided that the best course of action was to see if anyone was standing outside looking suspicious. Finding nobody out there, I returned to Linda. I was shocked to see the waiter filming the whole thing on his smartphone, and I told him, in no uncertain terms, that he should cease immediately before I lost my shit.

"Tell me again what happened," Linda said. She'd got the woman to sit down and had asked another diner to fetch her a glass of water.

"I was with my date," she said. "We'd just had a couple of drinks at the lounge bar on Maple Avenue, and Paul, the guy I was with, asked me if he could walk me home. I said, of course. I've known him since high school. I even know sister, his parents. Jesus—" she stopped herself mid-sentence and tried to compose herself. "His parents. What am I going to tell them?"

"It's okay," Linda said. "Other people will deal with that. You just need to worry about yourself for the moment."

The woman nodded and took a sip of her water. I noticed a long scratch on her forearm, like someone had dragged something sharp across her skin.

"Anyway," she continued, "we took the shortcut across Lincoln Park and stopped for a little while by the lake, you know, to talk and stuff. It was a bit cold, so Paul wrapped his sweater around me. He really was a gentleman." She stopped again, and I could see tears welling in her eyes. "Is someone going to get him?" she asked. "I can't bear the thought of him being out there on his own. Not with that maniac around."

"Don't worry," the waiter said, seemingly trying to redeem himself. "I called them just after you came in."

As if by magic, a police car pulled up outside. Sheriff Harris was the first to enter the restaurant, followed by his two deputies.

"Nancy," he said, racing over to the victim. "What the hell happened?"

The blond girl, Nancy, stood and collapsed into the sheriff's arms. "It's Paul," she cried. "I think he's dead."

An hour later, we were all standing in Lincoln Park, watching as the body of Paul Chase was examined by the only medical examiner the town had—an elderly gentleman with a white, handlebar mustache and checkered tweed suit named Doctor Brooks. I had my arm around

Linda because she was shivering from the shock *and* the cold. I knew how it looked, but I was beyond caring. Devil's Ridge was having an effect on me, and it wasn't a good one.

What we had learned in the intervening period between Nancy entering the restaurant and all of us heading down to Lincoln Park was shocking to say the least. After Paul had draped his sweatshirt around Nancy's shoulders, he'd decided to find himself a quiet spot among the trees to relieve himself. Nancy said she'd waited on the park bench for around 15 minutes before realizing Paul had either abandoned her or that something bad had happened.

She headed off in the direction Paul had walked and, after a little while, she heard a commotion. She said she initially thought it was just two men having an argument by the water fountain; but then, she realized that one of the men was Paul, and he appeared to be bleeding heavily from a head wound. Then, the other man, whose back was to her, pushed Paul to the ground and leapt on him.

To her horror, he then opened his mouth and plunged his teeth into Paul's neck, taking a bloodied chunk out of his flesh. She said she could see a jet of blood gushing from the wound like a geyser. It was at this point that she'd screamed, alerting the attacker to her presence. She said the light from the lamp was behind him, so all she could make out was a silhouette. However, she could tell the man was deranged because he was howling like a wolf or a coyote, and he was breathing heavily.

Nancy dropped Paul's sweater, which was branded with the Devil's Ridge football team logo—a comical depiction of Satan holding a burning football in one of his hooves—and ran for her life. However, the guy was on her before she'd even made it 30 feet, and she'd tripped and fallen face first into the gravel.

The man then pounced on her back, and she said she could smell his breath, which was coppery and warm. His fingers pushed into her shoulder blades like sharp daggers. She'd swung out an arm, but he knocked it away, causing the long gash that I'd seen earlier. Then, he'd tried to roll her over onto her back, but as he did so, Nancy brought her heel up into the guy's testicles and he'd crumpled into a heap on the floor. She said she then leapt to her feet, ran, and didn't look back—she just focused on the street lights from Governor's Boulevard way off in the distance and pounded her legs as fast as she could.

"You did a good job calming Nancy down, Linda," the sheriff said after he'd finished up with the doctor. "She's had a hell of a shock. We all have. Jesus, what a mess."

"Is he—" I asked, raising my eyebrows.

The sheriff nodded, his skin ashen. "Murdered in cold blood. The poor guy didn't stand a chance. Just bled out right there on the path."

"Who would do such a thing?" Linda said, her voice trembling. "And why?"

"Have you informed his parents?" I asked, searching for the right words.

"Not yet. That's a job I need to do myself. I've known Mark and Jen for 30 years, maybe more. I was at their wedding. Christ, I never thought the job would come to this."

"Can I do anything to help?" I offered.

The sheriff shook his head. "No, but thanks. This is one of those jobs I can't delegate, I'm afraid. I'll be needing a statement from both of you, of course. But, for now, that can wait."

He tipped his hat and headed off in the direction of his car. My mouth felt dry and my senses were numbed. First, I'd been confronted by a shadow creature right there in the park, then Zed had been attacked by some sort of ghost in the mine, and now this poor guy had been killed by a man who appeared to be thirsty for human blood. I wondered whether bad luck just followed me around like a bad smell. I thought I'd left all the bloodshed and violence in Fallujah, but somehow it followed me all the way to Chicago. Now, here it was once more, catching up with me as if we were old pals.

Linda shivered beside me. "I could sure use a drink," she sighed, her blue eyes gazing longingly into mine.

I could smell her perfume, her arm around my waist, and her hip against my leg. Every part of me wanted to be with her, but I knew that, right now, that would be one hell of a mistake. Something bad was going down in Devil's Ridge, and I couldn't rule out the possibility that I was the catalyst.

"Can we take a raincheck?" I asked, feeling my heart sink as her expression turned cold.

"Sure, of course you can. I—" she turned away, retreating from me. "It was only a drink."

"I know. Honestly, I do. Another time?" I offered. "I think I need some time to process what just happened."

She turned back to face me, her eyes damp. "I get it," she said. "I was too full-on. You must think of me as some sort of lonely, desperate woman."

"No, of course not."

"You don't like me that way, obviously. That's fine."

"It's not that. It's just—"

There was an awkward silence between us.

"I'll see you around," she said, and then she left.

CHAPTER EIGHT

An Attractive Offer

I woke the next morning to the sound of gentle tapping on my door. At first, I thought there were rats in the room; then, I thought someone was throwing pebbles at the window. Once I realized there was someone in the hallway attempting to get my attention, I threw on a pair of jeans, turned the latch, and opened the door.

Penny was standing there in a crimson dress, her hazel hair tumbling over her shoulders in thick waves. I checked my watch. It was a little after six in the morning, and yet the owner and manager of the Regal Hotel looked as though she was ready to go out on a dinner date.

"Penny," I said. "Is everything okay?"

"Yes. Everything's fine. I just—" Her eyes narrowed and she cocked her head sympathetically. "How are you?"

"I'm fine, I think."

"I heard about what happened last night. It must have been quite the shock."

Everything came back to me then—Nancy bursting into the restaurant, the guy with his neck torn out lying by the fountain.

"You've heard," I said.

She nodded sombrely. "Everybody has. It's all over town."

Jesus, I thought, *news does really travel at lightspeed in small town America.*

"That poor man," she said. "And Nancy, too. She'll need therapy after something like that."

"I guess she will. I hadn't really thought about it."

Penny grabbed my arm. "You might need someone to talk to as well. Don't dwell on these things on your own. You need to let it out."

I looked down at her hand and then up at her face, trying to figure out where she was going with this. Linda had told me not to trust Penny White, and I was starting to think she was right.

"I'm fine," I said. "Honestly. Is there anything you need, Penny? It's just that I should probably get up to the mine and see what's going on."

"Ah, yes. I forgot. You found all that gold, didn't you? The gold that's going to rescue this town."

I feigned a smile. "It wasn't just me. Little Bear was with me. I guess we just got lucky."

"Quite." Penny traced a finger along my forearm. "Anyway, a little bird told me that you were running low on cash and thinking about moving on from our little establishment."

I felt my mouth fall open. I had no idea how Penny had heard that. I'd literally only mentioned it to Linda the night prior.

"How do you know about—"

She held a finger to her lips. "I cannot reveal my sources," she said, winking impishly. "Let's just say, I have my ways."

I shook my head, realizing that there really were no secrets in this town. "Well, your sources are right. I can't afford to stay here for much longer."

"Well, we wouldn't want to lose your business," she replied. "You've been good to have around the place, so I want to make you an offer you can't refuse."

"I'm listening."

"How about we waive your fees for a couple of weeks, just while we wait and see how that deal up at the mine pans out. If it comes good, you can pay me what you owe out of your share. If it doesn't," she shrugged. "Then, I'll just write it off as a bet that didn't pay out. How does that sound?"

I was speechless, which was a rare thing for me.

"You look shocked," she said.

"I don't know what to say."

"Well, you could tell me you accept my very generous offer. Why don't you start with that?"

I thought of Linda, of how my snub last night had upset her. She hated Penny, I knew that much, but I also knew that I didn't want my kind of trouble to go knocking on Linda's door. She didn't deserve that. Hell, I didn't even deserve a woman like her.

"I accept," I said after a moment's consideration. "Thank you."

Penny patted my cheek and grinned. "Excellent. Most excellent. Don't forget, breakfast will be served at six-thirty on the dot." She turned to leave. "Don't be late."

CHAPTER NINE

Ghosts in the Darkness

The mine was busy that morning. With the entrance blasted, and most of the necessary reinforcements in place, prospecting had begun in earnest. There was a queue of men ready to go down into the hold, despite what had happened to Zed the day prior, and also what had gone down at Lincoln Park. It appeared that the lure of gold could ease the fears of even the most skittish of men. Neither Zed or Caleb showed up for work that morning, which I thought was odd, but I confess that I didn't give it a second thought.

"How's it going?" I asked Boomer, who was sitting in a folding chair and puffing on a pipe.

"Going pretty good, as far as I can tell. You got yourself into some mischief last night I hear."

"Yeah, I'm afraid so. Have you heard any more about it?"

"Only that the poor boy is dead and his parents want blood. It's a terrible thing, knowing that your kid was killed like that."

I nodded. I didn't have kids, but I'd lost a brother in a brutal fashion and knew that the Chase family would never heal from their emotional wounds. They would be etched into their skin like tattoos that could never be removed.

"You got someone covering for you at the train station?" I asked.

"My grandson, Scooter. His parents have been on my back for months about getting him some work. The lazy bastard spends most of his time on them video games and lord knows what else. This seemed like the perfect opportunity to get him up off his ass and earn himself a living."

I grinned. *At least something positive had come from me finding the gold*, I thought. That and meeting Linda, although I suspected I'd well and truly screwed that up.

"You want to take a look in the mine?" Boomer asked. "Seeing as you found the stuff to begin with?"

I nodded. I did want to take a look. I'd only ever seen a thin slither of gold that stretched into the mine's mouth, but I had no idea how much of it there was or how deep it went.

"Wayne!" Boomer yelled. "Will you get over here and show Mr. Carter what the guys are up to down in that hole?"

After a moment, a young man with long hair tied back in a band, his arms wiry, and his frame exposed as if he was in need of a good meal, walked across from the crooked wooden shack that had been erected as a headquarters.

"Sure thing, Boomer. You want to follow me, sir?"

Wayne led the way down the dusty path that snaked past Kiowa Rock into the mouth of the mine. I recalled what Zed said he'd seen down there, and what Nancy said had happened to her date. *Could the two things be inextricably linked? Or, were they just two coincidentally horrific events that had occurred within a few hours of each other, both of which involved me?*

"You're still thinking you're cursed, aren't you?" Bill asked as he walked alongside us. "When are you going to let that crazy notion go? I told you, I was blown up by insurgents in Iraq. That had nothing to do with you. The woman in Chicago was killed by Hogan's goons. Again, nothing to do with you. You're about as cursed as that tree," he said, pointing toward the forest.

"And what about what's gone on here since I arrived, smartass?" I hissed. "I suppose that had nothing to do with me either?"

"Exactly!" Bill exclaimed, clapping his hands. "Now, my little brother's getting it."

I moved out the way as three guys wheeled a barrow full of rocks past us, and I gratefully took the hard hat that Wayne offered me.

"You'll need these too," he said, handing me a pair of steel-toed boots. "I've taken a guess on your size. I hope they fit, because they're the last pair we have."

I pulled them on. They were a little tight, but I didn't complain. I was eager to see what was going on, and if wearing a few items of personal protective equipment got me my ticket in, then I was more than willing to comply.

"They're still clearing the tunnel so that we can get some of the bigger gear down into the mine," he said. "There won't be much to see yet, but you'll get an idea of what we're planning."

I followed Wayne as he led us past dozens of men who were already covered in dirt and grime, the crevices in their cheeks and foreheads thick with limestone, dust, and sand. I spotted several vaguely familiar faces from town: Dale Maybury, who owned the grocery store; Hester Smart, the butcher; Maggie Adams, who sometimes worked behind the bar at the hotel. I even spotted a homeless man who I'd seen sleeping in the doorway of the hardware store just days earlier. Everyone, it seemed, was keen to get in on the action, and they all had one thing in common: their eyes. They were wide and alive, as if these ordinary, god-fearing people were chasing a mind-enhancing high or running toward unlimited treasures that they'd been told were waiting for them at the end of some magical rainbow.

Not one of them mentioned the incident with Zed, or the murder of Paul Chase the evening before. It was as if they were living in a bubble—one that encased the town of Devil's Ridge in some sort of invisible skin. You couldn't see it, but it was there alright, and it arrived the moment the vote had been cast at the town meeting; a meeting that would never have taken place if Little Bear and I hadn't found what Bill had told me about all those years earlier. Namely, the band of gold in Kiowa Rock.

The entrance to the mine was quite small, and the lanterns that were being used inside provided only a little respite from the suffocating gloom. I sensed a presence as soon as I entered, and I glanced around at the others to see if they had noticed it too. No-one returned my gaze. Everyone was focussed on the job in hand: pickaxes clattering repeatedly into hard rock; boulders the size of office desks being hauled out; timber struts being erected overhead; long lengths of power cable being wound down the wine shaft to enable better lighting and the continued use of power tools.

"You have a real operation here," I said to Wayne as we continued down the tunnel. "You're really making great progress."

"Yep, once this tunnel has been fully opened up and power has been installed all the way down, the mining can start. Boomer reckons there's a weeks' worth of work before we can get to that, though."

I nodded in agreement. "Still, I'm mightily impressed."

I thought back to my time in Iraq and how efficiently my platoon had built our base in the middle of the desert. The command hub had been up and running in a little over a day, followed by the ammunition store, dorms, washrooms, fortifications, and most importantly, the kitchen. I had been amazed then, and I was equally amazed now.

My first impression of Old Boomer when I had arrived at Devil's Ridge train station had been all wrong. The guy might have been old and his joints might have been creaking, but there was nothing wrong with his brain. He knew his stuff, and he had the mining operation running like a finely-tuned engine.

The further we descended down the tunnel, the darker it became. There were fewer lamps down there and even fewer people, and the tunnel walls were rough and jagged. It wasn't long before we reached a wide open area that stretched 30-feet to either side of me. I couldn't see much further than the end of my arm.

"What's this?" I asked, reaching for my torch.

"We think this was where the miners that went missing all those years ago would have slept when they were working long shifts. We found a few tin cans, some leather holdalls, and what looked like a cooking pot hanging over the remains of some burnt coals. We call it the dorm."

I asked a question I wasn't sure I wanted to know the answer to. "Did you find any...bodies?"

Wayne shook his head. "Not so far, but we haven't really explored this area yet. We're still installing utilities, and until we do, this cave will remain untouched."

I peered into the gloom and imagined what it must have been like mining down there way back in the '40s and '50s. The conditions would have been cramped and claustrophobic, and the miners would have been forced to work long hours on meager salaries. I couldn't help but wonder what happened to them. Almost a 100 men had gone missing, leaving no trace. I wondered if their ghosts were with us now, lurking just out of sight, watching as men walked over the very ground they may very well have been buried beneath.

Suddenly, there was a loud clatter from further back along the tunnel, followed by the sound of people yelling, and the familiar scuffle of hurried feet and hands. I knew that sound well. It was a sound I'd become all too familiar with during our many weeks in the desert, miles away from home.

"Fight!" somebody yelled.

"Hit him, Ryan!" another voice added. "He can't talk about your girl like that!"

Wayne turned to me and rolled his eyes. "Wait here," he said, before disappearing into the darkness.

I sat down on a ledge and scanned the cave with the thin, blue beam of my torch. Dark shadows retreated from the light as if the illumination scalded them. In my mind's eye, the shadowy spirits of dead miners reached for me in the gloom, their long, thin finger silhouettes clutching at the air, attempting to drag me into the forever black that lay thousands of feet beneath the earth's surface.

"It's here," Bill said, sitting beside me. "Whatever that guy saw, whatever attacked the man last night, it's down here with us."

"Don't talk like an idiot, Bill," I replied. "I don't believe in undead spirits, and neither do you."

"Well, you're the one talking to his dead brother, not me."

I knew he had a point, but I tried not to show it. I listened in silence as the sound of the melee further back along the tunnel began to die out. Whatever Wayne had said to the others, it seemed to be working.

"I don't like it down here," Bill said after a moment. "Creeps me out."

"Yeah."

"Bad things happened down here."

"You may be right," I sighed. "But we've banked everything on this, so I'm afraid there's no backing down now."

Bill's image seemed to retreat into the darkness, and suddenly I was on my own in a cave full of memories.

"I think I'll go and see if everything's under control up there," I said to myself, standing and watching as my torch beam created sinewy shadow bodies in the gloom, their misshapen torsos tumbling over each other like a horde of crazed wildebeests. "The kid might need a hand."

Something cold slithered down my neck and I slapped at it unconsciously. My hand came away damp and I peered at my fingers which were covered in something black. I swung the beam of my torch, and once again a blackened figure retreated from the blue light, but not before I caught sight of a long, muscular leg which ended at a huge, wolf-like paw with claws as long as kitchen knives. It barreled into me, pushing me backward, and I cried out, automatically reaching for the hunting knife I carried in a concealed sheath tied to my calf. The wooden handle felt comforting in my grip, and I swung the knife in the darkness hoping to make a damaging strike on whatever it was that was toying with me. I felt a rage burning deep within my gut, and I channeled it.

"I know you're here," I growled. "I know you've been stalking me ever since I arrived in this town. Well, if you want me, I'm here motherfucker! Right in front of you. Why don't you just come and get me already?"

In the darkness, I could hear the sound of slow steady breathing, as if the cave walls themselves were inhaling and exhaling, inhaling and exhaling. I took a step forward, the knife held in a sideways grip, my wrist limber and loose. I knew how to fight up close and personal, and even though my attacker had the advantage of being able to see me when I could barely see three inches in front of my face, my instincts had been honed on the battlefield and my senses were keenly attuned to any noise, any movement.

I stood in the center of the cave and waited for the creature to make its move.

After what seemed like an eternity, I heard the sound of feet on the ground behind me, followed by heavy breathing and then a low guttural grunt up ahead. I was confused, disorientated. *Were there two attackers? Was I being outflanked?* I dropped to the ground, the knife held overhead in a reverse grip, ready to plunge the blade into the first thing that came within striking distance. But then, a light erupted from the tunnel and the slim silhouette of my beleaguered chaperone stepped out into the open.

"Sorry about that," Wayne cried, his hair unruly and his shirt pulled sideways across his body. "Took four of us to restrain the guy. I think he must have been draining a bottle of bourbon without any of us knowing. Anyway, he's been fired and the others have calmed down a little. It's amazing what the promise of a little bonus for their cooperation will do. You want to head back up?"

I wiped the sweat from my brow and stood, slipping the knife back into its sheath. My heart was still beating in my chest like a jackhammer on steroids.

"Yeah," I said, casting a sideways glance at the darkness as it moved like an organic form behind me. "I think I'm done here."

CHAPTER TEN

Hiding Out

Z ed sat crouched in the dumpster and picked at the
remains of a hamburger somebody had thrown on
top of him while he lay crouched among all the crap. He
was so hungry—starving hungry. Like those little kids in
Africa, hungry with the flies buzzing around their eyelids,
and their tiny little ribs all sticking out like drum sticks.
He needed to eat. He needed to eat, like, a lot. He was
famished. He could eat a 100 leftover burgers, possibly
even a thousand.

The vision of that undead ghost drifting over him like
the worst weed he had ever inhaled just wouldn't quit. It
was like a TV program on repeat, the pictures just playing

over and over in his head, again and again; repeat, rewind, *repeat.*

He used his fingernails to claw at his temples, as if there was some way he could reach into his brain, find the offending memory, and pluck it out like you might pluck out a stray hair or pop a zit. It was speaking to him, too. Some grainy, gargling voice. He couldn't make out what it wanted, but he knew it didn't want anything good. That much was obvious. Black, swirling spirits that emerged from the exploded wall of a long dead mine hardly ever did in his experience, although his experience was only really something he'd gleaned from the movies.

He swallowed the remainder of the half-chewed meat and peered through the gap between the dumpster and the heavy lid. The street was deserted, which was good. He didn't want to see anybody. He didn't want to speak to anybody. He'd seen the cop car outside his apartment, and he knew that wasn't a good sign. He'd heard the sirens blaring the night prior, and he'd guessed something bad had gone down in Lincoln Park. He wasn't an idiot, even though his father used to say otherwise. He had street smarts. He could sense when things weren't how they should be, and since he'd seen the Wendigo, nothing had been right.

He pushed his nose under his armpit and pulled it away sharply. He stunk. He stunk badly. He needed some soap, water, and a change of clothes, but more importantly, he needed to eat. He thought he had some chopped beef in the refrigerator and a couple of steaks in the freezer. The thought of those tasty, meaty morsels made his mouth water and his stomach hurt. He wasn't usually such a big eater, but these past couple of days—

He thought about the cop car some more, and then about his refrigerator. He thought about the Wendigo, and the vision swirling around in his brain. He thought about Caleb and how he'd screamed when he'd seen the ghost, and how the spirit had turned on him. He laughed as he recalled Caleb running like a scared little girl up the mineshaft while he'd lay there trembling and jittering. Caleb was a good friend, but he was the biggest scaredy-cat he had ever met. The guy couldn't even handle a tiny spider. *Jeez, Caleb was a douche.*

He looked through the tiny crack once more. As soon as the way ahead was clear, he pushed the lid open and hauled himself out, flicking cigarette butts and chocolate bar wrappers from his clothes. He'd slept in some shitty hotels before, but that dumpster took the biscuit. The cake, too.

The streets were quiet. They were always quiet in Devil's Ridge. He'd heard talk of people walking shoulder-to-shoulder down the streets of Manhattan, and wondered how anybody could stand to be so crammed into such a small space. He'd get claustrophobic. Damn, he'd get hungry. He thought of the skin-on-skin contact, and it made him kind of jittery. He could almost smell the flesh, taste the salty sweat, the iron in the meat. He slapped his own head and pushed such crazy notions away. *What the hell was he thinking?*

The Wendigo appeared in his mind's eye once more and he bent over double, waiting for the moment to pass. He thought he had some weed stashed under his mattress that he hoped would help with the flashbacks. Perhaps he had PTSD or something.

His apartment was three blocks away, so he quickened his pace. His stomach was aching with hunger, and his throat was dry and hoarse. He hoped that whatever had happened in the park had nothing to do with the Wendigo. He hoped that whatever it was had just gone back to its sleeping place in the mine. He didn't think he could cope knowing the Wendigo was out there, hunting for souls it could devour. Surely, it would come for him first. He had been the first one to set eyes on it, after all. Terror rose to the surface of his skin, and he felt its fiery heat dance in his blood.

He rounded the corner and spied the cop car. He could see the deputy leaning back in his chair. He was chewing gum. Zed could use a stick of gum too, only he would swallow it whole. He was so hungry.

He knew he would have to use his secret way in if he was going to get into his apartment unnoticed, but that was okay. He'd done it plenty of times before, especially when the landlord came collecting. He was practically an expert, like the Special Forces or something.

He ducked behind a hedge and made his move.

Zed swallowed the last of the raw steak, which still had a little bit of ice at its center. He didn't care. The taste of the meat, along with the dampness of the juice and blood that ran from his lips, was almost erotic to him. The chopped beef had been the perfect appetizer, but the two steaks had been the best main course ever. The only problem was, he was still hungry. *Shit, how could he still be hungry?* Also, what if he caught hepatitis or salmonella, or whatever else it was you got from eating undercooked meat. *Man, he*

could die right there in his room and nobody would even know. He couldn't think of anything more tragic than that.

He sat on his bed and laid back. The shades were partially open so he pulled them closed. He liked the darkness. It helped him forget about things, like seeing ghosts or having undesirable urges to eat human flesh.

Without realizing it, he drifted into semi-sleep. He dreamed of giant hamburgers, wolves roaming the streets, and the exposed throats of horny women. He could hear himself groaning, but it didn't wake him. In his sleep, he grabbed hold of a wandering goat and bit down on it with teeth that were as long as spears and as sharp as box knives. The goat was tasteless, but the meat satiated his appetite, but only for a moment. He was dismayed to find he was instantly hungry once more.

A cloud settled upon him as he lay gazing up at the blue sky. It was a gray cloud with a red center. It settled onto the Earth like a thick, dark fog. From within the mist, a man emerged. He was tall and lean, and covered with what looked like thick, squirming tree roots. They encircled his limbs and torso, but they moved with him, as if they were alive and a part of him. His head was merely a bare skull, with long, sharp antlers. His eyes were a gleaming red, and his teeth were long and hooked, like sabers.

The creature picked up the pace and started to run toward him, and Zed knew it was going to kill and probably eat him. He started to kick his legs and push himself backward across the grass, but the beast was too fast. And before he had a chance to react, it was on him, its claws tearing at him, its teeth ripping chunks from his flesh. The pain was unbearable.

He screamed.

Zed leapt from his bed and slumped into a ball in the corner of the room, sobbing. He needed to get whatever it was that had drifted into his subconscious and taken up a place in the farthest recesses of his brain out of him as fast as possible. He needed it gone. He couldn't bear it.

He glanced at the kitchen and thought of using a knife, but he knew that cutting it out wasn't an option. He needed an exorcist or a shaman—something. The only thing was, he didn't know any. But, he thought the sheriff might. Or the Indian. *Yeah, the Indian would know what to do.*

His stomach growled again. *Shit, how could he be hungry?* Maybe the Indian would have some food. Yeah, sure he would. *Indians eat all kinds of shit, don't they?*

There was a tap on the door and Zed glanced upward. *Who the hell could that be? Surely it could only be the deputy, but how would he know he was up here?* He hadn't seen him. No way had he seen him. Zed was good at getting into his apartment without being spotted. He'd made a habit of it, after all.

He slipped off his shoes and approached the door, his bare feet barely making a noise. He knew where all the squeaky joists were, and he avoided them like the plague. He raised his eye to the peephole and he let out a sigh. *Thank God. A friendly face.*

He reached for the chain and unlatched the door, opening it wide.

"Jesus, man," he said. "Where the hell have you been? I really need to talk to you."

CHAPTER ELEVEN

The Muddies

That night, I learned from Penny that the Devil's Ridge Police Department had made Zed Hardacre the prime suspect in the murder of Paul Chase. Something about that seemed off to me. Zed hadn't seemed like a murderer; he'd just seemed like a kid who was scared out of his mind, and based on my altercation in the darkness earlier that day, I could completely understand why he would feel that way. The only problem was, Zed hadn't been seen since his breakdown at the mine, and neither Boomer nor the sheriff had been able to reach him on the phone. It seemed like he'd just disappeared.

The other thing I learned from Penny—who really appeared to have her fingers in all the pies—was that the coroner had published his report. He concluded that the Chase kid had died from acute blood loss, caused by a severing of his carotid artery by a bite from a person or animal with extremely long incisors and an incredibly powerful jaw. That also didn't jive with Zed being the prime suspect in this case. From what I'd seen, he barely had a full set of teeth of his own, and his yellow and black molars were anything but sharp.

The whole thing didn't add up, and I became increasingly eager to speak with Sheriff Harris. Something was going on that I wasn't being kept apprised of, and I didn't like it. The only problem was, the Sheriff was out of town on an urgent personal matter, and my chances of getting anything useful out of his two deputies were close to zero.

That left me with one option that I didn't like: I needed to talk to Zed.

Zed lived in an apartment less than two miles away from the hotel, in an area of town that the locals called "The Muddies"; low cost, affordable properties that housed some of the less socially-attractive members of the Devil's Ridge population. It was a relatively warm evening, so I decided to walk. I hadn't been getting nearly enough exercise since I'd left the military, and the two-mile trek uphill felt like the ideal opportunity to make some of that right.

On the way there, I thought of Linda and the way I'd left things with her. It hadn't been one of my better moments—far from it, in fact. For some reason, this very attractive school teacher with a happy-go-lucky personality and brilliant blue eyes seemed to like me, and I knew that my rejection had embarrassed her. I wasn't happy about being the cause of that. Then, there was Penny's offer, which I'd decided to accept for all the reasons I mentioned earlier. Bad news seemed to follow me around like a storm cloud, and I didn't want Linda dragged into any of my shit. I needed to tell her about it, but I just didn't know how. I was acutely aware I would be giving her yet another rejection, and that could only further dent my chances of maintaining any sort of relationship with her—if there was still a relationship there to be had.

Plus, Penny had told me something about her. Something I didn't know what to make of.

"Ask her about her ex," she'd whispered after I'd told her about Linda's offer to let me stay with her. "Ask her where he is now."

"Her ex? She never mentioned anybody significant. He doesn't still live with her, does he?" I was a little offended that she thought I was the kind of guy who would pursue a woman who already had a live-in lover.

"No, nothing like that," she said, smirking. "But, just ask her about it. I'm sure she'll fill you in on all the details."

It had been a strange conversation and one that intrigued me, but I knew I needed to focus on what was going on up at the mine and what was causing these strange visions I was having. I didn't know if Zed had any answers, or if he was even responsible for the death of Paul Chase, but he and Nancy Ward were the only people still breathing who had seen this Wendigo, or whatever the hell it was. And by all accounts, Nancy was in no fit state to talk about what she saw.

By the time I reached Zed's apartment block—a concrete building surrounded by a weed-infested lawn that looked like it hadn't seen a lawnmower in the past decade—the sun was disappearing behind the horizon and the first silvery speckles of stars were beginning to show themselves from within the steadily darkening sky overhead. I spotted one of the sheriff's deputies hunkered down in his squad car at the end of the street, and I ducked behind a Dodge pickup before he had the chance to make me. I knew that me appearing at their main suspect's home would look more than a little suspicious, and I really didn't want to explain to Deputy Barns everything that had happened at the mine that day, or why I thought that he and his colleagues were completely wrong about Zed's involvement in Paul Chase's murder.

I glanced to my right and spotted the rusted metal fire escape, and I decided that sneaking in the backdoor was a much better option than getting spotted walking through the main entrance.

I looked up and counted the windows. I knew that Zed's apartment was on the fifth floor, number seven, meaning that, assuming the numbering went from left to right, that his window was the one in the middle. The lights were out, but that didn't mean that somebody wasn't home.

I reached up and pulled down the ladder. It let out a high pitched shriek as if it was startled, and I paused to see if anybody had heard me. Satisfied that my arrival had remained unnoticed, I started my ascent. I glanced back toward the parking lot, seeing that Deputy Barn's squad car was just visible around the corner of the building. I was relieved to see the police officer was fully-engaged in devouring a double cheeseburger, his head nodding along enthusiastically to some song that must have been playing through his AirPods. I continued upward until I reached the fifth floor, pulled open the fire escape door, and entered the building.

Inside, the corridor was dimly lit by fluorescent lighting overhead. The carpet was threadbare and the wallpaper hung from the walls. Dark patches of damp mottled the surface, and various items of trash were scattered across the floor: cigarette packets, empty cans of beer, condom wrappers, and discarded needles. I navigated my way around the debris and stopped in front of Zed's door. It appeared to be open and I approached it cautiously, craning my neck to peek through the gap in the door. The room appeared to be shrouded in darkness. I reached for my knife and tucked it in the back pocket of my jeans. I wanted it in easy reach if Zed was hiding himself away in there. I wasn't about to let him take a bite out of me.

"Zed?" I whispered as I pushed the door open. "Hey pal. Are you in there?"

There was no answer, but I was immediately hit with a dense, sickly odor that I recognized. *The scent of death.* Someone, or something, had died in Zed's apartment.

The living room was decorated with posters from various rap artists—Snoop Dogg, The Notorious B.I.G, and Lil Wayne—and the sofa was riddled with cigarette burns and empty papers. A carton of fries sat on the coffee table next to an open can of beer. If Zed had been here, he'd left in a hurry. The kitchen sink was piled high with dirty dinner plates and cups, and the water inside had turned a dirty brown, a thick layer of grease floating on the top like an oil spillage.

I heard a sound from behind the bedroom door, which caused my breath to catch in my throat.

"Zed!" I called out. "Are you in there?"

Again, there was no response. I reached for my knife, leaned forward, and held my ear to the door. I could definitely hear something moving around in there, as if someone was frantically collecting their things in readiness for a hasty escape.

"It's me, J.C. We met at the mine a few days ago. I was there when you had your little episode. Look, I'm not here to turn you in. I just want to talk."

The sound from within the room increased in volume and I backed away from the door. I knew there was every chance that whoever was in there was preparing to defend themselves to the death, so I decided to regain the element of surprise. I tilted my head, dipped my shoulder, and ran into the door at full speed, splintering the wood and sending shards of timber flying across the room.

The smell instantly increased in intensity and I held my hand to my nose to prevent myself from throwing up.

There on the bed, lying with his throat torn open and a dozen rats feasting on his decaying flesh, was the bloated, blackened corpse of Zed Hardacre.

"Jesus," I muttered under my breath. "What the hell is going on here?"

I left Zed's apartment block by the front door, half-expecting Deputy Barns to be waiting by the entrance, having belatedly realized that someone had managed to breach the impenetrable perimeter he'd set up around the building. Instead, his head was slumped sleepily against the side window of his vehicle, a thick smear of snot and saliva creating a trail where his face had gradually slipped further and further across its surface. When I tapped the glass, he leapt up as if he'd heard a gunshot.

"Mr. Carter!" he yelled as he lowered his window. "W-What are you doing out here?"

"Zed's been murdered," I said, the image of the oversized rats tearing chunks out of Zed's mottled cheeks still clearly depicted in my brain. "He's up there on his bed if you want to call the doctor."

"What? What do you mean?" He reached for his radio. "What the hell were you doing up there?"

"What the hell were you doing down here?" I sniped. "From the look of him, he's been home for a while, and he's been dead for most of that time, too."

"But, that's not possible. I've identified everyone going in and coming out of the building for the past three days. If Zed had gone home, I would have spotted him. Hell, I would've recognized him. We went to school together."

I pointed to the rear of the building. "How's your view of the fire escape?" I asked. "Because that's how I got in."

I turned and walked away as Deputy Barns radioed it in. I'd had enough of the Devil's Ridge PD's incompetence. My suspicions had been proven correct. Zed hadn't killed Paul Chase, but he had seen something in that mine—I was now more sure of that than ever. I was also sure that whatever he had seen, it had come for him, and it was thirsty for blood.

If I had any chance of getting my hands on that gold and paying off Hogan and his gang of cut-throat thugs, I had to put an end to the Wendigo. And I knew that there was only one person in town who could help me.

CHAPTER TWELVE

Cunning Wolf

That night, I dreamed of Linda. She was sitting by the lake and watching as a bald eagle glided across the surface of the water, eventually coming to land on the long branch of a narrowleaf cottonwood. She sat in the grass and gazed up at the bird. There were tears on her cheeks. It was then that I realized her clothes were sopping wet and her hair lay across her face in lank, wet strands. Her shoulders were slumped and her body was shuddering.

I went to her and put my arm around her shoulders. But when she turned to face me, it wasn't Linda's face at all, but the snarling, biting face of the Wendigo, its teeth snapping inches from my exposed throat. I turned to run, but the Wendigo clamped its jaws around my ankle and shook me like a rag doll. My foot was yanked free of my leg and tossed onto the grass like a discarded shoe.

I tried to drag myself away but my hands were cuffed in restraints made from pure gold. When I eventually managed to stand with my one good leg, I saw Bill. He was cradled in Penny's arms, his body a bloodied mess, his innards hanging from the jagged, scorched wound in his abdomen.

"Don't worry, my love," Penny said as she kissed his forehead. "He'll be coming home soon. So soon."

Bill turned toward me, and his eyes had been replaced with gold coins. When he opened his mouth to speak, black blood poured from him in sticky, thick torrents.

It was then that I cried out and threw back the sheets, my body covered in a slick sheen of sweat.

"Jesus," I said, my breath shallow and ragged. "I have to get out of this town."

It took three cups of coffee and a cold shower to bring me back to the land of the living. I decided that I needed to eat, and went downstairs in the hotel's restaurant to get some breakfast. Once more, the grumpy old lady—who I now knew to be a widow and devoted Elvis fan by the name of Sylvia—was on duty.

"I'll take an omelet," I said. "With peppers."

"Chef don't make them that way," she replied. "You want cheese, we got cheese. You want peppers, try Maud's across the street."

I smiled. I hadn't expected any less.

"Cheese it is," I said. "And tabasco if you have any."

"We don't," she said, and walked off.

My phone rang. It was an unknown number so I answered it with caution. As far as I knew, Hogan had no way of knowing that I had a new phone. "Hello? Who am I speaking to?"

"It's Deputy Barns, Mr. Carter. We need to speak to you down at the station, if that's fine with you."

"Well, I did have an appointment this morning. Can it wait until this afternoon?"

"I'm afraid it can't. It's about Mr. Hardacre. We need to take a statement from you."

I should have guessed as much. I had found the body after all. "Okay. Do I need a lawyer?"

"Not if you haven't done anything wrong."

There was something in the deputy's voice that made me suspect he wasn't sure either way.

"Okay. I'm just having breakfast. I can be with you in the next 30 minutes."

"That'll be just fine. See you then."

"Here's your omelet," Sylvia said. "And no calls while you're in the restaurant please. It's quite rude."

I ended the call, offered my apology, and glared at my coffee.

"You've gone and done it now," Bill said. "You've pissed her off and got yourself in a whole load of hot water with the police department."

"Hey," I replied. "I didn't do anything wrong. I just found the body. They could have done that if they'd been doing their jobs properly."

"Did you touch him?"

I nodded. I had. I'd wanted to get the rats off him, so I'd brushed them away with my forearm. "That doesn't mean anything. I was trying to be respectful to the deceased."

"And why were you there in the first place, Mr. Carter?"

"You know why I was there."

"I do, but they don't—and they'll be the ones asking the questions."

I took a mouthful of cheese and egg, and swallowed. It sank to the pit of my stomach like a lead weight. "They can't possibly think I had anything to do with this. What would I have to gain from killing Zed?"

Bill shrugged. "Beats me. But you were close to the scene of the crime when the Chase boy was killed. Is that coincidence or evidence?"

"Jesus, Bill. You really are something, you know? Linda will back up the fact that I was in the restaurant with her when he was attacked."

"Another person in the town who has a reason to dislike you."

"What?"

Bill sat back in his chair and folded his arms. "I'm just saying, you're not exactly making friends, are you?"

I hated to admit it, but he was right. *If I went to the station, what was I going to say? That I'd been attacked by the Wendigo at Kiowa Rock and wanted their prime suspect in the murder of Paul Chase to give my story some credibility?* It sounded pathetic, even to me. I needed to know what we were dealing with, and I needed to have some proof. I thought if I had those two things, I would be better equipped to talk to the police without looking like a lunatic—a lunatic who openly admitted to breaking into a murder victim's home.

"I need to talk to Little Bear," I said, throwing my fork onto the table and headed out.

"Are you going to pay for that?" Sylvia hollered.

"Add it to my tab!" I yelled back as I raced through the door.

I sat in Little Bear's trailer, Axle's huge head nestled in my lap.

"I did warn you," Little Bear said as he took a drag on his cigarette. "These things should be left to lay dormant. Now that it's awake, you can't just put it back in the box."

"I know," I replied. "But I need to know what it is we're dealing with."

"You've heard stories of the Wendigo, I presume."

I nodded. I had, but what I knew came from Wikipedia and chat rooms. I needed to hear it from someone who really knew the truth.

"Well," he began, leaning back in his chair and blowing smoke.

Legend has it that the Wendigo was created by my ancestors out of pure greed. The head of the tribe, a chief known as Cunning Wolf, had grown to become fearful that rival tribes would come to the camp in the dead of night to steal the many treasures that were stored in the caves."

Cunning Wolf consulted with a wise woman who lived in the forest surrounding the camp—a bruja that the other tribesmen called Whispering Wind. He told her about his fears, and offered to pay a handsome sum if she was able to cast a spell that would fend off his rivals. She considered this for many days, and after she had searched her many books, she called Cunning Wolf back into the forest and told him she might have the very solution he desired. However, her price was high. Whispering Wind demanded Cunning Wolf's soul in return for her help. Cunning Wolf was not happy about this at all, but he accepted her terms, planning instead to come back to the forest with an army once his little problem was resolved, and burn the bruja at the stake—thereby, releasing himself from her incantation.

Whispering Wind, delighted by the deal they had agreed upon and unaware of the Chief's devious plan, spoke of a spirit that lived in the forest called Chenoo. The spirit enjoyed watching the humans as they ate, drank, danced, and fornicated. He wanted to be able to enjoy these simple pleasures too, but his ghostly form meant that he was unable to. Whispering Wind said she had spent the past few days speaking with Chenoo, and they had devised a way for the spirit to possess a human body. This involved a sacrifice, the drinking of human blood, and the burning of a sacred charm.

Chief Cunning Wolf was overjoyed at the news and demanded that they cast the spell immediately. Whispering Wind asked the chief to remain patient for a day or two while she summoned the strength required to draw the spirit out from the afterlife and through the portal to the human world.

"We also need a host for Chenoo," she said. "You must find a willing subject." This did not concern the chief at all. He had a young son, Ahanu, who desperately wanted to gain his father's respect. He knew that Ahanu would do his bidding. "We also need a sacred charm," she added. "One that means more than life itself to you."

The chief gazed down at his chest, where the skull of a rattlesnake hung from a necklace made from cowhide. The snake had bitten his wife while she slept, killing her, and he had hunted it down over many days across the scorching desert, where he had eventually found its lair. He then killed the sleeping snake and tortured its children before eating them alive. "I have the very thing," he said, holding the snake's skull in his palm. "When the moment comes, I will throw it into the fire myself."

A week passed and, much to his disappointment, Chief Cunning Wolf hadn't heard from Whispering Wind. He became increasingly paranoid that his treasure would be stolen, and he took his frustrations out on other members of his tribe, killing one man for daring to look upon his gold. After a month passed, the chief decided that the bruja had deceived him, and he headed into the forest with three of his best soldiers to kill her. However, when he came upon her camp, he found Whispering Wind already dead, her body hanging from a tall pine, her eyes gouged out and her tongue ripped from her mouth. The chief became afraid for his life, and he sent his three soldiers into the woods to hunt down the killer.

That night, while the chief waited by the bruja's hanging corpse, a spirit appeared beneath the canopy of the tall pine.

"I am Chenoo," the spirit said. "And you are Chief Cunning Wolf?"

"I am," the chief replied, excited by the spirit's unexpected appearance. "This bruja promised that she would broker a deal between you and I, but as you can see, somebody has taken her life. Will you deal directly with me?"

The spirit thought about this for a moment, and then said, "Ordinarily, I do not make deals with humans who do not understand magic, but I would be willing to do so if you agree to offer me what you offered the bruja in exchange for her help."

The chief was taken aback by this. He had indeed offered his soul in exchange for Whispering Wind's assistance, but he had planned to kill her before his soul could be taken. "But the bruja told me that your wish was to possess a human body so that you could enjoy the pleasures of our world. I offered my son, Ahanu. He is a strong warrior and I assure you that he would be an excellent host, allowing you to partake in all the things that you desire."

The spirit looked around them. "And where is this Ahanu?"

"Well, he is back at the camp," the chief replied. "I had not expected to meet with you today."

"And how long would it take to travel to your camp, fetch Ahanu, and return him to me?" the spirit asked.

"One day and one night," the chief replied.

The spirit shook its head. "Then, we have no deal. The spell must be cast immediately or not at all. I am not in the mood to wait any longer."

As the spirit's translucent form started to fade, the chief began to imagine his gold being stolen by marauders, and fearful for what might be happening while he stood there bartering, he made a snap decision. "Okay," he said. "We have a deal."

Instantly, there was a loud clap of thunder as loud as the sound of the earth being ripped in two. A bolt of lightning the length of Colorado leapt across the sky, striking the base of the tree beside them and setting both the trunk and the bruja's body ablaze.

"Very well," the spirit replied. "And, do you have the sacred charm??

The chief, feeling the fierce heat of the raging inferno on his skin, ripped the snake's skull from the strap that was tied around his neck and held it out to Chenoo. "I do," he confirmed.

"Then throw it into the fire," Chenoo commanded.

The chief complied, tossing the skull into the roaring flames, and watched in horror as the skull turned black and the bruja's flesh began to peel from her bones. Suddenly, he recalled what Whispering Wind had said to him. "I thought you also needed the blood of a human," he said. "But I did not bring any with me."

Chenoo grinned and turned toward the darkness of the forest. Immediately, the severed heads of the chief's three best soldiers rolled toward them, bloody entrails hanging from their exposed necks.

"Is this the blood of which you speak?" Chenoo asked, laughing.

"You killed my men?!" the chief roared, a rage like no other burning in his belly. "That was not part of the deal!"

He drew his blade and lunged at the spirit, but realized, too late, that Chenoo did not occupy an earthly form like the foes he had battled in the human world. He passed straight through him as one might pass through smoke. As he fell for-

ward, he lost his footing and stumbled to the ground. Chenoo immediately wrapped himself around the fallen chief and commanded Cunning Wolf to drag the knife across his own throat. The chief fought with all his might but he was unable to disobey the spirit, and as the knife tore skin and sinew from his exposed neck, he watched in horror as Chenoo dipped his head, opened his mouth, and drank the blood that was spraying in a thick jet from his open artery.

"You will be a good host," Chenoo said as the blood created a large pool at Chief Cunning Wolf's feet. "For I now own your soul, and this blood that I drink is the life essence that will allow me to walk among others like you. Your blood will be the first of many gallons I plan to consume, for mankind has become full of greed and lust, and is blind to the spirit world and the magic that exists on Earth. The time has come for me to leave this ethereal plane and walk among you."

"And with that, Chenoo's spirit was absorbed into Chief Cunning Wolf's stricken body and the deal was finalized. As legend has it, to this day, Chenoo still dwells in these hills and protects the chief's gold as promised. But in order to do so, he hops among human hosts so that he may feed," Little Bear concluded as he took one more drag from the burning stick of tobacco.

As he stubbed out his cigarette, Axle jumped up from my lap as if he'd heard somebody approaching, and he headed out the door. I was still taking in everything Little Bear had said. I thought of Zed's throat torn open on the bed, and of Nancy's story about the strange man attacking her boyfriend.

"So, I'm guessing the Wendigo is this spirit, Chenoo, inhabiting the chief's body?" I asked.

"Something like that," Little Bear replied. "I'm not sure I believe everything that's been passed down through the years, but one thing I do know is that the Wendigo stories have persisted since way before you white folks landed on these shores. The miners who used to work up there at Kiowa Rock, they spoke often of seeing dark spirits lurking in the tunnels, and of a sense of dread that fell upon them as they dug deeper into the soil."

I stood and gestured toward the door. I needed something I could take back to the sheriff and his deputies. I knew that if I went back to town with nothing more than a Native American legend, I would end up behind bars before sundown. With Zed out of the picture, I suspected I was fast becoming a suspect.

"I need to see this thing for myself," I said. "Will you show me?"

Little Bear let out a long sigh and crossed his arms behind his head. "I can take you up there to where the legend says this whole thing took place, but it's no more than a bunch of rocks and a few scorched trees these days."

I nodded eagerly. "Okay. Well, it's a start."

"There's really nothing there."

"Come on, man. Humor me."

"You really wanna go?"

"I do."

He stood, his enormous frame towering over me, and shook his head. "Alright. But I pray to god that the Wendigo doesn't choose today to show himself."

I smirked and stepped outside into the hot midday air. "Well, it just so happens that in my current position, I'm wishing for the exact opposite."

We drove to a spot three miles out of town and parked by a rolling stream. Little Bear let Axle drink from the cool, clear water while he loaded his rifle.

"You expecting company?" I asked, checking that I'd brought my trusty knife.

"It's a four-mile trek up the mountain," he said. "We're apt to see a bear or two on the way. Maybe wolves, too."

"It's the middle of the day."

"Bears don't wait to be invited," he said. "And I don't take no chances."

Part of me wondered whether the whole bear story was to throw me off the scent, and what Little Bear was actually afraid of was the Wendigo in human form. I wasn't too proud to admit, I was a little afraid of that possibility, too.

We walked for an hour or more along an uneven path that snaked through the thick, densely-populated forest. The stream disappeared off to our left, much to Axle's annoyance, and the trees gradually thinned out, revealing a rocky incline that rose steeply ahead of us. The track soon disappeared, too, leaving us at the mercy of Little Bear's navigational skills. I decided to put my full trust in him, even though I knew my Native American friend was still pissed at me for convincing the whole town to once more mine gold from Kiowa Rock.

We walked in silence for a little while longer before I asked Little Bear the question that had been bugging me since we first met. "Why Little Bear?" I said. "Why were you given that name? You're not exactly small."

Much to my surprise, he threw back his head and laughed.

"What is it?" I asked. "Did I say something funny?"

He wiped tears from his cheeks and looked down at me, his eyes still glistening. "Oh, no. It's nothing. It's just that you're the first white man brave enough to ask me that question."

I held out my hands. "Hey, I don't mean any offense by it."

"Don't worry. None taken." He rolled himself another cigarette and grinned. "I was born in these hills. My mother and father lived a simple life out here. We didn't have any electricity, no TV, no internet. We lived together, as a community. My parents, my brothers and sisters, my aunts and uncles, my cousins. We looked out for each other, you know?"

I nodded. I knew exactly what he meant. I'd found that sense of family in the military. My brother and I often spoke about being a part of something bigger than the two of us, which was exactly what we'd needed after our parents had passed. The members of our platoon were like kin to us, which is why everything had been so painful after what had happened. I hadn't just lost one brother, but a whole brotherhood.

"Anyway, I was born eight weeks early. My aunt delivered me and, as she tells it, I was barely big enough to hold in her two palms. Apparently, I was also covered in thick, dark hair. When it came to the naming ceremony, which was attended by everyone from the village, a black bear and her cub appeared in the middle of our land and approached my crib. Rather than chase the bears away, everybody watched as the mother bear looked down at me, then looked from me to her cub, and then she picked her child up in her mouth so that he could see me. A bond was forged that very day. That young bear grew up around the camp and we became close friends. I called him Brother Bear. Until a few years ago, when he sadly passed, he would often come and visit me at the trailer."

I was stunned by his story. "Jesus, that's some tale. It sounds pretty out there."

"Yeah," Little Bear agreed, his expression solemn. "I know." Suddenly he slapped me hard on the shoulder and walked off. "That's because it is. I made it all up. You white people always think there's some special reason for the names we're given. Well, there isn't. It was probably the first thing that came into my father's head. I have no idea."

I decided that probing into the big guy's past was something I would save for another time.

After a heavy trek over rough terrain and up an incline that threatened to burst my lungs, we emerged on a plateau that looked out over a huge expanse of untamed land. It was a mountain pass that wound through the Rockies like a giant python. Ahead of us, the mountain fell away steeply, the ground over 3,000-feet below us.

"What a view," I said. "Is this the place?"

Little Bear shook his head and pointed at a spot higher up in the distance. "This part of the journey is dangerous. You need to stay close." He stooped down and tied Axle to a heavy boulder. "You stay here," he said to his canine friend. "The path isn't exactly dog-friendly."

We clambered over a rock face that seemed to rise almost straight up from the plateau. I knew the basics of free climbing, and thought I held my own, but Little Bear was something else entirely. Despite his size, he leapt from rock to rock like a teenager, his huge hands finding the unlikeliest of crevices to jam his cigar-like fingers and the tiniest of ledges to slide his oversized feet. I found myself struggling to keep up, but I did my best.

Beneath us, the plateau seemed tiny, and beyond that, the ground looked a million miles away. The wind up there was strong, and Little Bear's long, dark hair swirled around his head like the mane of a thoroughbred. I struggled to catch my breath as the wind pounded us, and I felt the muscles in my biceps, chest, and calves begin to throb as the climb became more and more treacherous. It seemed the peak that lay above us was moving further and further away with every foot we climbed and every rock we traversed.

With the wind in my ears, I thought I heard the faint strain of somebody calling my name. The sound was faint, barely a whisper, but it sounded like my mother's voice calling me back inside for dinner. I hadn't heard that sound in such a long time that every word struck a painful blow to my gut, as if I'd just been punched by a prizefighter.

"You hear that?" I yelled to Little Bear.

"Hear what?"

"I don't know. A voice, somebody calling us."

"Ignore it," he hollered back. "It's the spirits. They're messing with you."

As we continued, the voice faded away. But I was left haunted by the sound of my mother, the parent I hadn't seen in over 15 years. Even back then, she had been a shell of her former self, the cancer eating away at her like some murderous creature, hellbent on causing as much pain and destruction as possible.

"We're here," Little Bear cried. "Come on. Get a move on, won't you. I thought you were a soldier."

"Used to be," I said, hauling myself up onto the summit. "But that was a long time ago." I looked past the big guy's shoulders and took in my surroundings. "Holy shit!"

Little Bear had brought me to what looked like an ancient settlement made from limestone blocks. So high up in the hills, this tribe had clearly foregone more temporary dwellings to make permanent stone structures. I could make out the remains of a stone wall, several small buildings that were constructed in a wide circle, surrounding a much larger, central structure. Nothing remained of the roofs of the buildings, which I guessed had been made from branches and foliage from the forest floor, but the walls and doorways were clearly evident.

"Cunning Wolf's tribe?" I asked.

Little Bear nodded before leading me deeper into the compound. We passed what would have been a cooking area, the ground excavated to accommodate a fire above which meat could be cooked and vegetables could be prepared. A ditch was dug further along, which I suspected was some form of bathing area, and at each of the four corners of the village were stone pillars, which I assumed had been used as lookout posts.

We entered the large structure at the center, which led to a spacious room that I supposed had been used as a banquet hall. I pictured Chief Cunning Wolf seated at the head of the table and commanding his subjects. The whole thing seemed surreal.

"We'll stay here tonight," Little Bear said, gazing up at the sky. "A storm's rolling in."

"What?" I replied. I hadn't planned on camping out. "What about Axle?" I pictured the poor dog on the plateau below, tied to the rock.

"He'll be fine. It's just a little wind—he's slept through worse—but it's too risky for us to climb back the way we came with the gales coming in from the northeast like that." Little Bear sat on one of the low walls and took out his pipe. "You wanted proof of what happened. Here's your proof."

I looked around me at the well constructed stone dwelling. It was like something from a movie, but it wasn't the kind of proof I was looking for. Little Bear must have seen the uncertainty in my eyes.

"Sit back and relax. All we gotta do is wait it out."

Overhead, the sky had turned black and the clouds had built into tall pillars of swirling gray cotton. The wind screamed like a banshee between the remains of the building, as if the spirits themselves were running from door to door, looking for the treasure that Chief Cunning Wolf had left behind.

Little Bear stuffed his pipe full of dried leaves and lit a match. "This will help," he said, sucking on the pipe and blowing out a thick plume of yellow smoke. "Here." He passed it to me.

"What is it?"

"A little herbal remedy, is all. Take a draw on it and maybe you'll find what you're looking for up here after all."

I didn't know whether to trust the big guy or not, but he'd brought me this far. I took the pipe from his hand, the scent of opium heavy in the air. I'd smoked quite a bit of weed when I was a kid, much to my brother's annoyance, but I'd never partaken in anything stronger. I preferred alcohol, even though I could barely control my consumption of the stuff.

"Is this going to spin me out?" I asked.

"It'll only do what you let it," Little Bear replied, leaning with his back against the wall.

I placed the end of the pipe to my lips, took a moment to steady myself, and inhaled deeply. The acrid smoke hit my throat almost immediately, the bitter taste burning all the way down. I could feel it swirling around in my stomach like a fiery worm, its tendrils snaking through my veins and reaching out the very tips of my nerve endings. When I let it out, it was as if my spirit was leaving my body.

"Woah," I said, and closed my eyes. "That stuff is weird."

"It will open your mind, my friend. Just give it some time."

I passed the pipe back so that Little Bear could take another hit. He looked like a sleeping dragon sitting beside me, his nostrils like caves to his soul, his eyes like giant globes of black ash. He breathed in the opium as if he was sucking on oxygen, his whole body expanding to take in

the mighty volume of poppy scent into his lungs. When
he exhaled, it was as if his whole body was on fire, and the
smoke billowed from his mouth, nose, ears, and eyes.

"Try some more," he said, passing the pipe back to me.
"The more you take, the better you will feel."

I gripped the pipe tightly, my knuckles white, and
took another lungful of the pungent smoke. The world
swirled into a chaotic storm of colors and sensations before plunging me into a suffocating darkness. When my
vision cleared, Bill was standing—or rather hanging—before me. His guts were spilling out like grotesque tendrils,
his mouth gaping in a silent scream as he coughed and
gagged, droplets of dark blood splattering all over the floor
and onto my clothes and face.

"Bill! Jesus, what is going on with you?" My voice was
trembling, my throat ragged.

He tried to speak but no sound came out. Black blood
poured from his lips and nostrils like thick syrup. All he
could do was extend a blood-soaked finger to a spot behind me, his arm shaking with the momentous effort. My
stomach churned with a sickening dread as I twisted my
neck to see what he was pointing at. There, emerging from
the darkness like a blackened monstrosity, was a thing with
teeth that oozed festering flesh, eyes that were as black as
coal, and claws like serrated blades. Its hair was tied back

in long braids, and he wore a headdress of charred feathers and scorched beads.

"Chief Cunning Wolf?" I cried, but the words barely came out.

I turned but Little Bear was no longer there. In his place was a dark vacuum, as if the Earth had been sucked into a giant black hole, within which we were now spinning and swirling like tiny flies. As I watched, the thing before me twisted and convulsed as its head grew in length so that it was almost equine in nature. Its eyes were dark voids in a cracked, gray skull. Long antlers sprouted from its scalp, twisting and bending at obtuse angles until they jutted out like long, reaching limbs. Roots sprouted from its angular torso, winding themselves around its body like ivy, its arms encased in dark bracken and thorny shoots. Its breath smelled like the rotting corpses of a thousand lost souls and its voice came from the very pit of the Earth, as if the soil beneath our feet had been cleaved in two and molten rock was now spewing from a mighty ravine, encasing us in its basalt crust for all eternity.

"You have no business here," it snarled, its finger tracing a long line down my trembling cheek. "You have no business meddling in what you do not understand."

I spun back toward Bill, praying he was still there, senselessly hoping he could offer some form of salvation, some way out. But he was gone. The blackness had consumed us all.

I whirled back toward what I now knew to be the evil spirit—the Wendigo—and this time, its face was so close that its fetid breath enveloped me like a toxic stench. Before I could scream, it seized my throat in a grip so powerful I could feel the vertebrates crumble in my neck. It lifted me off the ground as easily as a ragdoll.

My vision narrowed to pinpricks as I clawed at its grotesque skull. Its antlers pierced my cheeks and eyes, and I felt its claws penetrate my skin, separating my flesh from the bone. I knew that whatever I had confronted, I had lost. *This was it. Everything had been for nothing. My parents' deaths, everything that had happened in Iraq, my brother's murder, the horrendous acts I committed for Hogan, my growing affection for Linda. Nothing. I was nothing.*

Just as the edges of my consciousness faded to nothingness, as if someone had simply flipped off my power switch, I was suddenly slammed back into reality. I came to under a dark swirling sky, the air around me thick with the scent of opium and sweat. I rose to my elbows and looked up. There was a dark shadowy creature looming before me. It stooped down and slapped my face.

"Are you awake?" the shadow said. "J.C., are you there?"

I realized it was Little Bear standing in front of me.

"Yeah, yeah." I was trying to come to terms with what was going on. *I wasn't dead. The Wendigo hadn't attacked me. I wasn't covered in Bill's undead blood.* "What's going on?" I asked, trying to shake off the last remnants of the hallucination.

"Someone's here," Little Bear whispered. "Something followed us."

I swiftly rose to my knees, my head still swimming. I reached for my knife but Little Bear raised a finger to his lips and gestured toward the room's tiny annex. I followed him as he hunkered in the darkness behind a wall. I crouched beside him, watching as the sky overhead continued to swirl in an ever increasing cyclone, and what little light penetrated the thick blanket of cloud above us cast long, snaking shadows across the ancient stone.

After a moment, a figure emerged in the doorway. It was thin and ragged, like it had been out in the wilderness for too long. It moved with a fast, jerky motion, as if it was blessed with too much pent up energy. A hand quickly reached in, gripping the wall and feeling for purchase, and then a leg stretched across the dust-covered floor like a thick tentacle. It leaned forward, revealing a blond head of hair and a thin face with narrow lips. Its pearly white eyes opened and closed rapidly, and it glanced around the room, as if searching for something it had lost.

I recognized the face. It was Zed's friend, Caleb. The last time I had seen him, he was emerging from an underground tunnel while Zed lay on the ground, screaming about being visited by the Wendigo.

I was about to step out from our hiding place to ask him what the hell he was doing all the way up here, when I saw the slick, glint of blood on his lips, and the dark crust under his fingernails. He turned his head in our direction, as if he sensed our presence, and I instantly felt a chill race through me, as if I had just swallowed a thousand ice cubes. I could see his pupils were narrow slits, like those of a cat, and his tongue flitted across his lips like that of a serpent. A low mewl emanated from his throat and he sniffed at the air, stooping down to collect Little Bear's pipe. He raised it to his nose and sniffed furiously at it before tossing it against the wall.

I glanced at Little Bear, who was looking increasingly anxious. His hands moved toward his rifle which lay between us. I looked down at it and wondered how this was going to unfold. As far as we knew, Caleb wasn't guilty of anything, and we weren't in any danger. However, something about the way he looked, along with the way he was acting, made me think that something evil was at play here.

Had Caleb had anything to do with Paul Chase's murder? Did he know anything about what had happened to his friend Zed? Where had he been since the incident at the mine? And what was he doing miles away from home in the mountains, coincidentally at the exact place Little Bear had brought me to find proof about the existence of the Wendigo?

This time, I grabbed my knife and gripped the handle tightly. If Caleb was coming for us, I planned to be armed. Little Bear raised the rifle and pressed the stock into his shoulder. He quietly pulled back the bolt and rested the barrel against the wall, aiming it at Caleb's skull.

Caleb dropped to all fours and raced around the room, inhaling the scent in every corner, licking the ground at his feet. He was acting like a feral dog, as if he had lost all his senses. In an instant, he was crouched by the annex door and peering into the gloom as if he could see Little Bear and I hiding in there like naughty school kids. He seemed to scan the room, his eyes narrowing, his tongue once more licking at the air. He gnashed his teeth together, which appeared far longer and sharper than ordinary human teeth, and I thought I saw the hint of flesh hanging from them.

He grunted and scratched frantically at the earth, and for a moment I thought he was going to launch himself at us, snarling and gnashing like a wolf, clawing and biting as he tried to tear out our throats. I gripped the knife and clenched my teeth preparing for the inevitable, but in an instant, he turned and ran, disappearing into the swirling darkness of the night.

We stayed silent and motionless for a few minutes, listening for his return; but when it became obvious he wasn't coming back, I sat back on my haunches and let out a long breath. I could still feel my heart pounding in my chest and my senses remained tuned on high alert. Beside me, Little Bear lay the rifle on the ground and grunted. He walked out into the main hall and stooped, picking up a small, rectangular piece of plastic that appeared to be covered in blood and grime. He held it out to me and I waited for my eyes to adjust before reading the embossed inscription. I gasped. It was a Wells Fargo bank card, made out in the name of one Z. Hardacre.

"Well," Little Bear said, his lips curling at the corners. "Is this proof enough for you?"

CHAPTER THIRTEEN

An Undesirable Arraignment

I headed back to town, buoyed by our dramatic find, but also hesitant about how I would present my case to the sheriff's department. I went back to my room at the Regal, avoiding Penny's gaze as I raced hurriedly through the foyer. I took a long, hot shower, the heat turned up until it was on the verge of becoming unbearable. I needed to wash off the stench of that ancient citadel and my burgeoning fear.

Something had happened to Caleb, I was sure of that. He wasn't the person he had been before his visit to the mine. Friends spoke of him as being a quiet, humble person who struggled to make eye contact. This could only mean that something had turned him into the snarling, spitting creature we'd seen in the mountains; the creature that I was now convinced had killed both Zed and Paul Chase.

I dressed, left the hotel, and crossed the street, the bank card held in a clear baggie I was clutching tightly in my hands. I knew that Deputy Barns was going to be pissed about me bailing on him the day prior, but I felt sure I had all the ammunition I needed to clear my name and point the police in the right direction.

"Well, look who it is!" Deputy Mckinley yelled as I opened the door. He was an older man with a pencil thin mustache and a deep mistrust for, what he called, outsiders. "We've been looking for you, Carter. Hell, we've been out scouring the streets all night. I didn't get to spend any time with my kids because of you."

Deputy Barns emerged from the interview room to my right, holding a set of cuffs. "Hell, Carter. You sure do make things hard for yourself."

I turned around and held my hands together while the deputy cuffed me. I'd come prepared for this.

"I get it," I said. "I know you have to do this. But do yourselves a favor and take a look at the contents of the bag in my hands, won't you?"

Deputy Mckinley came around the counter, bent down, and gave the baggie a look of sheer contempt. He avoided touching it. I could almost hear the gears in his head turning. "Is that...is that what I think it is?"

"Well, that depends on what you think it is," I replied, before shooting him a glance over my shoulder. "But, I suggest you get the good doctor to run some DNA tests on it, pronto."

He glanced over at Deputy Barns and they shared a glance that I didn't like the look of. I realized, with some anxiety, that they thought I'd murdered Zed and stolen his bank card, eventually realizing how it would look before bringing it in.

"Oh, wait a minute—" I began to say, but before I could utter another word I was being thrown across the room and pinned to the floor. Deputy Barns ran his hands roughly down the length of my body where he recovered my knife, pulling air through his teeth before dropping it into an evidence bag. He practically screamed my Miranda Rights in my face before picking me up and shoving me unceremoniously into a holding cell. As the metal door slammed, I heard a loud screech as the deadbolt slid home.

The feeding hatch opened and the two deputies stood there, glaring at me with trepidation as if they were looking at some crazed madman.

"Oh, you done it now, boy," Deputy Mckinley snarled. "You're in a whole world of trouble, son."

"Okay, Jason," Sheriff Harris said, his voice calm and quiet. We were sitting alone in the interview room. My hands were chained to the desk and I sat in a flat chair that was about as comfortable as sitting on cold steel. "This is how it's gonna go. I'm going to ask you some questions and you're going to answer them as honestly as you can. If you want a lawyer, that's perfectly fine by me, but bear in mind that most people in this town knew and loved Paul Chase. So, basically, finding representation that doesn't want your murdering ass hung up in the town square and flogged until your skin is hanging off your bones like strips of raw chicken is about as unlikely as finding a Republican at Joe Biden's birthday party. In any case, all you gotta do is play nice, tell us the truth, and hopefully we can get to the bottom of this awful mess as quickly as possible."

"I didn't do it, Elijah," I said, looking the sheriff squarely in the eyes. "But I know who did."

"Well, now see there's a thing, right there," he replied, chewing on a toothpick. "You can't be calling me by my first name. You gotta call me Sheriff. Be respectful, goddammit."

I grunted and folded my arms like a petulant child. I didn't care. I was pissed. "Sorry, I meant Sheriff Harris." I was hot and frustrated, and I was using all my remaining energy to keep my temper in check. I felt like the whole field trip with Little Bear had been a complete waste of time. These people already had their minds made up about who killed those two men, and as the "out of towner," I was squarely in their sights.

"And you gotta lose the attitude, too. You're not the only one who's having a bad time of it, you know?"

I didn't know where the sheriff had been for the past couple of days, but there were dark patches beneath his eyes and he looked like he hadn't slept at all. "Okay, okay. I get it."

"Alright, that's good. Now, I'm going to call Deputy Barns in, and we're going to record this thing. If you get outta hand at any point, we're gonna stop and start all over again. You get it?"

I nodded. I got it, but that didn't mean I had to like it. I leaned back in my chair and exhaled slowly. "I've got nothing to hide."

The interview lasted for three excruciatingly painful hours. The heat in the room was almost unbearable, and the repeated tedious questions being thrown at me by the sheriff and his goon felt like blunt daggers being driven into my eyeballs over and over again. I was being prodded and pushed. I knew the drill and I knew this kind of interrogation was by the book, but it didn't make it any less painful. It also didn't prevent me from wanting to break free from the desk, reach across the table, and plunge my thumbs into the eye sockets of the stupid, incompetent deputy sitting there with a look of smug, dumbass satisfaction on his face.

When it was over, the sheriff spoke to me alone in my cell. "Look, I have no choice but to charge you. Of course, we'll get the DNA checked out on the bank card, but it could take a few days. We only have one qualified doctor in town and, of course, he only has limited access to the labs upstate. But we'll also go check in on Caleb, find out where he's been. However, I gotta say, right now, all the evidence is pointing in your direction. You were in the vicinity when both crimes were committed, you were the one who found Zed dead in his apartment, and now you have Zed's bloodied bank card in your possession."

I knew it would be fruitless to point out that I had led the police to Zed's whereabouts when they'd drawn a blank, and had brought the bank card in voluntarily. I also had an alibi for when Paul Chase had been murdered, although they appeared to be suggesting that there was a window of opportunity between when I'd said I'd entered the restaurant and when I'd actually met with Linda.

That was clearly ridiculous, because I would have had to have been the world's fastest distance runner to get from the restaurant to the park, kill Paul Chase, and get back before Linda noticed me sitting there alone. I'd been over and over all of those points in the interview room to no avail. As I said, they'd already made up their minds.

"You'll be arraigned in the morning. I've arranged for you to have counsel. It's a guy I know who works for the state. Name's Gordon Thatcher. He's a good man; a little disorganized, but he'll do right by you, I'm sure of it. That is, unless you have somebody else in mind, of course." I shook my head. I could barely afford to feed myself, let alone pay for an expensive defense attorney. "Look, J.C.,

I don't know what to make of this. You seem like a decent guy, but all the evidence adds up. I hope I'm wrong, I really do."

He headed out and left me alone in my metal-encased coffin. I wished to god I'd never listened to my brother and headed down to Colorado. I'd been faced with one disaster after another since I'd set foot in this town. Compared to what was happening to me in Devil's Ridge, being beaten to a pulp by Hogan and his enforcers seemed like a picnic in the park.

"What are you going to do now?" Bill asked.

I held my head in my hands and groaned. I had no idea.

"Looks like they're out to get you," he said. "Seems pretty unfair to me."

"You think?"

"Gonna lock you up for a long time, I reckon."

"Fuck you, Bill."

I sat there in silence, pondering my chances of walking away a free man. I thought they were slim, unless something came back on the bank card quickly. I'd gambled on Caleb's fingerprints being all over that little morsel of evidence, but I'd grossly underestimated how slowly things turned down there in the boonies, and how badly the sheriff's department wanted me to be guilty.

"Hey, you don't think they're setting you up so that they can keep all the gold for themselves, do you?" Bill asked, suddenly standing and pacing the room. I hadn't thought of that possibility, but now it seemed entirely plausible.

"You think they might be?"

Bill nodded, his expression grave. "Yeah, I think they might."

"Shit," I said, "I didn't even think the gold would mean that much to them."

"Come on now, J.C. Have you seen this town? It needs every cent it can get."

"But, why not just take it? We don't have a contract. I couldn't prove that we agreed on a split over a handshake."

"And risk a lawsuit?" Bill cried. "They need that gold now. They don't want to wait for years of legal proceedings to conclude before they can get their hands on the stuff. Did you see the mayor when we were up at the mine? Did you see the look on his face? He's a guy that's used to getting what he wants whenever he wants it, and what he wants is for you and Little Bear to be out of the picture while he pockets the loot."

It was all beginning to make sense now. Sure, I'd found the gold which, if the townsfolk had been less hung up about superstitious mumbo jumbo, they would have surely found for themselves a lot sooner. But, me being in the picture meant a complication that the town couldn't afford.

The murders of Zed and Paul Chase had created an opportunity for the town council, and one which they couldn't pass up—frame me for the murders and get me out of the way before any of the gold was successfully recovered, and I'd willingly obliged by sticking my nose where it didn't belong. Once again, I'd made a series of dumb decisions, ensuring I snatched defeat from the jaws of victory, just when things were starting to look a little less depressing.

"We need a plan," I said as the realization set in.

"Brother, you need a miracle."

The arraignment took place at noon. The courthouse was a small building three blocks down from the police station. We left the cells and walked along Governor's Boulevard while the whole town looked on, or at least it seemed like it. My hands were cuffed behind my back. The deputies kept pace beside me and the sheriff strode purposefully ahead of us. I couldn't help but think the whole thing was being put on as some kind of show, but I held my head high as we walked. I wasn't about to be bullied into submission. I needed everybody to see that I had nothing to be ashamed of.

My counsel was waiting for me as I arrived.

"Benjamin Hardy," he said as he shook my hand. He was a short man with a stout face, but he had the air of someone who didn't take any nonsense.

"Oh, I thought I was being represented by a guy called Thatcher."

"Change of plan," he replied. "Don't worry. We have this all under control."

The courtroom was packed with onlookers. To my right, I spied Penny. She was wearing a tailored suit, her hair elegantly curled, and her lipstick just so. She winked at me. I looked for Linda but I couldn't see her. Part of me hoped she would never learn of my arrest. I didn't want any of this to come back on her.

Judge Barbara Dexter was an older lady with short hair in tight ringlets and thick glasses. She spoke with a Bostonian accent and had fingers that looked like they'd held about a million cigarettes. When she entered, everybody stood.

"Welcome," she said, addressing the crowd. "I note this is a very full room for what will be a very short arraignment hearing. I do hope that everybody in here knows how to behave themselves in my courtroom." There was a murmur of agreement and then a hushed silence. "Mr, Jason Carter of Chicago, Illinois. Well, well, well. You're a long way from home, aren't you, sir?"

I nodded. That had never felt more true than right at that very moment.

"You're here before me on two charges of first-degree murder. Namely, that of Mr. Zedekiah Hardacre on May 22nd, 2023, and that of Mr. Paul Chase on May 24th, 2023."

"Hope you rot in hell!" a gruff sounding man yelled angrily before a commotion erupted in the stalls.

"Silence!" Judge Dexter hollered. "I will have order in my courtroom or you will all be removed! Do you understand me?" The cacophony of raised voices died down to a low murmur. "Might I remind you all that Mr. Carter here has not been found guilty of committing an offense. This is the start of a process, not the conclusion." There was another low murmur from the amassed crowd, before things returned to a modicum of calm. "Now, Mr. Carter, how do you plead?"

I once more held my head high. I glanced at Penny, who I guessed had had something to do with my change of attorney, and spoke. "Not guilty, Your Honor."

Once again the room erupted in a crescendo of animated noise.

"Quiet!" Judge Dexter yelled. "Quiet or I will have all of you ejected. This is a courtroom, for heaven's sake!" The noise died down, but it took a little longer for silence to resume. "Very well," she continued. "While we await a trial date, I've decided to allow bail at the very persistent and most convincing request of Counselor Hardy—"

Now, the noise in the courtroom became almost deafening, and an overweight looking security guard and the sheriff's two deputies were forced to intervene in what looked like a scuffle at the back. When I glanced at Penny, she shot me a smug, knowing look.

"But—" the prosecuting attorney cried out. "Your Honor, this man stands accused of the vicious and callous slayings of two respected members of our society. There is no guessing what he might do if he's allowed to roam our streets once more."

"I am the presiding judge, Mister Underwood, am I not?" the judge yelled. She had to raise her voice to be heard over the ruckus that was threatening to descend into a full blown riot.

"Yes, Your Honor."

"Then, what I say goes. The bail is set at $50,000. These proceedings are now closed."

I was pushed urgently through the crowd, the two deputies shoving people away and hollering instructions as we made our way to the squad car. Sheriff Harris had deemed it too dangerous to walk back the way we had arrived, and so they drove me the short distance before hastily pulling me into the station house. I felt completely deflated, like an aging birthday balloon. I didn't have $50,000—not even close—so the setting of bail was a moot point at best. The judge may as well have refused it and saved herself a whole load of abuse. I couldn't complain. Penny had tried, and whatever strings her attorney friend had pulled, they had worked. They just hadn't worked for me.

When I stood in my cell with the door locked behind me once more, I realized I was going to be spending every single day and night right there in that tiny six-by-eight foot room for the foreseeable future. If the mayor and the other members of the town council were dead set on keeping me out of the way, all they needed to do was continually push the court date back, and there wasn't a damn thing I could do about it.

"Well, that went well," Bill said, leaning back on my bunk and picking at a fingernail. "I'd say you've succeeded in making a whole bunch of friends down here."

"Just leave me alone, won't you," I replied, slumping onto the hard mattress. "I need time to think."

"Think about what? About how there's a vengeful, Native American spirit out there murdering people for the fun of it while you sit in here on trumped up charges? Or, how there's millions of dollars worth of gold in that mine that you're never going to see a nickel of?"

I whirled on him. "Jesus, Bill. Just give me a break!"

"If I'd have been alive, none of this would have ever happened!"

"But you're not, are you?!" I screamed. "You died out there in Fallujah. I wish you hadn't! I wish that, every single day! I would have traded places with you in a heartbeat, Bill—you know I would—but it's too late for that now, isn't it? It's just too late!"

I closed my eyes as my head pounded and my body shook, and I waited for the stars and the shapes to stop swirling and blinking behind my eyelids. I must have drifted off, because the Wendigo was back in my cell, but this time it was in the guise of my old boss, Frank Hogan, and he was spitting with rage.

"You owe me, J.C.," he sneered, his ebony skull hanging with festering flesh. His antlers scraped plaster from the low ceiling, leaving long, diagonal depressions. "And I've come to collect. Do you have what I need?"

He reached for me, his clawed hands carving the shape of a pentagram through my shirt and into my chest. I could feel the blood seeping from the wounds and soaking through my clothes. The pain was excruciating. It felt like every nerve in my body was on fire, as if my skin was bubbling like melting plastic. Hogan drew closer to me and I tried to pull away, but the room was too small and I was cornered like a caged animal.

"Time to pay up," he said, before opening his mouth and plunging his teeth into my trembling throat.

"Time to go, J.C."

I opened my eyes, but the light from the overhead panel was blinding.

"What? Where am I?"

"You're in the cell, but you gotta go."

I shook my head until my vision cleared, and I eventually came to realize it was the sheriff who was standing over me.

"Gotta go where?"

"Today's your lucky day, soldier. Somebody paid your bail."

I sat up and waited for the stars to dance away from my eyes. I paused to wonder whether I was still dreaming, or if this new reality was in fact the dream, and my body was lying unconscious and being repeatedly subjected to a vicious assault by a possessed crime boss.

"Who paid?"

The sheriff stood aside to let me pass. "Looks like you have a friend in this town after all."

I walked along the corridor where I was handed my things by a pissed looking Deputy Barns. "If I had my way—" he grumbled, before turning and pushing his way through to the offices out back. I got dressed in the restroom, checked myself in the mirror, and realized that I looked like I needed a shave and a good shower.

Heading out into the street, I half-expected a baying mob to be out there, waiting to strip me bare and drag me through the town behind a speeding wagon. Instead, standing in front of her car and shooting me a beaming smile, her brilliant blue eyes shining like the sweeping beam of a lighthouse in raging waters behind her, was the one person I hadn't expected to see.

"Well, hi you," Linda said, pulling the passenger door of her Toyota open. "What took you so long?"

CHAPTER FOURTEEN

A Painful Option

S heriff Elijah Harris sat back in his chair and thumbed through his phone. He was fed up with everything that was happening in the town. *His* town. Goddammit, he'd been raised in Devil's Ridge, had spent every year of his increasingly miserable professional life serving the people that he'd grown up with while not expecting a word of thanks or even a pat on the back to acknowledge his not inconsiderable efforts. But, he was starting to question why.

Why had he agreed to arrest Carter with what could only be described as circumstantial evidence (and even that was a stretch)? Why had he allowed the mayor to go against decades of warnings not to mess with what was very possibly a cursed mass grave at Kiowa Rock? And why had he allowed himself to get into such a grotesque, out of character, extremely embarrassing and compromising situation that now meant he'd become exposed to bribery and threats against his good name and the name of his family? What the hell had he been thinking?

Sure, he'd paid for sex before. He was a divorced, single man with needs, and he was either related or was good friends with most of the women in town. His options were limited. But, when the woman with the long red hair and narrow, pink lips had approached him at the bar and suggested he go back to her place, he'd had no idea the whole thing was being secretly recorded by the very people who now had him hanging over a political furnace, with the flames of infamy burning a hole in his pants.

He thought about his kids. His son, Dwayne, was a successful property developer in town—not that there was a huge amount of property to develop—but he was doing okay, and managing to support his wife and two young girls, Hazel and Violet. His daughter, Rebecca, was more of a loose cannon, but she was artistic and inciteful, and despite her piercings and tattoos—which he hated—she was kind-spirited and had a lot of friends. They were doing alright, the pair of them. They didn't deserve to have such a mess up of a father.

He often wondered, usually over two or three glasses of bourbon, whether they would be better off not having him around. Not that he was suicidal or anything—far from it—but he knew he wouldn't be able to bear it if the photos of him in that hotel room with that feeble excuse for a honey trap were released to the press. It would be a blot on their reputations that would never fade. Like a hot brand in their skin, the mark would always be there. And his ex-wife and her new husband? They would have a field day with it. He would never be able to get away from it. He would be forced out of job, that much was for sure—and probably out of town, too.

And now, with a double murder enquiry on his roster and the press hard on his case, he was under increasing pressure to find the culprit using any means possible—hence the whole Jason Carter debacle. Except he knew what many other old-timers in the town knew. It was as obvious as smearing butter on your pancakes. They'd awakened something up at that mine—something evil. Something that had already taken so much from the town, but now wanted so much more. And whether the murders of Zed and the Chase kid had anything to do with it or not, it didn't matter.

The fact remained, there was an evil spirit wandering their streets, and they now had two dead bodies in the town morgue to show for it. If he was a betting man, and he was—another thing his ex-wife held over him, and one of the reasons things had become tense between them in the first place—he'd lay a $100 down on there being more to come. *Lots more.*

He wished that Carter had never shown up in the town; that he'd stopped him hiking up to Kiowa Rock with the Indian; and that he hadn't bought into it by taking the news of that faint slither of gold to the mayor. It was as if he'd loaded his own gun with the very bullet that was destined to put him in his grave.

When he'd got the message, he'd taken some time out. Just a couple of days. He'd almost left town for good, figuring that if he wasn't there at all, the pictures would lose any street value. But then, the people behind it all—people he'd considered to be his friends, and wasn't that just the biggest joke of all—had gotten really nasty with him, stating that if he didn't return, they'd post the pictures all over the internet. Then, wherever he was, the people he was with would know what kind of lowlife, pussy-hunting pervert he was. He was cornered like an alleycat, and there was no way out.

So, now here he sat, alone in his office, reading a text message from the people that were bribing him. The message clearly stated that, in no uncertain terms, was he to sort out the one person who was staking a claim on their gold or else. And out there in the streets, something malicious and terrifying was wandering the very streets he was duty bound to protect, waiting to find its next victim.

As he saw it, he only had one option, and it was a painful one. He had to hunt down the Wendigo, and he had to get rid of Jason Carter.

CHAPTER FIFTEEN

Pandora's Box

I sat in Linda's kitchen while she made us both coffee and eggs. I'd taken a shower as soon as we'd arrived back at her place; a tidy, little three-bedroom duplex with a neatly trimmed front lawn, a healthy sized living room, a kitchen diner, and a bathroom that housed an enormous walk-in shower. Linda had been right, she did have plenty of room.

I sat there bare chested, my hair dripping onto a towel that was draped over my shoulders, and watched as she maneuvred herself expertly around the kitchen. She really was something, and I found myself staring without even realizing I was doing it. I silently wondered whether she knew about the agreement I'd struck with Penny White regarding me staying at the hotel for free, and if so, why she'd so generously posted bail. I also wondered how the hell she'd found that amount of money in such a short span of time.

"You know," she said. "They really have no evidence against you. I told them time and time again that you were with me at the restaurant, but no matter what I said, I could see that imbecile, Danny Barns, already had his mind made up."

"I think he was just doing as he was told," I replied, thinking about my discussion with my brother. "I think somebody wants me out of the picture."

Linda spun round, a pan of steaming eggs in her hand. "And why would somebody want that?"

I watched as she scooped a generous helping of huevos rancheros onto my plate before I answered. "People do some pretty weird things when money's involved. Particularly when it comes in the form of a mountain teeming with gold."

Linda's mouth fell open. "So, you think that's what all this is about?"

I chowed down on my eggs and nodded. "Yeah. That would be my guess."

"But I didn't think you had anything to do with that!"

I swallowed my mouthful, realizing that now would be as good a time as any to fess up. I told her about my trip to Kiowa Rock with Little Bear, how we'd uncovered the gold in the mine, and how I'd convinced the sheriff to take it to the mayor. She took it all in her stride, but I could see she was a little put out that I'd kept her in the dark.

"So, what you gonna do about it?" she asked, forking some eggs into her own mouth before washing it down with her coffee.

"I need to find Caleb Foster. I think he's the only one who can help me." I recalled the image of Zed's old pal scurrying around on all fours in the dirt, his breath coming in ragged, hurried gasps.

"What about that bank card you gave to the sheriff's office?"

I grimaced and shook my head. "I think that whoever was behind my arrest will bury whatever secrets that card holds as soon as the good doctor publishes his report."

Linda slammed her hands on the table. "That's not fair!" she cried. "People have been murdered—real people—and they're just going to pin it on an innocent man!"

I finished my eggs and sat back in my chair. "Not if I have anything to do with it."

Linda grunted as she ate her breakfast. Her cheeks were flushed with a smear of scarlet and her dimples trembled as she chewed. I could see she was angry, but I didn't know if it was about what was going on with the murder investigation, or if it was about Penny. It was clear she didn't like the brash and frankly flirtatious hotel owner, but I suspected her disdain for her was caused by more than just Penny's outspoken personality.

On the way back from the courthouse, Linda had barely said a word to me. I could sense the tension in the car as soon as I'd closed my door, but I hadn't expected to be given the silent treatment. When we pulled into her driveway, she paused to speak, but she appeared to think better of it before heading inside.

"Bathroom's second door on the right," she had murmured. "Help yourself to towels."

When I emerged, clean and feeling something a little closer to normal, she'd been cooking eggs and sounding more like her old self. However, I suspected that she was building up to something. I'd guessed the dam would burst sooner rather than later.

"She's married, you know," she said eventually. "Penny, I mean. She's been married to the same man for the past 10 years, although you'd never know it. He's a resident of some significant wealth and influence in these parts. He owns that hotel, as well as several other properties in the center of town."

I sat back in my chair, shocked. She was right. There was no sign that Penny had a husband. No ring, no mention of a man in her life, nothing. "Wow, that's news to me."

"Does it make a difference to what you think of her?"

I thought about that for a moment. "No, not really. It's her business, I guess."

"You don't think her offering you free accommodation and providing you with her own, very expensive lawyer is a little odd, then? Given that she's a married woman and all?" I held back a grin. There it was. The thing that had been pissing Linda off.

"The accommodation isn't free. I promised her I'd pay her back when the whole gold thing plays out."

"And if it doesn't?"

"She said she'd wipe the slate clean."

"So, as I said. Free accommodation, then."

She'd maneuvered my king into check without me noticing. *Damn, she was good at this.* I decided my only way out was to go on the offensive, which I also knew was an equally risky move.

"Look, Linda," I said, trying to sound annoyed. "I don't know what's gone on between you and Penny White, but I do know that I don't have the time or the inclination to get caught in the crossfire. In case you hadn't noticed, I've been charged with a double murder. If I don't find a way out of it, I'll be spending a long time in accommodation that is also free, but nowhere near as comfortable." I stood for added effect, shaking the towel from my shoulders. "So, you want to fill me in on what's going on?"

Linda set down her fork and began to nod slowly. "Okay, okay. You want to know? Here it is. Penny and I went to high school together. Her parents lived in the hills, and mine lived down here in the valley. But there's only one school in Devil's Ridge, and it so happens to be the one that I now teach at. Anyway, I was dating this guy, Travis Newsted, who played for the high school football team, and Penny was dating another guy, Buck Overton."

"We used to double-date together, go to the movies, do all that teen stuff, you know? The problem was, Penny was ambitious, even back then, and Buck wasn't on the sports team. He also wasn't exactly setting the world on fire with his grades. He just wasn't "Penny material." Travis, on the other hand, went on to get a scholarship out of state and I went to WCU to get my Bachelor's in English Literature. Penny, however? Well, she ended up staying here. She said she wasn't interested in college. She wanted to start earning money—quickly, too—and she thought she wasn't ever going to be able to do that while hunkered over some books and writing crappy college papers."

"Anyway, me and Travis carried on seeing each other. I'd travel to his college on the weekends, or he would come to mine, and we even started talking about getting engaged after we graduated. At the time, I thought I loved him, and I thought he loved me too. Little did I know, right? After a year or two, Travis started claiming he had football practice on some weekends and he wouldn't be able to see me, which I thought was fine. He was on a football scholarship after all. But then, the weekends we actually did see each other became fewer and fewer until I saw him maybe once a month. Eventually, I'd had enough, and I decided to go see him anyway."

"I turned up at the college and headed straight for the football field, but to my surprise the whole place was empty. I found the janitor and asked him if practice had finished already, and he said that practice was usually on Wednesday and Thursday nights, and that it only happened on the weekends if there was an exhibition game on. You can imagine how I felt after he told me that. Part of me thought the janitor had made some mistake, but another part of me knew that something was going on. I headed straight for the house that Travis shared with three of his teammates, but when I got there, he wasn't home. I asked his friends where he was and they said he was out of town. I asked them what for, and they were so coy with me, I got that sinking feeling in the pit of my stomach. I thought I was going to be sick right there on the spot."

"So, that afternoon I called Penny and told her what had happened, and she convinced me to head back to Devil's Ridge. She was throwing a party for a few of our high school friends that, like her, had decided that college wasn't for them. She said it would help take my mind off everything. I didn't like the idea, but Travis wasn't picking up, and I was on my own with no boyfriend to hang out with."

"I managed to get the next train, and I arrived at Devil's Ridge at around 7 p.m. I headed straight for Penny's parent's house. They were out of town and her brother was away with work, so she had the place to herself. It was so busy. There must have been over a 100 kids there: high school seniors, ex-high school students, and some freshman's. There were so many kegs of beer you wouldn't believe. I grabbed a drink and asked one of the party-goers if they'd seen Penny, and they asked me who Penny was."

"I was there for maybe 30 minutes before I needed the restroom, so I headed upstairs. I knew my way around Penny's house so I didn't wait to be shown, but when I made it to the upstairs hallway I noticed the door to

Penny's parent's bedroom was open and there were noises coming from inside. Worried that one of the kids had decided to take something that wasn't theirs, I burst through the door, only to be confronted by a scene that I will never forget."

She paused, her face red with rage and her fingers gripping the edge of the table. Her knuckles were white. I knew enough about Penny to guess how this story was going to end, but I let Linda finish without interrupting. "There she was, lying beneath Travis, her fingernails digging into his shoulder blades—his pelvis thrusting into her. And, do you know what she did when she saw me walk into the room? Her parent's fucking room?" I shook my head. "She smiled. That bitch grinned at me as if the whole thing had played out exactly how she'd planned it."

My eyes fell to the floor. I didn't know how to look at her. I just didn't have a clue. I knew now why Linda had been so cold toward Penny, and also why Penny was so keen to keep me there at the Regal. I was just a pawn to her, a piece on a board she controlled, a footsoldier she could sacrifice for her own precious advantage. She'd obviously been playing Linda since high school, manipulating and using her to make damn sure she always won. Whether it was the job, the money, or the man—Penny wanted it all.

"I'm so sorry," I said. "I had no idea."

She turned her head and held a hand to her face as if she wanted to hide. "Oh, it's not your concern. It's just a petty, small town squabble. I didn't want to burden you with it, but, you know? You asked."

"Yeah," I said, wanting to hold her but not knowing how to make the first move. "Yeah, I did."

I cleared the plates from the table and went to the sink. I felt so bad for the way I'd treated her. I'd misinterpreted the situation, and I'd become close to the one person who had caused her so much pain. I knew I needed to make it right somehow, but my confidence just seemed to evaporate. I became clueless, thoughtless.

I turned to her then, and was shocked to find her standing right behind me. I could smell how clean she was, could see the freckles on her cheeks, and the way her mouth curled up at the corners. She had the soft sheen of restrained tears in her eyes and they glistened with a brilliant blue, as if the ocean itself was behind her stare.

She touched my hand and I moved it across her shoulder blades. She leaned into me and I pulled her forward, dipping my mouth to hers. We kissed then; a kiss full of longing, hurt, and unsuppressed desire. After I pulled back slightly, she peered up at me with those unmistakable eyes, and she silently took my hand in hers. She turned and headed toward the hallway, her bare feet hardly making any sound on the cold tile. I knew she was leading me to the one place I shouldn't go—a Pandora's box that once opened could never be closed—but at that exact moment, it was the one place I longed for more than anywhere else in the world.

CHAPTER SIXTEEN

Bait

We were lying naked in each other's arms, half-asleep in Linda's bed, when there was a loud hammering on the front door. I leapt up and grabbed my clothes instinctively while Linda bashfully pulled the sheets up over her chest. I raised an eyebrow at her.

"Someone I should know about?" I asked, as the banging became louder and more persistent.

"I think that question is better directed at you," she said. "Now, are you answering that or am I?"

It wasn't my house and I felt pretty uncomfortable answering the front door of someone else's home, but it sounded like, if I didn't hurry, whoever was out there was going to kick the door down. I pulled on my shirt, which was crumpled and dirty, and peered out the window. Little Bear was standing outside and he was looking pretty agitated, which was understandable. We'd both seen the same terrifying thing up in the mountains, and stuff like that was difficult to get out of your head.

"Don't worry, I'll deal with this," I said, forcing a smile. "It's a pal."

"I didn't think you had any in this town!" she called out as I approached the door and turned the handle.

"We need to talk," Little Bear said, pushing past me. Axle followed behind.

"Hello to you too," I replied. "You know I don't live here, right?"

"I guessed you'd be at the schoolteacher's house. She bailed you out, after all."

I closed the door and turned to him. He slumped onto the sofa and Axle curled up at his feet. Little Bear didn't look like his usual, stern-faced self. His hair looked lank and his skin was ashen. There was also the faint scent of stale body odor, which I'd never picked up on him before. He kept glancing around the room as if he suspected someone was watching him.

"They dragged me in last night," he said after a long silence. "Seems like if they can't get you, they're going to come after me."

"They can't do that," I replied. "They don't have any evidence."

"Maybe they don't need any. Maybe they just think the Indian living on his own in the hills is the obvious culprit. Hell, most people in this town can't even bring themselves to say hi to me. Why do you think I live all the way out there? Most of the people in Devil's Ridge are bigoted assholes."

Maybe he was right, but that didn't mean the sheriff's office had the right to drag him to the station in the middle of the night to question him. It was a flagrant flouting of authority. I knew it did mean one thing though, although the thought didn't bring me any real joy. If they were going after Little Bear, that meant they had realized they really had no case against me. Unless, of course, they were going after both of us. We each had a stake in the gold, after all.

"This is ridiculous," I said. "Don't worry. We'll sort this out."

"And how do you suppose we do that?"

Linda entered the living room. She was dressed in tight blue jeans and a white tee. She looked every bit as stunning as when I'd first met her. She gave me a look that was a mixture of coy, sheepishness, and confusion.

"T-This is Linda," I said, gesturing toward her. "And this is Little Bear, the friend I told you about."

"Pleased to meet you," Linda said, holding out her hand. After Little Bear shook it, she stooped to the ground. "And who, may I ask, is this beautiful boy?" Axle groaned as she moved her hands behind his ears and began to tickle them furiously.

"That's Axle," Little Bear replied. "He's my old buddy."

"Well, I bet he's a good buddy, too," Linda replied. I could see that she was really taken with Little Bear's sleepy bloodhound. "I bet he's a real good boy."

"Linda," I said. "Would it be okay if you keep Axle company while Little Bear and I have a conversation in the yard?"

She looked up at me. I could see she was curious. "I guess," she said. "You two keepin' secrets?"

"No," I replied, holding up my hands. "Nothing like that. It's just that we have some business to deal with. You know, about the gold?"

She shot me a knowing smirk and raised her eyebrows. "Fine. Go ahead."

I showed Little Bear the way, and after we stepped outside, we took a seat on a couple of lawn chairs. Little Bear's chair creaked audibly under his substantial size.

I leaned forward and half whispered. "As I see it, if we want to clear our names, we have to find Caleb."

"You saw him," he replied. "If we find him, we better be armed, because that guy is not currently in his right mind."

I knew what he meant. I felt sure that Caleb was the one who had killed Zed and Paul Chase, and I knew the bank card I had foolishly handed over to Deputy Barns carried the proof.

"We will be," I replied. "We'll have to be."

Little Bear thought about this for a moment. "And, where do you suppose he'll be? You think we should head back up into the mountains?"

I shook my head. "No. I think he was only up there because that's where we were headed. I think the Wendigo wanted back up, which is why it dragged its minion up there with us."

"Well, if that's the case, maybe Caleb will come looking for us in town."

I'd been thinking the same thing. We'd found the gold, we'd convinced the town to open up the mine, and I'd been the one to find Zed's remains. We were a threat to the Wendigo, and our trip to the ancient settlement proved that to him. But, even so, I didn't think Caleb would be bold enough to come hunting for us in a residential district. He was still at least semi-human, after all, and I reckoned that that part of him would know that hunting in a crowded area was a bad idea. Of course, that meant I really had no idea how to find him.

Suddenly, a thought occurred to me.

"I think we should stake out Lincoln Park tonight," I blurted out. "We know he's killed there before, so there's no reason why he wouldn't do it again."

Little Bear nodded. "That sounds like the makings of a good idea."

"We take a couple of rifles with us, and we set up camp by the lake. If he really is hunting for us, we'll be ready for him."

He seemed to consider this, his hand resting beneath his chin. "You know, I think we stand a better chance of him coming to us if one of us is unarmed and alone."

I cocked my head. I knew he was getting at something, but I wasn't sure what. "What do you mean?"

He pointed at me and winked. "It means that you, my friend, get to be the bait."

After Little Bear left, I collected my things. I wanted to head back to the hotel and get some rest before I headed to the park and sacrificed myself to a rampaging cannibal.

Linda watched me as I collected my wallet and keys from the bedroom floor, her arm resting on the doorframe. She was tapping her foot on the floor.

"So, that's that, is it?"

"So, that's what?"

"You get what you want here, and then you ride off into the sunset?"

"No," I went to her, slipping my arm around her slim waist, but she pulled back. "It's not like that at all."

She turned away and I could see that she was upset. I couldn't escape the fact that I had my way with her, a fact I wasn't proud of. It was the very reason I hadn't wanted things to move so fast. Everything I touched seemed to be turning to shit, and I didn't want her downstream of that. She didn't deserve it.

"Look, I need to get to the bottom of what's been going on in town, and Little Bear's agreed to help me. For whatever reason, the sheriff has it in for the both of us, so it's in our best interest to stay ahead of this thing."

"Can't you just let the police do their job?"

"Not when the job they're doing involves trying to put me behind bars."

She turned her back to me then, her cheeks flushed once more. "What the hell are you planning, J.C.?"

I held her face in my hands and kissed her forehead. "It's better that you don't know," I replied. "Just trust me."

Linda wasn't enamored with me heading back to the Regal, where I'm sure she suspected Penny White would be lying in wait for me, her claws sharpened and at the ready. However, she had papers to mark and I was adamant about going ahead with my plan. I'd agreed to meet Little Bear at a little after 9 p.m. at the monument. I didn't know if Caleb would take the bait, but I hoped that with me on the end of the line, we were giving ourselves the best chance.

I decided to eat dinner at the hotel restaurant before we left, treating myself to a hearty last supper.

I was halfway through eating my thick ribeye steak when Penny took a seat at my table. "You're welcome," she said, shooting me a winning smile.

"Yeah, about that," I replied, chewing down my mouthful. "What the hell happened there? One minute I was due to be defended by some guy on the town council's payroll, the next thing I know, I'm standing next to a polished guy in a tailored suit who I assume had a quiet word in the judge's ear."

Penny shrugged and flicked a curl of hair from her face. "I have my uses."

"And thank God you do. Really, thank you."

She touched my hand, her gaze never leaving my face. Her expression suddenly became serious, and she idly wiped lipstick from the corner of her mouth with a long nail. "Let's hope that friend of yours can pay back the money she borrowed," she said. "I mean, lord knows how she'll do it when you consider the pitiful teacher's salary she gets, but," she winked, "here's hoping."

With that, she stood and left, leaving me to wonder who Linda had borrowed the money from and how she was going to clear the debt. *Shit, not only had I brought bad luck to her door, I'd also just put her in $50,000 worth of debt.* Suddenly, the rest of my steak looked like nothing but ash on my plate, and I pushed it away. My appetite had evaporated. Linda was right. Penny knew how to manipulate a situation to her advantage with little more than a few carefully placed words.

When I arrived at the monument, the sun was falling below the horizon and there was a chill in the air. I stood there alone, watching as the shadows elongated to nothingness, and the darkness crept in from the east, pushing all semblance of light from the wide expanse of lawn. The trees became giant statue silhouettes all around me, their long obsidian fingers reaching for me in the deepening gloom. Every sound became a booming thunderclap in my ears, every movement a marauding pack of animals racing toward me with their claws drawn.

"You okay there, J.C.?" Little Bear said as he approached from my rear. I whirled on him, ready to draw my knife and plunge it into his throat. "Woah there, soldier! Friend! Friend!" he cried.

My muscles were so tense I could feel them straining against every fiber in my body. I took three deep breaths and gripped Little Bear's shoulder. "You ready?" I asked, trying to sound commanding.

"Are you?" he replied, swinging the rifle from his shoulder.

I nodded. I was as ready as I would ever be.

"I suggest you sit over there," he said, pointing to a wooden bench that was placed on the edge of the lake. "That way, I'll have a clear shot from my hiding place just beyond the tree line."

"We don't want him dead," I replied. "We need him to confess, not wind up lying next to the other two men in the morgue. We already have the sheriff's department trying to pin those murders on us. We don't need a third."

Little Bear grinned. "Once you have two, you may as well have three," he said, laughing. "What harm will it do?"

I shook my head. "Not funny."

"Anyway, don't worry. I'll just give him a little knick in the thigh to bring him down. After that, he's all yours."

I hoped Little Bear was right. I still couldn't shake the image of Caleb peering into the darkness while the two of us hid in the shadows. He'd looked hungry, unable to control his desires. His teeth had been elongated, his eyes dark slits. I knew that if Caleb caught me off guard, and if Little Bear's aim wasn't true, then I'd be number three on his list of victims.

I made my way to the park bench as my protector disappeared into the darkness. A young couple walked past as I sat there with my heart pounding in my chest. The water was still, like smooth glass. The moon reflected off its glistening surface, creating an eerie, ghost-like glow that painted silver leaf across the treetops. The stars were out, too, like little droplets of white paint on the rolling black canvas of the universe. If I wasn't waiting for a demonically possessed lunatic to attack me, I might have thought the evening to be beautiful.

"This is a bad idea, you know?" Bill said, seated next to me. "I mean, as far as your ideas go, this is as bad as it gets. You realize you're just a slice of carrion waiting to be picked off by the next buzzard?"

I didn't answer. Bill knew he was right. He didn't need my acknowledgement.

"He kills you, he kills me too. You understand that, yeah?"

Of course I did. I wasn't an idiot. Bill was me and I was Bill. That much was obvious.

"Then, what are you doing just sitting here? You need to get away, like, now."

"This is the only way," I said. "I'd rather die here than spend the rest of my life in a prison cell."

"Oh, that's easy for you to say. You're not already dead. If your dumbass plan backfires, I get to die a second time. You get me? I get to die twice!"

I didn't answer, and that seemed to infuriate him.

"Fuck you, J.C.!"

I concentrated on everything around me: the darkness, the trees moving in the slight breeze, the low hum of traffic running down Governor's Boulevard, the cry of a coyote somewhere up in the hills. The park was deserted. I was alone on that bench with only the moon and my dead brother for company. I felt like I was back in the desert, my rifle site aimed at a spot in the distance, and wondering where the hell the next insurgent assault was going to come from. We knew as little then as I knew now. We were reacting, just as I was reacting. I was a passenger, a servant.

There was the sound of movement behind me and I glanced over my shoulder. Something shifted among the trees around 15 feet away from my right hand shoulder. It was low to the ground, as if it were crouching. There was the glint of moonlight on two flitting irises, and then it was gone.

I turned to face the treeline in the distance, which was now just a black line against a dark backdrop, and I hoped that Little Bear's aim was true. I suddenly didn't care if Caleb was taken alive. I just didn't want to be ripped to pieces and laid out like a slab of raw beef.

The noise returned and this time it was closer and immediately behind me. Caleb knew that I had seen him and had adjusted his position. He was smarter than he looked. My knife felt heavy against the inside of my right leg, but I didn't reach for it. *Not yet.* I needed him closer, much closer. I needed to be able to smell the reek of his breath, to feel the evil permeating from him.

There was a rustle of dry leaves, and the sound of a foot being depressed into hard soil. A twig cracked and the thing seemed to retreat, but when I closed my eyes I knew it was still inching closer. I wondered if Caleb was now completely at the mercy of the Wendigo, or if there was still a little of his soul left. I felt sorry for him. He had been a mere spectator as Zed uncovered the lair of the undead spirit, but it had somehow affected him more.

I could hear heavy breathing, as if the creature crouching behind me was drawn to something so powerful, he couldn't resist it. It was the sound that people make when they are approaching a powerful climax, or when they are so hungry they would eat rotten meat from the slaughterhouse floor. Whatever was compelling Caleb to do its bidding, he was powerless to fight it.

The ragged breathing stopped and so did the sound of movement in the undergrowth, and I began to think that Caleb must have spotted Little Bear waiting with his rifle in the distance, and he'd backed off. Then, there was a horrifying shriek, followed by the sensation of something large hurtling through the air behind me.

I moved instantly, rolling to my right hand side, and at the same time reaching for the knife that was strapped to my leg. I found the handle and pulled it from the sheath, just as I heard a loud crack from the treeline. A bullet embedded itself in the bench, just above where I was lying, sending sharp splinters into my face. Caleb came over the spine of the bench like a ravenous wolf, his lips pulled back, his obscenely long teeth drawn, and his clawed hands tearing chunks of timber from the wooden structure. He lunged for me, his teeth snapping in the air just inches from my face. I brought the knife up, but his arms were powerful, and he flung me down onto the ground, dislodging the blade from my grip. It went sliding into the lake and I watched as it disappeared beneath the water.

Unarmed, I leapt to my feet, but Caleb was on all fours and ripping the Earth up as he raced toward me. I backed off and set my feet, my hands ready to strike. As Caleb leapt into the air once more, his claws aimed at my face, I swung a left hook which struck him on the cheek. I felt something give in his face and he tumbled onto the ground. He flipped onto his back and pushed himself up, once more striking at me with his strong arms. I dodged, but a sharp claw tore at my chest, ripping my shirt open and drawing blood. I ignored the pain and danced away from him, just as another loud retort sounded from the treeline and a hole appeared in the branch to my right.

I glanced at the water and saw my blade lying in the reeds behind Caleb. I knew I needed to maneuver him away from the water, so I skipped to my left and stepped toward him, aiming a kick at his midsection. I was too slow, and Caleb saw it coming. He rolled away from my leg and pounced on me, pushing me to the ground. I went sprawling onto the hard earth, my head connecting with the concrete path. I saw stars for just a second, and that was all it took for Caleb to be on my back, his teeth snapping beside my ear. I spun onto my rear, hoping to dislodge him, but he clung to my chest like an excitable chimp. I held up my hands, but he was way too strong, and I realized that my plan had completely backfired. *Bill was going to be so pissed.*

Just as Caleb's eyes glistened with the heat of the chase, and he bared his teeth, ready to rip out my pulsing throat, his head exploded in a flurry of bone and brain matter. It rained down on me, some of it falling into my open mouth. I instinctively dry-heaved onto the grass.

Caleb flopped to the ground, his eyes now vacant and unseeing. I kicked myself away from him, as if I thought that at any second he could jump back to his feet and renew his frantic assault.

I looked down at the blood on my shirt and on my hands, and I knew then that we were in big trouble. *The town of Devil's Ridge now had its third victim.*

CHAPTER SEVENTEEN

Face Off

We had limited options in a sea of no options, so I chose the one that came to me first. I washed the blood from my face and shirt in the lake, retrieved my knife and headed to Little Bear's trailer, leaving Caleb where he lay. I felt really bad about that. He didn't look like an undead creature, hellbent on feasting on human flesh. He looked like a kid, fresh out of college and looking for his first big break.

We stopped off at a phone booth and I placed an anonymous call to the sheriff's office, tipping them off about the body. I added that I thought I'd heard a commotion in the park, like a fight or something, and then the sound of a gun going off. I wanted to plant the seed that there had been at least two people in this fight.

Neither of us spoke as we drove up into the hills. Our plan was in ruins. The only person who could testify to our innocence was now lying in the park with his brains leaking from a hole in his head the size of an eight-ball. There was no coming back from that.

"You couldn't hit him with the first two shots?" I asked as we sat outside in the car, waiting for someone to speak first.

"He was moving too quickly."

I exhaled. He was right. Caleb had been like a wild animal, moving with the speed and agility of a leopard. I didn't know what was controlling him, but it was as if he had transformed into something quicker, something stronger.

"What are we going to do?" he asked. "How the hell do we get out of this one?"

We headed inside and Little Bear poured us both a large glass of bourbon. I knew it was a bad idea, but I knocked it back without even thinking about it. Little Bear did the same. We had just killed a guy, after all. It gave you a bad case of the whinnies, and then some.

"If they pin this on me, Linda's going to lose her $50,000," I said. "I can't let that happen."

"So, you want me to take the fall?" Little Bear said, his voice tinged with acidity.

"No, I never said that."

"So, what's your big plan?"

I shook my head. I didn't have one. I knew that three people were now dead, two killed by Caleb, and one killed by the two of us, and I also knew there was something in the hills that had controlled Caleb's actions. And now, with Caleb now out of the way, it was going to be looking for its next puppet to control.

"We need to get the mining work shut down," I said eventually. "We can't risk anybody else ending up like him."

"And how do you suppose we do that?" he asked. "You've already been charged with a double murder, and my neck is next on the chopping block. What's more, the bullet that killed that kid is somewhere in that park, probably embedded in a tree or something. Sooner or later they're going to trace that back to me."

I knew he was right, but it didn't make my idea wrong. We had to cut this thing off at the source. We couldn't keep killing the possessed victims of a demonic spirit. The Wendigo had to be stopped.

As we sat there, pondering our predicament while the smoke from Little Bear's cigarette wafted toward the ceiling and the sound of Axle's thunderous snoring reverberated around the tiny trailer, the front door opened.

Little Bear leapt to his feet, grabbing his rifle. I pulled my knife, stepped to the side of the door and flattened myself against the wall.

I watched as a man's boot came into view, stepping tentatively onto the carpet, followed by a pair of blue jeans, a brown leather jacket, and a face that I knew only too well.

Sheriff Elijah Harris stood in the doorway, his face a mask of solemnity and mistrust.

"Hello boys," he said, before removing his hat. "The three of us need to have ourselves a little talk, don't you think?"

What we hadn't known—what we couldn't have known—was that the sheriff had been trailing us since Little Bear had left the interview room that morning. It seemed that he had gambled on the Native American coming to me, and he also knew that bringing Little Bear into the station, unsettling the big guy, would compel the two of us to act.

As he spoke, I silently wondered how the chips would fall. On the upside, the sheriff had to have seen the way Caleb was, the way he had attacked me, and the super-human way in which he was able to outmaneuver and overpower me. That was on the upside. On the downside, he would have also seen how we lured Caleb into the park before putting a bullet in his skull. You say tomato, I say tom-ah-to.

The sheriff leaned back in his chair and glared at each of us in turn. I was trying to work out his play, but I had to give it to him—his poker face was a good one. Little Bear glanced up at me, but I didn't avert my gaze. I'd learned in the military that if somebody decided they wanted to stare you down, you just went ahead and stared right back. The sheriff had put me in court on some trumped up charges, and I hadn't forgiven him for it. Being locked in a cold cell for two nights straight will do that to a guy.

"I'm guessing you guys think you're going to get away with that little shit show back there?" he said eventually, laying his hat on the table. "You realize I witnessed you kill a man in cold blood, right?"

I felt my throat tighten. Hearing the sheriff mouth the actual words somehow made the whole thing appear more real. Maybe, up to that point, I had been hoping it had all been a dream—I don't know. What I did know was that

I was sitting in front of the head of the local law enforcement, and I was once more being accused of murder.

"I don't know what you think you saw," Little Bear said, interrupting the silence.

"Oh, I know what I saw."

"But I'm guessing you saw a little more than you anticipated," I said, finally finding my voice. "Otherwise, you wouldn't have come here alone. There'd be a whole bunch of squad cars out there, and a whole load of guns."

The sheriff's eyes shifted for just a second, and I knew that my observation had hit home. There was no way two guys suspected of triple murder would be brought in by a lone gun. This wasn't the 19th century.

"Well, let's see," he began. "From my perspective, I witnessed you, J.C., brawling with a man we've been searching for, for some days. And I saw you, Little Bear, fire three shots from a spot around 200 feet from this little squabble. While your aim was a little off, shot number three hit the jackpot. Does that about sum it up for you, Carter?"

I held his glare and chose my words carefully. I knew that what I was about to say could be considered crazy talk, but it was all I had. I glanced at Little Bear, who stubbed out his cigarette, before nodding for me to go ahead.

"I think you saw much more than that, Sheriff. We both know that Nancy Ward's account of her boyfriend's murder stated that he was involved in an altercation with another man, and that this man tore a chunk out of Paul Chase's throat with his teeth, causing him to bleed to death. Am I right?"

The sheriff gave a hesitant nod. "She was a long way away, but that is what she thought she saw."

"And I assume the forensics back that up?" This time the sheriff was unmoved. "In any case, let's assume she was right. She was the only witness, after all." I paused to gather my thoughts. "You would, I presume, have seen me sitting alone on a park bench before Caleb arrived in the park."

"You were luring him in," he replied. "The Indian had already taken up position at this point."

"Be that as it may, I was alone, and at no time did I incite a quarrel with Caleb. You'd agree with that, yes?"

He shrugged. "As far as I could tell."

"That's right. So, when Caleb emerged from the treeline to rush me in the way that he did, what did you think he was doing?"

"I presumed you two had already had some sort of communication while he was apparently in hiding."

"And why would he be in hiding?"

The sheriff picked at the rim of his hat. One of his eyes closed as he considered the question. "That I don't know."

"Because he was the killer, Sheriff. Can't you see that?"

"Caleb's a good kid." He glanced at Little Bear. "*Was* a good kid."

I set my elbows on the table and leaned forward. "That wasn't Caleb who attacked me."

The sheriff let out a snort. "Sure as hell looked like him."

"But, it didn't move like him. Didn't act like him. You must accept that."

I could see the sheriff was uncertain of his position, and he stood up, grabbing a glass from Little Bear's kitchen and pouring himself a large bourbon.

"Didn't move like any man I'd ever seen," he said, taking a large sip. "Jesus, he looked like a wild animal."

I approached him. "You didn't want us to blow that mine. Neither did Little Bear, here. I was new in town and I didn't understand, even though you tried to tell me. I wouldn't listen." I peered out the window, half-expecting to see an inhuman creature, its skull flayed to the bone, leaning toward the glass, its inflamed eyes glaring at us, its teeth gnashing together in a frantic rhythm of desperate hunger. "We've woken something, Sheriff, and Caleb became its host. Zed saw it first, which is why it killed him, but then it got hungry and it killed the first passer by that it chanced upon. Me and Little Bear went to its home in the hills to find it, and now it's coming for us too."

"That's crazy talk," the sheriff said, but I could see doubt in his eyes. "That legend's been around for centuries, but that don't make it real."

"It was real enough for Caleb," Little Bear said, lighting another cigarette. "For Zed too."

"And it's the very reason you came here alone, isn't it?" I said. "You know what's going on. You just wanted to hear it from someone else. Maybe you thought you were going insane, but this insanity's spreading, Sheriff. It's spreading fast."

He leaned against the kitchen counter and let out a long, slow breath. "Shit, I'd hoped that this wouldn't go down on my watch."

"But here we are, all the same," Little Bear replied.

The three of us stood in silence while the wind outside rattled the walls of the trailer and somewhere in the distance a coyote cried out, its sad, lonely mewl drifting down from the hills.

"Yeah, well I guess we have a problem," he said eventually. "We have one hell of a problem."

I nodded, thinking of Hogan and Bill, of Linda and Penny. Above all, I thought of Caleb. He hadn't chosen this, but it had come from him nonetheless.

"What do we do now?" I asked.

The sheriff leaned across the table, collected his hat, and placed it back on his head. "We hunt."

CHAPTER EIGHTEEN

The Possum

L inda sat alone in her apartment and sipped a large glass of Malbec. *What the hell had she got herself all tangled up in?* She was supposed to be a respectable school teacher, goddammit, and yet here she was hooking up with the ruggedly handsome, new face in town. She didn't even know the guy, and yet within two weeks of him showing up, she'd already gone to bed with him? Oh, and let's not forget, bailed him out of jail with money that was not hers. As holes went, she'd dug herself a pretty big one.

Then, Little Bear had knocked on her door and J.C.'s mood had changed. Now, they were out there in the darkness doing God knows what to heaven knows who, and if it was something illegal—which she couldn't rule out because, duh—then didn't that make her an accessory?

She sipped some more wine and stood at the open back door, breathing in the night air. The wine had distorted her senses a little, which was a good thing. She was all over the place. The thing with Penny had really affected her. How dare that bitch of a woman start playing cat and mouse with J.C. like that. And she was only doing it because Penny knew she liked him. She was as sure of that as she was sure that J.C. wasn't exactly who he said he was. But that excited her a little. Did that make her a bad person? Maybe, but she'd spent her life toeing the party line and doing what was expected of her, and how far had that got her? Not very far at all.

She lived in the same town she had always lived in, apart from her short spell at college; she taught in the same school she went to when she was a kid; and she lived two blocks away from where she grew up. Oh, and by the way, she was flat broke too. How about that? Didn't she deserve a little excitement in her life? A little bit of devilry to spice things up a bit? And the sex had been good too. *Like, real good.*

She topped her glass and headed out into the yard, sitting on a lawn chair and gazing toward the mountains that lurked out there in the distance, their outline just visible beneath the glittering stars. She wondered if there was anybody up in those hills, keeping watch on her. She hoped so. She needed a guardian, a friend. She needed a miracle, that was what she needed, except miracles were hard to come by and even harder to afford.

She hadn't been completely honest with J.C.. Travis had been her true love, but not in the way that she'd told it. Not that it mattered, as she was sure that J.C. hadn't been honest either. He had the face of someone who was running from something or someone, and he reeked of desperation. She suspected that Devil's Ridge was his one shot at redemption, which is why he was so set on mining that gold. And look what trouble that had brought him.

There was a noise from the end of her yard, just out of sight, and she set her glass down. Her head was even fuzzier now, but wine always seemed to give her courage, so she stood and stepped onto the lawn.

"Is somebody there?" she said in little more than a whisper. "Hello?"

There was no response, but she did hear that sound again, as if someone was shuffling in the dirt. She thought about going inside to get her flashlight, but she didn't want whatever it was to get away before she had a chance to see it. She thought it might be a possum, hedgehog, or something of the sort. Maybe it was a cat. Perhaps she could feed it.

"Hey," she said, bolder now. "I won't hurt you. Don't worry. I just want to make sure you're okay."

The sound was louder now, closer too, and Linda thought she could hear something breathing. She crouched down and looked deeper into the darkness. She could see two eyes close to the floor. They were staring up at the sky, the starlight glistening off their gleaming surface.

"Well, hello there," she said. "What are you?"

Suddenly, her screen door slammed shut and she leapt up, stifling a scream. She whirled toward the door, and she saw a shadow move from within the kitchen. She almost stumbled over her own feet as she staggered backward. *What the hell was it? Who was it?*

"J.C.!" she cried out. "Is that you? Stop fooling around. You're scaring me!"

The shadow moved through the house. She saw it stumble into the living room as it passed the window, and then upstairs where it stood in her bedroom, its shape visible through the shades. It was watching her through a small gap. She could see its eyes. They were unblinking.

"What the—" she said, but she tripped on an object behind her and fell onto something soft that was lying motionless on her lawn. She rolled over to see what it was, but her hand slipped in something warm and wet, and she fell face first onto the thing beneath her. She glanced at her fingers and they were painted in a deep, sticky redness. She raised her head to look at the bulging shape she was lying on, and everything she knew about her world evaporated in an instant.

"It can't be!" she cried. "No, it can't be!"

She pushed herself away, her hand making contact with her own face, wiping a smear of blood across her cheeks and lips. She looked down at herself as if she was inhuman, ungodly, and then looked again at what she had fallen onto.

The two eyes she had seen weren't from an animal at all. They were from a human; a lifeless, motionless human—someone who had once been so full of life, who was the life and soul of the party—every goddamn party. Someone she had known since she was a kid. Someone she had shared laughs with, tears with, men with.

She didn't know why, and she didn't know how, but there on her lawn lay the body of Penny White, a ragged wound in her throat and bite wounds on her face and chest. A chunk was missing from her abdomen, and her innards lay in tangled entrails on the grass.

As the shadow lurking behind Linda's shades evaporated into the night, and her body became ravaged by icy daggers of utter, unabated terror, she raised her head to the sky and screamed.

CHAPTER NINETEEN

The Husband

The next day, the charges against me were dropped and Little Bear was formally removed from all enquiries. Not only could the sheriff testify that I had been assaulted by Caleb and that Little Bear had acted to protect me, we also had a solid alibi for the brutal murder of Penny White. Not that it was any comfort to me. Penny did not deserve what had happened to her, but I was also only too aware that Linda could have been hurt. Also that I'd left her on her own, knowing there was a killer in our midst.

"This is really bad," the sheriff said as his deputies cordoned off Linda's yard. "Four murders in two weeks. That's more than this town has had in the last 10 years or more."

"These aren't your usual homicides," I said. "The only way this stops is if we find that thing and send it back to wherever it came from."

Linda sat outside with a thermal blanket over her shoulders. I went to her.

"How you holding up?" I asked, knowing the answer to my own question.

"I can't believe she's gone," she said. "I was so horrible to her, too."

"This wasn't your fault," I replied, grabbing her hand, which trembled beneath my fingers. "Somebody, or something, was sending a message."

"But why me?"

I knew the answer to that one, too, but it was almost too terrible to say out loud. I'd let the very thing I'd been trying to avoid happen, and all because I wanted to get the girl. "Because I was here," I said, hating the way the words spilled from my mouth. "This thing is after me, Linda. It was sending me a message, not you."

Her eyes narrowed as she tried to comprehend what I was telling her. At that moment, I felt sure that she would tell me to go to hell, and who would have blamed her? Maybe I was already there.

A car pulled up on the street. It was an expensive looking Tesla, its chrome wheels polished, its gleaming red exterior glistening in the morning sunshine. A broad man with sleek, dark hair and a black goatee emerged. His eyes were red, his cheeks puffy.

"I want to see her!" his voice boomed as he approached the sheriff.

"That's not a good idea, Travis," the sheriff said, holding out his hands. I jerked at the mention of the newcomers name, and I felt Linda's body stiffen beside me. *Wasn't Travis the guy that had an affair with Penny behind Linda's back?*

"Goddammit, Elijah, she's my wife!"

The sheriff blocked the taller man's path and placed his hands on his thick chest. "That's not your wife anymore. She's gone, Travis. She's gone. I'm so sorry."

The man started to sob then, tears running down his cheeks and into his neatly trimmed beard. Linda stood and went to him, her arms outstretched. I felt a pang of jealousy jab at my insides. This was supposedly the man that Linda had almost married, but apparently for the past 10 years he'd been Penny White's husband? That was one important detail Linda had left out of the synopsis she'd given me. *Why would she do that?*

Travis stooped down and gave her the sort of embrace only ex-lovers give. She was practically absorbed into him like water, and she gave herself willingly. The jealousy swirled like bitter acid in my gut.

"I'm so, so sorry," I heard her say.

"I know our marriage wasn't perfect," he replied, gripping onto her like she was his only salvation. "And I know that what happened between you and I didn't help any—"

My mouth fell open while I listened. What happened between the two of them? The way Linda had told it, she had been the victim, not Penny.

"Hush now," Linda said. "That's all in the past. That was finished before it had even begun. You loved her, Travis. Anyone could see that."

I began to walk away. I'd heard enough. It seemed like nobody in the town of Devil's Ridge told the truth the first time they were asked.

"Is this the guy I'm paying for?" I heard him say. "Is this the guy the sheriff thought was the killer?"

I kept walking, although I now knew where Linda had got the bail bond from. I instantly felt dirty.

"Hey, killer!" Travis yelled. "Did you murder my wife?"

"No!" I heard Linda shout, but I could tell that Travis wasn't used to listening to the women in his life. The sound of his footsteps boomed as he headed toward me and I turned to him, intending to face him down. Then, I realized my head only reached his neck and I reconsidered my options.

"Did you kill my wife, you son of a bitch?"

"I did not. But I'm terribly sorry for your loss."

"You bastard!" His fist connected with my jaw, and I dropped to the ground, stars flashing before my eyes. "I ought to put you in the ground, right here, right now!"

He was on my back before I had time to move. He was a large, bulky mass and I struggled to get out from under him, despite having had plenty of hand-to-hand combat training in the military, including some Brazilian street fighting lessons. I pivoted my hips, bringing my legs around and scissoring his left leg until I was able to pull myself over him and gain the top mount position. The maneuver caught him off guard and he looked up at me in surprise.

He tried to throw me off him, but my knees gripped his ribs tight and I raised my fist, not wanting to strike him but knowing that I would have to if it came to it. His face grew redder and redder with each urgent movement, and he grunted with frustration. Eventually, all the energy went out of him, and he slump back onto the lawn like a fallen giant.

"I told you I didn't do it!" I hollered, dropping my fists. "Ask him!" I pointed to Sheriff Harris.

"He's right," he replied. "He was with me."

"Then, who the hell did?"

I could see the man was hurting and I reluctantly rolled off him, rubbing my tender jaw. His wife had just been brutally murdered, and here I was rolling around in the grass, fighting with the guy.

"We don't know yet, Travis," the sheriff replied. "But I swear to you, we'll find out. We'll catch this sick sonofabitch."

I walked away from the melee and headed up the hill toward the hotel. I had no idea if the place was open after the tragedy that had just befallen its manager, but all my stuff was in my room and I needed time away from Linda.

I heard her call out to me, but I wasn't in the mood to listen. I felt like I'd been deceived, which I sort of had. I wanted to leave town and get as far away as possible, but I knew that option wasn't open to me. I'd started something, and I had to see it through.

We all did.

CHAPTER TWENTY

No Escaping the Past

L ittle Bear sat on a chair outside his trailer, Axle eating dog chow from an enormous bowl. It was mid-morning and the sun was already hot. He dabbed at his forehead with a napkin and rolled himself a cigarette. The doctor said he needed to quit, but what the doctor didn't know—what Little Bear could never tell him—was that contracting lung cancer, or any other form of cancer for that matter, was way down his list of things to worry about.

He'd just received a call from J.C. who sounded like he'd just been on a long run, or in a wrestling match with a bear. He'd told him about what had happened to the hotel manager, and how she'd been gutted and tossed on the schoolteacher's lawn, as if the killer was bringing him some sort of sick gift.

Little Bear had heard about things like that from his ancestors. They told of the Adlet, a half human-half dog creature which was created by the cross breeding of humans and canines. Horrified by the birth of such grotesque creatures, the distraught father would throw the Adlet into the wilderness to fend for itself, hoping the unnatural abomination would perish in the cold. However, if the pup survived, it would often scavenge in the forest for fresh meat, hunting rabbits and young deer. It would then bring the bloodied carcass back to the family home as a gift for its mother, who would find it in the morning, festering outside her front door. The father, angered that his mutated offspring had returned, would confront the Atlet, chasing it away. But, as the pup grew older and much stronger, it would return to the fold, only to slaughter its father and mortally wound its mother so that she may never abandon it again.

He sipped his coffee and shook his head. He couldn't believe that he'd allowed this to happen. His father would often tell him never to trust the greedy white man, for they would do anything for a nugget of gold and the kiss of a beautiful woman. He knew he should have done more to stop the mining, but maybe he wanted some of that gold, too. *Maybe he wanted a better life for himself.* He looked back at this trailer with a door that barely closed properly, and a roof that leaked when the heavy rains came. *Why shouldn't he want more for himself? Damn it, he deserved it!*

Little Bear had grown up in the hills with his family—that much of his story was true—but he'd left out a lot when he'd given J.C. his potted history. Hell, he'd left out the real juicy stuff.

Little Bear had done jail time. The sheriff knew that, which was part of the reason why he'd brought him in for questioning after J.C. had been bailed out. Not the only reason though. The gold had a big part to play in it—he knew that—but his eight year spell in Colorado State Penitentiary had come into the equation, too. Of course, it had. Little Bear had been convicted of second-degree murder, and that was a fact the sheriff just couldn't ignore.

That had been a long time ago, and Little Bear had been trying to push the memory of that fateful October night out of his head since it had gone down. He'd spent a lot of time ruminating on it as he sat in his six-by-eight cell with only a tiny window and a bunk you could use as a launchpad. He hadn't meant to do it, but at the age of 18,

Little Bear had been an angry young man with a temper that was apt to blow at any second.

His dad had been a hard man to please. Not that that was an excuse for his actions, but hell, he couldn't ever remember his father ever telling him he liked him, let alone loved him. Everything Little Bear did was too slow or too clumsy, or maybe the fence wasn't painted properly, or the plates weren't scrubbed just right, or the rabbit meat hadn't been cleaned thoroughly enough. And his mom? Well, she just went along with his dad. She didn't want any upset in the family. There were eight of them in that house, after all. She had five other kids to think of.

He had been 15 when he left home. He couldn't stand it in that house any more. He was big enough to stand up to his father now, but not big enough to win. He thought if he didn't leave, they would end up killing each other. He headed for the city, hoping to make something of himself, but not counting on his lack of an education being a factor, or the racism that seemed to bubble unseen beneath the glittering lights and pounding music. He hustled himself a job as a doorman, working at a busy club for minimal pay, and it was enough for him to rent a one-bedroom apartment above a casino.

It was during this time that he found alcohol, and more problematically, cocaine. He became hooked in a matter of days, and the sharp spike in adrenaline that the little lines of white powder gave him only served to fuel his burgeoning rage. He found that it had its uses though, particularly when he was dealing with particularly aggressive customers at the club. Little Bear had always thought of himself as a big guy. His dad was big, and so was his grandfather, so it was hardly a surprise. But some of the guys in the city, they made him look like a Nirumbee.

One afternoon, he took a call from his dad.

"Your mother is sick," his dad said. "You need to come home."

"How sick?"

"You need to ask? Why does that matter? Don't you want to see her? She's your mother, for God's sake!"

Little Bear did want to see his mother—he missed her—but he was already on his third line, and he'd sunk a quart of Jack Daniels. When your mind was as frazzled as his, everything seemed just about as fine as wine.

"I can be there next week."

"She might not make it that long." Little Bear thought his dad sounded strange, as though he'd shrunk somehow.

"Well, I can't get there until next week. She'll be fine. Tell her I love her."

He'd hung up the phone, thrown on his jacket and headed to work. Didn't his dad realize he was busy? He'd told him to get himself a career, to find something he was good at. Well, guess what, that was exactly what he'd done. He had a career and he was damn good at it. He could crack heads together better than most, and he'd even learned a few new moves from some of the other doormen, like how to take down a big guy with just three fingers jammed expertly into the solar plexus.

Three days passed. Friday came around pretty fast that week. Little Bear had been pounding the powder pretty hard. He could barely remember waking each morning, and the evenings? Forget about them. He got by on instinct and muscle reflex. As long as he got his paycheck each week, who cared, right? He was even getting laid, something else he could barely remember.

When his phone rang and he saw it was his sister, he thought about not picking up.

"Hey," he said. "How you doing, little sis? How's those kids of yours?" He knew she had kids, but he couldn't remember how many or what their names were. There was an awful sound from the line, like an animal in horrible pain. "Everything okay?" he asked. "Hinto, what's going on?"

"He said he called you," she said through heavy sobs. "He said you wouldn't come."

Little Bear was momentarily confused, but then he remembered the call he'd taken from his father. He also recalled telling him to basically go to hell.

"Is it mom?" he asked. "Has she gotten worse?"

Hinto didn't speak, but he could hear the sound of her heart breaking from 500 miles away. He could have heard it without the phone. He knew then. He knew she was gone.

The news sent him into a tailspin. *How could he have been so stupid? How could have he ignored what his dad told him?* He had been so selfish, so self-consumed. He was a terrible son, he was a horrible human. He deserved the worst punishment for his lack of empathy, lack of care. He had abandoned his own mother at the one moment she had needed him. *The one time.*

He snorted everything he had, drank all the bourbon in the apartment, and headed to work. He was in a foul mood from the get-go, and had knocked a man out cold before the club had even gotten busy. Then, *they* showed up. The three guys with loud mouths and pumped-up bodies. They looked like they'd stepped off the stage at a Mr. Universe competition and injected themselves with a truckload of steroids.

"Hey there, Geronimo," one of the guys said. He had spiky blond hair and a barbed wire tattoo around his bicep. "Hey, Tonto, you got a light?"

"Back off fella," he said, feeling the rage bubbling in his gut. "You don't want none of this."

"Woah!" another guy with a jet black mohawk hollered. "We ain't lookin' for no trouble, Crazy Horse. We are just looking to pah-tay!"

His shrill, nasally voice made Little Bear want to punch through his face. He pictured his fist leaving a football-sized hole in the back of the guy's skull.

"Ignore them," the other doorman said, turning to Little Bear. He was a bulldog of a guy called Ren. "They're just flying high. Probably so pumped up on steroids, they're not sure whether they want to fight or fuck."

"Hey, I'll do both," the third guy said. He was bigger than the others with a high and tight buzz cut. "I'm up for both, man. I'm always up for both. How about you, Cochise?"

Ren put an arm out. "You guys aren't coming in. You got me? Now, move along before my friend here loses what little temper he has left."

"Aw, come on, man," the guy with the blond spikes cried. "We didn't mean to offend the big chief. We just want to come inside, get a couple of drinks, and hit on some hot ass."

"Yeah, man. We want some hot ass. That's all we need."

"Well, you're not getting it in this club," Ren replied, shoving the guy with the buzz-cut back. "Now, get the hell out of here. We've got people waiting in line."

"Hey, don't touch me man," buzz-cut hissed, slapping Ren's hand away.

"I wouldn't do that if I were you," Little Bear said, stepping forward.

"Oh yeah? And, what you gonna do about it, Sitting Bull? You want some of this? Do you?"

He thought the three of them looked ridiculous so he laughed, and that was the tiny, innocent sounding spark that ignited the whole thing. At least, that was what blond spikes and black mohawk said in the courtroom. Maybe they were right. Little Bear didn't remember. All he did know was that buzz-cut came in swinging, and while Ren pushed the other two guys away, he had plowed into him. All he could see was a swirling red mist, within which his mother was lying in her bed, her body frail and emaciated, her cheekbones standing out like sharp blades in her face. His father was beside her, glaring at him, calling him a failure, a let-down, and other names that he didn't recall. His sister was there too, pointing a finger in his face; jab,

jab, jabbing at him. When he stopped punching, he looked down at the bloodied mess on the asphalt and knew he was in trouble. *Big* trouble.

He ran, but not far. It was as though he wanted to get caught. He went back to his apartment to flush his coke, and that was when the police came crashing through his door. You would have thought he'd committed an act of terrorism, there were so many of them.

The judge gave him 10 years, and he used the time wisely, getting off the coke and studying engines and mechanics. He wanted to better himself. He had to. The parole board let him out after eight, and when he left the prison, he just grabbed his things and returned home—his real home. The house was empty, except for his dad, but when he found him working on an old station wagon out back, he looked like a shell of the man he'd once thought could crush mountains in his bare hands. His wife's passing had broken him.

"Here, let me help with that," Little Bear said, reaching for the wrench, but his dad pushed him away.

"You're not welcome here," he said. Those four little words still felt like sharp pins in his heart. He knew he would never be able to forget them, and neither did he want to. They helped him maintain focus.

He looked up as Axle growled menacingly at something in the forest. He hauled himself out of his chair and went to him, stroking his back, soothing him.

"I know," he said. "The ghosts are coming after us, old boy. We can't escape them."

CHAPTER TWENTY-ONE

Unresolved Issues

I sat in my hotel room and packed my things. I knew I couldn't leave, but I also didn't want to be at the Regal any more. It felt like I was dishonoring Penny. I planned to settle up my bill, which I knew would leave me with only a couple of hundred dollars to my name, but I guessed I'd have to figure it out. I always did.

I'd heard there was a place six blocks down that was letting out rooms for $50 a night. I thought I could make up the difference by working behind the bar or cleaning dishes—anything. What I couldn't do, what made my gut churn and my head hurt, was stay in a hotel room that was being rented to me for free by a woman who'd had her guts ripped out, and by a man who evidently had cheated on her with the woman that I'd literally just got into the sack with. The whole thing was messing with my head, which had been messed with enough.

"Oh, things just keep on getting better around here, don't they?" Bill scoffed. He was perched on the window ledge and looking down onto the street. "I told you you'd like it in Devil's Ridge."

"I hate it," I said. "Trouble's been on my back since I arrived."

"Oh, I think trouble was on your back long before then, my brother." Bill leaned out the window and breathed in the fresh air. "I wish I could smell that," he said. "The scent of the mountains, of freshly cut grass, of newly flushed exhaust fumes."

"You're not missing much."

"What are you going to do?"

"I'll work it out," I said, throwing my underwear into my suitcase.

"There's that whole thing with the Wendigo. You going to turn your back on that, too?"

"Nope. I'll see that through." *If it kills me*, I thought, which I guessed it most probably would.

"And the gold?"

I'd lost all interest in the shiny stuff. It was the last thing on my mind. If it hadn't been for the gold, I would have never come to this God forsaken town, and I would have never set foot up at Kiowa Rock. I wanted to settle the score with whatever it was that was killing people and haunting my dreams, and then get on the first train out of here. I would take my chances with Hogan. Compared to what was happening in Devil's Ridge, getting roughed up by a bunch of career criminals seemed like a small price to pay.

"You can't do that!" Bill cried, leaping down from the ledge and getting in my face. "J.C.! Jason! This is what we dreamed about. We're so close. You can't back down on me now."

"No!" I hollered, slamming my suitcase shut. "This is what you dreamed about, going on and on and on about it until you were blue in the face. I was never interested, but I listened anyway because you're my brother. I humored you. I never wanted to come here! I was happy in Chicago!"

"You were miserable in Chicago!"

I took that one like a man. He was right. I was miserable in Chicago. I'd been miserable since Fallujah. There was no denying it.

"Look, I just want out," I said, turning to the door.

"You mean you want to quit!"

I held my breath and closed my eyes. Perhaps I did, but who cared? I'd been attacked by a ghost, walked in to find a mutilated body, banged up in a jail cell for a crime I didn't commit, and almost eaten alive by a maniacal cannibal. *What did he expect?*

There was a knock on the door and suddenly everything was back in focus. I thought it was either the sheriff or Little Bear, so I opened it in a hurry. I was shocked to see Linda standing there. She'd been crying.

"Can I come in?" she asked. She sounded like a little mouse, and my stern demeanor crumbled.

"Yeah, sure."

She walked in on those tiny feet of hers and I gestured to the bed. "Take a seat."

"I'm okay standing," she replied, still meek and timid. She looked like someone who had taken a beating and was afraid there was more on the way.

"You want a drink?" I said. "I've got water or scotch."

"I'll take a scotch," she replied, her eyes puffy and waterlogged.

I turned my back to her and grabbed a glass. I poured us both a drink and wondered where this was headed. I was still angry at her. She had lied to me, and I had no idea why. And the way she'd reacted when Travis had shown up had really gotten to me—and not in a good way. I hadn't felt that jealous since I'd been in high school.

I handed her the glass and she took it, taking small sips and peering up at me with those gorgeous blue eyes. They were my weakness. I just couldn't resist them.

"I wanted to explain," she said. "To tell you why I lied."

I exhaled churlishly. "Huh. Why did you?"

She started to cry but I stood my ground. I wasn't going to be taken in by tears, crocodile or otherwise. *Those eyes though.* I had to avert my gaze.

"Travis and I did date in high school, and he did stand me up when I went to his college, but we'd already broken up by then. I was doing all the chasing. He'd made it clear that once he went away to university, he didn't want to see me any more, but I couldn't take it." I turned away. *This wasn't helping.* "Anyway, I came back to Devil's Ridge to live with my parents, and Penny was still here, lording it over people like she always had. We'd known each other for such a long time, and she'd always been the same. I feel terrible saying it now, what with everything that's happened, but I hated her for it. I hated the way she made me feel."

She set her glass down and sat on the edge of the bed, her hands clasped between her knees as if she was praying. "Anyway, after Travis got injured playing college football, he came home. I thought maybe we could reconnect, but after I'd put on my little stalker show, he didn't want to. A couple of months later, his dad loaned him the money to buy into his first business—a real estate agency in town. When that took off, he bought up a couple of other businesses, including The Regal Hotel. Penny saw how well Travis was doing and made a beeline for him, of course. She knew how I felt, but what did she care, right? She was Penny White. Most of the men her age wanted her. Who wouldn't? All you had to do was look at her."

Linda was right. Penny had had a presence in more ways than one, but that didn't make her appealing. She was friendly, she was helpful, but I always knew that the only person Penny had ever really looked out for was Penny.

"They got married six months later and I couldn't take it. I went on a six week summer vacation with my parents to California during the school break, hoping that by the time I got home, my feelings would have changed and I could move on."

"And, had they?" I knew the answer to this, but I felt compelled to ask.

She shook her head. "By this time, Travis had realized who the real Penny was, what she was all about, and we bumped into each other at The Prospector. He was sinking his fourth or fifth drink, and I was looking to take my mind off things. He told me that he'd caught Penny flirting with one of the hotel staff in a store cupboard, and it wasn't the first time. He also said they'd been fighting a lot. About money, mostly. Penny had thought Travis was worth a lot more than he actually was, so when she looked into his accounts she'd gotten a nasty shock. He was in debt up to his neck, and his father was constantly bailing him out of trouble. He was never a businessman. He was just an ex-football player whose father had deep pockets."

That little revelation made me feel a little better, although the guy had put up my bail, so I had to be grateful for that.

"We got talking and one thing led to another. We spent that night together."

"Spare me the details."

"It was just one night," she said. She couldn't keep her hands still, as if she was trying to wash something off. "I promise. The next day, I knew we'd made a mistake and I broke it off."

"But Penny found out, right?"

Tears welled in the corners of her eyes again and she nodded. "Nothing got past Penny."

"Tell me about it."

"She came after me, of course. Not head on—that wasn't Penny's style. She had a word with her friend who sits on the school's governing committee. I was kicked back from my upcoming promotion to deputy principal, and was sent back down to assistant teacher. I'd worked so hard to get myself in a promising position, and just like that, I was at the bottom of the ladder again."

"I'm sorry," I said. "I didn't know." I turned away, wondering if this version of events was the truth or yet another lie. "And Travis?" I asked. "How did he feel about all of this?"

She dabbed at her damp cheeks with the back of her hand. "He moved on," she said. "We both did. It had been a stupid mistake, and it had cost me my job."

"But you still have feelings for him?"

She let out a sharp exhale. "He was my first true love. I guess you never forget those."

"No, I guess you don't," I turned my back and went to the window. "But, why lie? Why not tell me this to begin with?"

"Because I was ashamed," she said, the words barely escaping her lips. "Because I knew that Penny would try to get her hooks into you. Because I thought that if you knew the truth about me, then you'd turn your back on our friendship. And because I hated her." She took a long breath. "Shit, I still hate her, even after what happened. Does that make me a bad person?"

I thought about that for a moment, but if Linda was bad then what did that make me? Her one little act of misjudgement against a person that had been a constant thorn in her side since childhood paled into insignificance compared to the things I'd done for Hogan. If Linda was hellbound, then I'd be waiting in the penthouse suite. Still, that didn't mean it didn't hurt.

"Should have told me," I scowled under my breath, but it didn't sound convincing, even to me.

There was a long silence between us as I gazed out the window and she sat on the edge of the hotel bed, sniffling. Finally, I heard the unmistakable sound of muted resignation before she stood. I didn't turn until she was almost at the door. She reached for the handle and opened it, glancing back before she left.

I thought of how I'd felt when I'd learned that somebody, or something, had been in her home when she was there, all alone, and that Penny's mutilated remains had been discarded in her yard. I thought about the way she'd made me feel when we'd spent that one unforgettable morning together. Despite what had happened, I couldn't let her walk out of my hotel room without saying something.

"Don't go," I said. "I don't want you to go."

"I don't want to go either."

I went to her and took her hands in mine. "Then, we're agreed," I said, before wrapping her in my arms and running my fingers slowly down her spine. "Neither of us are going anywhere."

Afterward, we lay in bed while I filled her in on what had gone down with Caleb and my subsequent rendezvous with Sheriff Harris. With each word that came out of my mouth, the look of horror on Linda's face became more and more exaggerated. It was as if I was describing the plot of some movie I'd seen to her, or recounting a horror story I'd read.

"Holy shit," she said, which caught me off guard because I think it was the first time I'd heard her cuss. "So, it was Caleb all along?

I nodded, although I knew that Caleb wasn't the architect of what had been going down. That was something else entirely.

"I teach his younger brother at school."

I huffed. In a small town, nothing went down without somebody knowing or being the family of one of the victims.

"But, wait a minute," she said after a moment. "If Little Bear killed Caleb when you said he did, a little after 9 p.m., then Caleb couldn't have killed Penny, or even been in my house around midnight that same evening."

I knew she was going to get to this point pretty quickly, and I'd decided to divulge what I knew, no matter how ridiculous it sounded. There was no way that I could avoid it. She'd been confronted by the Wendigo, which meant she deserved to know everything, or as much as I understood anyway.

As I told her all about what I'd learned about the demon spirit, followed by the trip Little Bear and I took to the ancient city in the mountains, the vision I'd had after inhaling from Little Bear's pipe, and Caleb's subsequent arrival, I expected the woman lying naked beside me to scoff or laugh out loud. But, then I realized, that was because it was what I would have done. But, I hadn't lived in Devil's Ridge all my life with the shadow of those missing miners hanging over me. Linda had heard these kinds of stories a hundred times before and they didn't seem to phase her in the slightest.

As she took in everything I said, she sat up, as if a terrible thought had occurred to her.

"So what's next?" she asked.

"What do you mean?"

"Well, this Wendigo, or whatever it is we're dealing with, clearly still has business with you and probably a dozen or so others in this town."

I nodded sombrely. She was right. I suspected that the creature had me in its sights, as well as Little Bear, the sheriff, Old Boomer, and anybody else who had been involved in waking it from its long hibernation. "Yeah, I guess so. But you don't have to worry about it." I ran a finger down her arm. "The sheriff, Little Bear, and I have already decided. Tomorrow, we're going on a little expedition into the hills and settle this thing once and for all."

She whirled on me then, her eyes ablaze. "But you don't even know anything about this thing? How do you even kill a demonic spirit?"

"I think it has a host," I said. "I think it inhabits humans, like Caleb and perhaps even the person who visited your home last night. But, I think it also has a parent host, the thing that maybe most resembles its true form in the spirit world." I recalled my vision in the mountains, of the skull face and the long antlers, the tall muscular form encased in the thick, writhing roots. "I think—and Little Bear agrees—that if we kill that, then the Wendigo will be sent back to wherever the hell it came from in the first place."

"But, you don't know your plan will work."

I shook my head. "We have a good feeling about it, but there's no guarantees."

She glared at me, her mouth open, her eyes disbelieving. After a moment of apparent indecision, she reached for her phone and frantically typed a message. Once the message was sent, she tossed her phone on the bed, leapt up, and collected her clothes.

I glanced at the phone. She'd sent a message to the school principal.

"Everything okay?" I asked, watching as she pulled on her jeans and shirt.

"Yep. I just told the principal there was a family emergency and I was going to be away for a few days."

I shook my head, confused. "What? Where are you going?"

She went to the mirror and ran a hairbrush through her shoulder-length hair.

"This thing came for me last night, J.C.," she said. "If you think I'm going to let you go out there on a hunt without me, then you've got another thing coming." She turned to me, her expression one of grim determination. "This Wendigo and I have some issues we have to work through."

CHAPTER TWENTY-TWO

Moral Compass

T he six-wheel, gunmetal gray humvee rolled into Devil's Ridge a little after mid-day. The sky was a brilliant blue and the digital display in the vehicle registered the air temperature outside at somewhere approaching 90-degrees, not that it mattered to the vehicle's occupants.

The driver had the air conditioning cranked all the way up, just like his boss liked it, and the bottled water was chilled to just above freezing. Including the driver, a broad shouldered guy with a square jaw and short crop of dark hair, there were four people in the car, including a thin weasel of a man with a pencil thin nose named Ethan Crane. There was also an ex-Special Forces soldier with a gleaming bald head and tattoos named Britt Steel, and the man they all referred to as "boss"—a tall man with a well honed physique, neatly trimmed blond hair, alabaster skin, and round-rimmed glasses.

Frank Hogan glared out the tinted windows and watched as the residents of what he considered to be Hicksville, USA walked idly by. He thought how easy it would be to push the muzzle of his Heckler and Koch 2000 to the window and blow one of those sleepy asshole's brains all over the street. It wouldn't take much, just a little squeeze and *poof*. Bye-bye baby. Most likely, no one would even care.

What did these people even have to offer the world? No one even knew this place existed. It was literally in the middle of nowhere, with no landmarks or monuments to speak of. It was as if life down there had stopped somewhere in the mid-20th century and had forgotten to restart. Why the hell Jason Carter had taken it upon himself to abandon his role working for his organization and run to the boonies was beyond him, but run he had. And as far as Frank could work out, he hadn't wanted to be found either.

"You want to stay here while I check things out?" Britt asked, pushing a handgun into the holster beneath his jacket. Britt had been a loyal servant to Hogan's cause for approaching five years, ever since he'd come back from his time overseas. He was a stone-faced killer and had a reputation for getting the job done, no matter the cost. If Steel came knocking on your door, you knew your time left on this Earth was short. *Like, very short.*

"Nah. I could use a coffee," Hogan replied. "Why don't we just leave the car here and walk down to that place." He gestured toward a sign hanging above a quaint little building nestled between The Prospector and a hair salon. The sign read "Cherry's On Top." "Sounds kinda nice," he said. "You guys want a little pie?"

The driver, Scott Campbell, answered first. He'd only been in Hogan's employ for a little under two months, and he'd never been offered pie by his boss before. "Sure thing, boss."

"You think this is a good idea?" Ethan said, peering through the window. "We're not exactly sure of Carter's whereabouts. He could be out there, lurking around some corner somewhere, and if he sees us, he could do something rash."

Hogan opened the door and stepped outside. "Well, then at least we would have found that low-life, backstabbing son of a bitch." He hauled himself out of the car and then leaned back in, jabbing a heavily-ringed finger at the three men. "Come on, I'm hungry."

They sat in the coffee shop, which was only half full, and sipped their drinks in silence. Hogan had ordered a cappuccino with everything, including whipped cream and chocolate dusting. He wiped froth from his upper lip and watched as people passed by. He thought of Carter and how he'd been during that last week before he'd disappeared. He'd appeared distant and distracted, like something had been gnawing at him. Hogan hadn't thought anything of it at the time. You didn't get to quit his organization, after all. The only way out was if the organization quit you, which almost always meant a visit from Steel.

Carter had come to him well recommended by none other than Steel himself. They'd served some time together in Iraq, and while Steel had been in a special ops unit, Carter's reputation as a no nonsense, no backing down kind of guy had made it back to Steel's unit. Since his brother had been blown to smithereens in Fallujah, it seemed that Carter had taken it upon himself to become a one-man crusader, storming into buildings full of enemy soldiers, risking the lives of the other members of his platoon while they fought to back him up. It was almost as if his brother's death had left Carter with nothing to live for. It was sad, really, but Hogan knew he could use it to his advantage.

"I need you to do a job for me," Hogan had said to Carter while they sat in a bar run by his organization. "It should be an easy one. Five-grand bonus in it for you if it's done right."

Carter had slowly swirled his whiskey, watching as the ice cubes clinked. "Sure thing, boss. What you got?"

"How's your moral compass doing these days?"

Carter shot his boss a furtive glance before returning his gaze to his ice cubes. "So so."

Hogan nodded. "Good, because this one might test it."

Hogan went on to fill Carter in on the details. One of their employees, a chancer named Tom Malone who thought of himself as a bit of an up and comer, had been leaking information about the Hogan Gang's business dealings to a rival organization run by the Pollacks. Consequently, one of Hogan's men had been ambushed on the east side of town. The guy hadn't been killed, but he was never going to walk in a straight line again. The worst thing was, the drugs that the guy was trafficking never made it to their intended destination. In fact, they'd gone missing, costing Hogan a little over two million dollars.

"You want him dead?" Carter asked, almost nonchalantly.

"No, death's too good for this deceitful bastard. My guy, Razor, has a wife and young kids, and now he can't provide for them like he used to. Just because Malone got greedy."

"I don't get it," Carter said. "So, you want me to do the same to him? Mess him up just like the Pollacks messed up Razor? Isn't that letting him off a little lightly?"

Hogan laughed out loud, making everyone else in the bar look up sharply. "Well, look at you, eager to get all murderous with one of his own. I thought you were the guy who preferred to scare people rather than put them in the ground. Well, anyways, turns out Malone's been seeing one of the god-daughters of one of these stinking Pollacks. Apparently, he's got himself loved up real good, so my thinking is, why not kill two birds with one stone?"

Carter didn't seem to understand, so Hogan put it in plainer language. "We kill the girl to send a message to both Malone and the Pollacks. You don't fuck with the Hogan gang. Not now. Not ever!"

Carter seemed pretty unsettled by the suggestion. "Woah, there boss. Has this girl actually done anything bad against us?"

"Yeah, she fucked a traitor."

"Besides that?"

"She was born into that family. Look, what does it matter? It's an eye for an eye."

"I'd prefer to take out Malone."

Hogan slapped Carter on the back and grinned. "Because he's a guy? It's the 21st century, Carter. This is an equal opportunities country."

"Yeah, but—"

Hogan leaned in and pulled Carter close. He could smell Carter's cheap cologne and see the hatred that burned somewhere behind his eyes. Hogan knew Carter didn't like him, but that was okay. To be a true leader, you didn't need your team to like you. You needed them to fear you.

"Look, pal. I want this job done, and I want it done soon. You work for me, so I expect you to do exactly what I ask without question? You get me?"

Carter tried to stare him down, but Hogan knew he had the jump on him. He always carried a blade tucked beneath the sleeve of his shirt on a spring-loaded mechanism. If Carter got the notion to do something stupid, he'd get a knife in his belly for his troubles. He didn't want to kill him, but if it came to it, he wouldn't hesitate. It wouldn't be the first time he'd had to make an example of a valued team member. Carter was replaceable. Everybody except Hogan himself was dispensable.

Eventually, Carter averted his eyes. "Yeah, I get you."

Hogan reached into the pocket of his jacket and pulled out a crumpled piece of paper. "Good. Here's the address. She gets off her shift at 10. I suggest you do the deed when she gets home. Make it look like a robbery gone wrong. I'll make sure Malone knows it was us."

Two days later, not only was Malone still fat, dumb, and happy, but the broad was still alive. What's more, Carter was nowhere to be seen, and his phone line was dead. When Hogan and Steel went to his apartment to find out what the hell was going on, they found it cleared out, along with almost $1500 of up-front money. They checked the bars he hung out in, along with the strip joints and movie theaters. Nobody had seen him. It was like he'd vanished into thin air.

It had taken them two week's of knocking heads together and checking CCTV footage from bars along the strip to find out where Carter had gone. He'd been spotted entering Chicago Union Station dressed like a much older man. The disguise hadn't fooled Hogan. He'd know Carter's slight limp anywhere. It was the last remnants of an old war wound, caused by shrapnel fragments from when he and his brother had been ambushed in the abandoned school.

When one of Hogan's guys had checked in with a contact they had in the office, they found out that he'd bought a ticket to Denver, Colorado. One way. From there, they'd traced him to Devil's Ridge, and the rest, as they say, was history.

Back in the coffee house, Hogan leaned over and cut a slim slice from his cherry pie. It looked delicious, but something about what was going on outside the shop window was bothering him. Many of the men looked like they'd been working long hours in a quarry or a construction site; but as far as Hogan could tell, there wasn't anything like that going on in the town. The place looked like it hadn't had any construction since the early settlers happened upon the place.

He watched as a man with a grimy face and scuffed knuckles approached the counter and ordered a black coffee. He gave off an odor, like gunpowder and dust. Outside, a woman got out of her car and headed for the grocery store. She too looked like she'd been rolling around in the dirt. She appeared exhausted, too, like she'd spent a long shift heavy lifting.

"Hey, you, over there," Hogan called out, putting on his best winning smile. "Hey, sir. You wanna come and join us over here? We have pie."

The guy at the counter turned, the lines in his face thick with dust and sweat. He looked angry, exhausted, and more than a little confused. He also bore the look of someone who was regularly suspicious of others and less inclined to chat to strangers than most.

"Do I know you?" he grunted, approaching with an air of caution, as someone might approach a rattlesnake or a discarded backpack.

"You don't. Name's Henry. I'm traveling on business with my colleagues. We're just passing through on our way to Denver."

"What kind of business?"

"Resource management," Hogan said, barely blinking. "It really is quite boring, I can assure you."

The man eyed each of them in turn, slowly sipping his coffee. "Yeah, I guess it must be." He held out a hand. "Name's Jerry."

"It's a pleasure to meet you, Jerry. Please," Hogan gestured to a chair that Britt Steel dragged across from the adjacent table. "Won't you sit?"

"I don't have long," Jerry replied. "I've just finished a long shift, and my wife's expecting me. I just came in to grab a coffee because I'm not supposed to drink caffeine. But what she doesn't know won't hurt her, right?"

"Right," Hogan said, forcing a laugh. His three compatriots joined in. "I get it. Well, she won't know about you eating some of this delicious cherry pie either. We won't tell, if you won't." Hogan slipped the plate across to the newcomer and handed him a fresh fork. "Go ahead. Dig in."

"Don't mind if I do," Jerry said, setting down his takeaway cup and forking in a huge mouthful of pastry, red cherry, and cream. "I haven't eaten a thing all morning and my wife's been serving me garden salad and fresh fruit all week. She says she's looking out for my heart, but my stomach isn't too happy about it, let me tell you that."

"I hear you, friend. We've all been there, right boys?" The others all nodded their enthusiastic agreement. "You mind if I ask where you work?" Hogan continued, pressing his advantage. "You sure look like you've been getting your hands dirty, if you don't mind me saying."

"Ain't that the truth. I haven't worked this hard in years. I usually spend my time in an office—all day behind a desk with my fat ass resting on an ergonomically-designed chair because of my bad back—but my boss allowed me to take a month-long sabbatical to help out with the dig."

Hogan's eyes narrowed and he leaned forward, placing his elbows on the edge of the table. "The dig?"

"Yeah," Jerry said, swallowing another large slice of pie. Cream dribbled onto his chin. "They only discovered it a couple of weeks ago. A new guy in town and the Indian found it, or so they say. Who'd have thought it, right? All the riches in the world, hidden up there in the hills all this time, and yet it took some guy from Chicago less than a day to realize it was there. How dumb were we?"

Hogan eyed Ethan Crane, who's narrow nose twitched furiously, as if he'd suddenly noticed a satisfying odor in the air. "Sounds fascinating," Hogan said. "But I don't understand. Riches? What do you mean by that?"

Jerry glanced around the room, finished the last of the pie, and shuffled his chair forward. "Well, I'm not really supposed to say, but as you fellas have been so nice and all."

Hogan gestured for him to continue. He could barely contain his anticipation. "Please, go ahead."

"Well, it turns out this guy—J.C., I think they call him—well, it turns out he hit the jackpot on day one."

"The jackpot?" Hogan replied, grinning.

"That's right," Jerry whispered. He looked at them each in turn. "He found gold."

CHAPTER TWENTY-THREE

The Moonlit Body

Sheriff Elijah Harris showered, packed his bag, and spent the next hour cleaning and servicing his Browning X-Bolt rifle. He didn't know exactly how long the three of them would be up there in the mountains searching for whatever the hell it was that was terrorizing his town, but he'd allowed himself enough provisions to get him through three nights. If they hadn't accomplished what they'd set out to do in that time, then the chances were their plan had either failed or they were dead. Either one of those options were distinctly possible.

He'd already briefed his two deputies that he would be out of town for a few days. They didn't need to know what he was planning, and he never gave them any indication of what it was. Barns in particular seemed curious, perhaps even suspicious, but he knew better than to pry. The sheriff's office could barely afford both guys, and Barns was only too aware that the sheriff had the sole say on who would be cut if it came to it. The kid had a young family and couldn't afford to lose his job. That suited Harris. It was the kind of situation that kept the young police officer compliant.

He'd then had to field a call from a very upset mayor who considered Travis Newsted and his father, Mac, as personal friends. The fact they'd almost entirely funded the mayor's last run for office hadn't escaped the sheriff's attention.

"We need to get to the bottom of this and fast, Elijah," the mayor said, his voice shrill and agitated. "Penny White was a wonderful woman, and to think of her being butchered in such a horrific way. It's little wonder that Mac and his son are so distraught. We need to find the killer and bring him to justice."

"We're working on it, sir, believe me," he'd replied, fighting his natural instinct to throw in a caustic comment.

"I'm sure you are, but we need results–and fast."

The sheriff chewed his pen and grunted down the line. "Uh-huh."

The line had gone quiet for a moment, and then the mayor said. "I hear you've dropped the charges against Carter."

The sheriff had known this was coming. "Well, I could hardly arrest him for a crime he couldn't have committed now, could I?"

"And you know this because—"

"Because he was with me at the time of Mrs. White's death."

"Could he have had an accomplice?"

"I don't think so. He doesn't really know anyone in town, other than the Indian, Penny herself, and Linda Thornton, the schoolteacher."

There was silence again. "I hear he's also on good terms with Hank "Boomer" Windell."

"You want me to bring in an 80-year-old man for questioning? I hardly think he was the one who ripped out Penny White's lower intestine, do you?"

"No need to be so crass!" the mayor hollered. "May I remind you that our mutual friends have some information on you that would hardly make your family proud."

The sheriff clenched his jaw and counted to 10. He could feel his pulse pounding in his temples, as if something powerful was trying to crawl out of his skull. He wanted to reach down the phone line and rip out the mayor's vocal chords with his bare hands. "Yes. I'm well aware."

"The killer has to be caught," the mayor hissed. "And this Jason Carter, along with his Indian friend, need to be dealt with. No excuses."

The call had ended abruptly, which had suited the sheriff. He hadn't enjoyed the conversation anyway.

As the sheriff set down his rifle and pulled on his hiking boots, there was a knock at the door. He opened it to find Carter, Little Bear, and the schoolteacher standing there, dressed in walking gear.

"I thought it was just the three of us," the sheriff said, looking at the much smaller woman. "This isn't going to be an easy trip."

"Well, that's good then," Linda said, pulling back her jacket and revealing the bowie knife sheathed in her belt. "I'd hate to get bored."

They rode in Little Bear's truck to the foot of the Sawatch Range of the Southern Rocky Mountains. Mount Elbert rose up like a giant monolith in the distance, its peak covered in a thick mist that seemed to hang in the air like cotton. The air had turned a little colder and there was a cool dampness that clung to Linda's cheeks and hair. She didn't know why she'd decided to come on this trip with J.C. All she knew was that she couldn't bear to be in the house on her own after what had happened, and she hated that. She hated being scared, and she hated the thing that had made her feel like that.

"Which way we headed?" the sheriff asked, his rifle hanging diagonally across his back.

"I say we go north," Little Bear said. "Through the forest, toward the peaks. I think the Wendigo prefers the altitude."

"It sure would be easier if he stayed down here on low ground," the sheriff replied, eyeing the incline with obvious trepidation. "I don't like the idea of him having the advantage of being able to see us coming."

"I don't think it matters either way," J.C. replied. "He's had the advantage all along. Can't see that changing."

Linda felt her pulse quicken as she listened to the conversation. Hearing three grown men talk about the Wendigo as if it was a real, living, breathing thing seemed absurd to her, even though she believed everything J.C. had told her, and she'd witnessed first hand the kind of things it was capable of. But the fact remained, she'd been told numerous tales of the Wendigo and what it may or may not have done to nearly 10 miners almost 80 years ago when she was a kid. It had always felt like a grim fairy tale to her, like stories of the Krampus or the troll under the bridge.

Little Bear pointed toward a tall forest in the distance. "There's a trail that leads across the valley floor and over that incline to Monarch Pass. I suggest we head that way, keep walking until early evening, and set up camp at the foot of the mountains."

Linda's eyes followed the line of his arm. She thought the mountains looked a long way off, maybe 15 miles, and the path rose and fell quite sharply. She looked down at her boots and was grateful she'd worn her sensible shoes.

"You don't have to do this, you know?" J.C. said, keeping his voice low. "I can take you back and then catch up with the others."

Linda shot him a sharp look of indignation and hitched her backpack onto her shoulders. "You don't have to worry about me," she said, setting off toward the path. "Just concentrate on keeping up."

The forest was a lot thicker than Little Bear had had us believe. As we descended deeper into the belly of the valley, the trees seemed to close in around us, as if they were guarding something; a secret maybe, or hidden treasure. I got the sense pretty early on that we were being watched, but I knew from experience that your mind could play cruel tricks on you when it was deprived of the everyday trappings of civilization. I'd experienced the Wendigo up close, and even though it was in its guise as a young, confused kid, I didn't think it would waste time toying with us. If the Wendigo wanted to pick us off, one by one, it would. We had to be ready.

My brother walked with us, of course. I knew he wouldn't miss the opportunity.

"Exciting, isn't it?" he said. "A real life ghost hunt." I shrugged. "Reminds me of our time hunting down that sniper that fled across the Euphrates. Do you remember?" I nodded, of course I did. I remember everything about my time in Iraq. *Every damn thing.* "We went building to building, searching for that son of a bitch, but do you think we could find him? It was as if he'd evaporated or something. I've never known someone just vanish like that."

I knew where Bill was headed with this, and I didn't like it. I glanced at the others, but fortunately they were lost in their own thoughts, the vapid nothingness of the forest shrouding them in its all consuming veil.

"Two days we searched, and both days we headed back to our base, empty-handed and despondent. The captain had almost given up all hope, which was hard to believe. That guy was like a hunting dog with a rat most of the time. Then, we got some intel from a market trader on the other side of town who said he'd spotted the guy living on a rooftop by the river bank. I was so pissed because I'd searched that area myself. Anyway, we headed back and surrounded the building. It had been a post office or something, as I remember it. I went up there, and you came too, didn't you?"

I had. I'd been on my brother's shoulder the whole time, fearing the whole thing was an ambush.

"I was so afraid that we were going to get picked off as we climbed that staircase. We were sitting ducks. All it would have taken was for that bastard to lean across from the upstairs doorway, and *putt, putt*. Two shots later, and you and I would have been nothing more than dog chow." Except that hadn't happened at all. "We got to the roof, kicked open the door, and headed out, guns at the ready. But, despite what the intel had said, there was no sign of anyone ever being up there. And do you know why? Do you want to know why?"

I wanted to tell him of course I did; of course I knew why the sniper the guys had nicknamed "Viper of the Euphrates" had disappeared from that rooftop. In the corridors of military intelligence, they spoke his name as if he might overhear them even from miles away. He was a sniper, one so precise and stealthy that his victims often seemed to drop from the mere sound of his name. Bullet casings were recovered, but the man himself remained an elusive enigma, blending into the harsh landscape as effortlessly as the desert swallowed the dusk.

"Because he was the next rooftop over," I said, "and before we'd even had the chance to think, he'd opened fire on our unit down at street level and killed three of our men."

Yeah, he had, and what made it worse was he got away. We never caught The Viper. Never even got to lay eyes on him. He'd done what he set out to do, and then he just vanished into thin air.

"This could end up the same way," Bill said. "This Wendigo could just pick you off one by one, and you wouldn't even know what hit you."

I swallowed cloying saliva. I couldn't let the Wendigo be our version of The Viper. I just couldn't. I'd unleashed this murderous creature, and I had to make it right. For me, for Linda, and for those who had already been killed.

"Wait," Little Bear said, holding up his hand. He slid his rifle from his shoulder as he lowered himself into a kneeling position, placing his rifle sight up to his eye. The three of us crouched behind him. I peered into the gloom, wondering what the hell had caught his attention. I couldn't see anything, just densely-packed trees with foliage-covered ground and a thick canopy overhead.

"He was there," he said. "I'm sure of it."

We sat in silence for a few moments, listening for a sound that would give away our prey's location. There was the repetitive thrumming of a woodpecker someway off in the distance, and a small animal rummaging in the undergrowth to our left, but otherwise the forest was silent.

"Probably just seeing things," the sheriff said, hauling himself to his feet. "It happens to us all."

"He was there," Little Bear repeated, before standing and pressing on.

I gleaned at Linda who looked a little unsettled by the near encounter. I'd wondered whether she'd really believed my story, or whether she had decided to come along simply to humor me. From the look on her face, she was now under no illusion that we were serious.

The Wendigo was out there, and come hell or high water, we were going to find it.

That night we set up camp at the foot of a hill where a narrow stream tumbled lazily between the trees. The sun was dipping between the mountains, giving the sky an eerie red glow. The temperature had also dropped quite significantly, and Linda and I hurried to collect enough dry timber to build a fire. Little Bear sat on the ground, his back to a tree as he sharpened his knife, while the sheriff checked his rifle.

"You worried that thing won't work?" Little Bear asked.

The sheriff looked up from his task. "What's that?"

"You've been cleaning, loading, and reloading that thing all day long. It's like you don't trust it."

"You take care of your firearm, it takes care of you," the sheriff replied brusquely.

"I've never known a firearm that needed so much care to begin with."

I struck two flints against the kindling and dried grass that Linda and I had piled beneath the larger twigs, and waited for the flame to ignite. Within a few moments, the sight of an orange flame emerged, followed by a thin stream of smoke that grew into a thick shaft.

"Hallelujah," I said, grinning at Linda, noticing how tired she looked. "Here," I said, pulling a log toward the edge of the flames. "Why don't you sit here and I'll prepare something for us to eat."

Linda shook her head. "I'm okay, I'm fine. Here, I'll help you."

Between us we rustled up a bean stew, thickening the broth with a little ketchup and some chopped beef. It really wasn't bad. Little Bear had even brought along some fry bread, and we each dipped the doughy pastry into the broth and devoured it while our campsite filled with the sound of slurping and satisfied groans.

With our meal finished, we sat there, allowing the darkness to keep us company.

"So, why?" the sheriff asked eventually. "Why did you come out here, J.C? What was so interesting about Devil's Ridge that made you want to travel all this way from Chicago?"

The question caught me off guard. I spied my brother sitting a little way away in the gloom, his pale face barely visible among the trees.

"I grabbed a map, closed my eyes, and stuck a pin in it," I said, smiling at Linda. "It was just a chance thing, really."

"I don't believe that," he replied. "You came here for a reason. You don't want to tell us, that's fine, but in my experience, a man suddenly shows up in town having traveled such a long way, he's either looking for something or he's running from something. Either way, you got a secret you ain't telling."

I didn't break his gaze. I knew if I did, I'd be giving away more than I was prepared to. I sensed Linda watching and waiting to see what would happen next, but I wasn't going to tell them all about how my brother was blown to pieces in Fallujah after giving me the details of the gold he'd found in the hills above Devil's Ridge. Nor how when I'd returned from the military, a dejected, broken man, I'd fallen in with a dangerous gangster, becoming one of his most effective enforcers.

"There's nothing to tell."

We sat in silence for a while longer before Little Bear stood and headed for his tent. "I'm turning in," he said. "Long day ahead of us tomorrow."

"Yeah, me too," the sheriff added. "I'm beat. How about you two?"

Linda yawned beside me. "I'll sit out here and keep watch a while," I said. "If that thing's out there, I don't want it catching us with our pants down, so to speak."

"There's nothing out there except the owls," the sheriff said, although his eyes betrayed him. I could see he didn't truly believe he would be getting much sleep that night. Perhaps none of us would. The ghost of the Wendigo was heavy on all our minds.

Linda and I sat by the fire, listening to the wood crackle and the forest creak and sway.

"Do you really believe what you said?" she asked after a while. "Do you really think it's out there?"

I let out a long breath and hoped I could keep the lure of exhaustion at bay. "I don't know, but I'm not taking any chances. Why don't you get some sleep? Don't worry, I'll wake you if I hear anything."

Before long she'd curled up into a ball by the fire, her sleeping bag pulled up to her chin. I watched her chest rise and fall, rise and fall. I kept my ears tuned to every rustle in the leaves, every snap of a twig, every sigh as the breeze kissed the top of the canopy. I peered into the darkness, half expecting a monster standing seven feet tall with a bare skull for a head and with thick, curved antlers to come charging toward me—its hot breath steaming from its nostrils, its legs pounding like pistons beneath it—but all I saw were fireflies and mosquitos.

I thought of my brother, who I missed dearly, even though his memory taunted me daily. I also thought of all the mistakes I made, of which there were too many to count. Above all, I thought of the woman lying asleep beside me by the fire. I wondered what I'd begun down there in Devil's Ridge, and whether I had the courage and the fortitude to see it through.

I could see my parents. My mother, as she lay dying in a hospital ward. My father, who I had little memory of, throwing me a ball and laughing while my brother tackled me to the ground. I thought of my first love; a girl I'd been pursuing at high school since ninth grade. Her name was Bethany and she was just about the most beautiful thing I'd ever seen at that young age. She made me feel like my heart would burst and my head would explode.

Then, I thought of Hogan and Steel, and all the people I'd hurt for them. I knew Steel was a bad guy from the get-go. I'd seen what he'd done in Iraq, the terrible war crimes he'd committed. I'd always known he enjoyed inflicting pain on others, no matter how innocent they might be. He didn't care. Then, all my memories seemed to blend and merge into one, and my mother was now throwing me the ball, except the ball was now a grenade and it was heading straight for Bethany. I dived to catch it, but I only succeeded in pushing it into the forest where my brother was hiding from Steel, who was convinced Bill was an insurgent.

When the grenade exploded, I jerked awake and that was when I realized we were not alone. Something was standing behind me in the forest.

The fire had burned down to nothing more than glowing embers and ash. Linda was still curled in a ball, but she appeared restless, as if something was gnawing away at her from inside her brain. I reached for my knife and slowly turned. I could hear something breathing behind me, as if a bull had crept into the woods and was now preparing to charge me, gorging me to death with its razor-tipped horns.

I could feel my heart pounding in my chest, but I knew I needed to react before whatever presence was with us out there in the darkness made the first move. I steadied myself and then rolled to my left, springing to my feet and bringing the knife upward in a jabbing motion, expecting that whatever was coming for me would find itself impaled on its sharp steel.

There was nothing there, but I instantly heard movement at my back. Realizing I'd been outflanked, I slowly turned my head and watched in horror as Linda pulled back her sleeping back and sat up. Her head was no longer where it should be. It was lying in what remained of the fire, finger like flames spurting from her eyeballs which had burst with the heat. Her mouth was drawn down in a sneering, grotesque arc of what must have been horrendous pain. I turned to her bloodied body which was now somehow rising to its feet. There, in the place where her head had once been, was the bare skull of the Wendigo, its mouth open, revealing long, bloodied fangs, and raw flesh hanging from its enormous jaws.

"J.C." it whispered to me. "You need to wake up."

I shook my head. "What?"

"You need to wake up, J.C. I heard something."

When my eyes opened I was staring at Sheriff Elijah Harris. He was shaking my shoulders and peering anxiously toward the hills. I looked down at Linda, and was instantly grateful to see her sleeping head back in its rightful place.

"Jesus, I'm sorry," I said, pulling myself upright. "I was supposed to be keeping watch."

The sheriff held his finger to his lips. "Be quiet," he whispered. "I think I know where it is."

He stooped down and collected his rifle before moving toward the stream. I was still collecting my thoughts, but

I was conscious enough to know that he couldn't go out there on his own. I also knew that there was every possibility that the Wendigo was trying to lure some of us away from the camp so it could prey on our two sleeping campmates. I wasn't about to let that happen.

I shook Linda awake, holding my finger to my lips. "It's out there," I said. "At the base of the hill. I'm going after it."

"What? What do you mean—"

"No time to explain," I said. "You need to wake Little Bear. The two of you keep watch here. I'll be back soon."

As her dreamstate faded from her mind like an alcohol-fueled fog, she seemed to realize what I was trying to tell her, and she reached behind her for her bowie knife. I kissed her before I turned to follow the sheriff, who was already climbing the shallow incline that led toward the top of the slope. I had no idea what time it was, but the darkness was still thick and suffocating. I suspected it was the early hours of the morning. The moon wasn't visible through the canopy, but the leaves overhead were painted with the milky white sheen of an invisible moon.

The sheriff turned, saw me and gestured to my right, clearly intending to try to outflank the beast. I had no idea what he thought he'd seen or heard, but his eyes told me all I needed to know. The sheriff truly believed the Wendigo was with us. You couldn't fake the kind of fear I could see etched onto his expression like a hot brand.

I scrambled across the soil and mulch, my knife in my hand and my handgun pushed into my belt. A branch snapped up ahead and I stopped dead in my tracks. I knew the sound had been too loud for it to be made by some sort of small forest animal or a deer. I drew my handgun and pulled back the slide slowly and deliberately to avoid making any noise. I didn't want to give away my location.

I'd lost sight of the sheriff some moments ago as he headed to his left so I continued to climb. It was so dark, I was literally moving through the forest on instinct, and I didn't like it. If there had been one thing I'd learned in the military, it was to always be one step ahead of the enemy. We were three steps behind, and that was being generous.

Suddenly there was a loud cry up ahead, like the sound of livestock being slaughtered. It was the kind of shrieking wail that made your blood turn cold. I could feel nervous perspiration gathering in the indentation between my throat and my chest, which was ridiculous because the air was cool. I headed toward the sound, hoping and praying that the beast wasn't following my every footstep, its hooked claws mere inches from my spine. There was another shriek and I quickened my pace, reaching the top where I looked down on a small clearing.

The moonlight shone down on the bare earth like a beam from heaven itself, but what I saw lying on the ground was anything but godly. The sheriff stood over it, his rifle hanging from a strap that was hooked over his shoulder. He looked as though all of his strength had left his body, as if finding this thing had taken what was left of his resolve and shattered it into a billion tiny fragments.

There on the ground, naked, his arms and legs outstretched in the shape of a star, a crude pentagram drawn in the earth around him in his own blood, was the ravaged, mutilated corpse of Travis Newsted.

"Holy shit!" I cried, scrambling down the slope. "What the fu—"

"Shh," the sheriff said, once more holding a finger to his lips. He pointed to the western edge of the clearing and there, cloaked in the darkness with just its crimson eyes visible, was the Wendigo. It was watching us. It wanted us to find Travis. It was bringing us a gift. I felt my stomach twist into a thousand knots, and my chest compressed as if there was a heavy weight pressing down onto it, squeezing every last ounce of air from my lungs. I could feel the malevolence in the beast, the insidious hatred that occupied every ounce of its being. I knew then that the grim reaper itself was there with us in that forest, and it had come to collect.

"We don't want this!" I tried to yell, my voice hoarse and cracked. "We're not afraid of you! Do you hear me, you sick son of a bitch!"

The sheriff reached out and grabbed my shoulder, hauling me back, but before I had a chance to resist, the Wendigo was gone. The space where its gigantic black shape had once stood was now just a slither of gray among the tall, dark silhouettes of ancient pines.

We stood there alone with Travis's moonlight kissed body. His throat had been torn open, just like the others, and just like Penny, his innards had been removed and scattered. There was something different though. Travis's eyes had also been torn out and taken, as if the Wendigo had wanted a trophy for this kill.

"How the hell did he bring him all the way out here?" the sheriff asked, shaking his head. "And why? It just doesn't make sense."

"Nothing about this makes sense, Elijah," I replied. "But that doesn't mean it isn't happening. It's right here in front of us."

"Jesus," he said, stooping down and peering at Travis's gore-covered remains. "Why rip out his insides? And why his eyes? I mean, what the hell are we dealing with here?"

There was a cry from behind us and I turned.

"It's coming from the camp," I said, my breath hurried. "Linda!"

We ran toward the slope, clambering upwards as fast as we could. I ran down the other side, crashing into thick branches and heavy trunks, but I needed to get back to our campsite. I'd already left Linda alone with the Wendigo once. I'd be damned if I was going to do it again.

I could see what was left of our firelight in the distance, and as I approached, there was another cry, followed by the loud rapport from a discharged rifle. I drew my own gun, and beside me, the sheriff shouldered his own weapon. We leapt over the stream and came barreling into the campsite, our guns aimed and ready. Little Bear was leaning against the trunk of a tree, smoke drifting up from the barrel of his rifle. Linda was by the fire, a gun in her hands. She was pointing it toward the darkness beyond the tree line, but her arms were trembling and I could hear the sound of soft sobs escaping her lips. I went to her.

"Linda. Are you okay?"

She nodded, but her eyes never left the trees.

"Thank God. What the hell happened?"

She never broke her gaze, but she spoke through her clenched jaw in a hissed whisper, the sheer terror resonating off her every word.

"It...was...here. That thing. *It was...here.*"

I looked into the distance. There was blood on the ground, but whatever had been there, it had made its escape.

"Little Bear!" the sheriff cried. "J.C. He's injured."

I went to him. Immediately, I could see the ragged wound in his side, and the blood seeping through his shirt.

"I'm okay," Little Bear said, but the pain was evident in his face. His skin had turned gray, and sweat was trickling from his forehead.

"The hell you are," I responded. "Linda. I think we have some cleaning fluid and dressings over there. Can you grab them?"

She looked down at me. I could see her thoughts were still focussed on their attacker. I needed to shake her out of it. "What?"

"Dressings!" I yelled. "Little Bear's losing a lot of blood."

She shook her head, breaking the trance, and she fetched what I needed.

"Caught me off guard," Little Bear said through gritted teeth as I poured the antiseptic fluid on his open wound. "Stupid of me. I should have been ready."

"Don't worry," I said. "You'll have a chance to get your own back."

"Sure will," Little Bear replied. "When it came at me, I looked into its eyes, and I saw something it didn't want me to see."

I glanced at the sheriff, who shrugged, and at Linda who was crouching nearby.

"What?" I said. "What did you see?"

Little Bear forced a smile through his pained expression. "I saw the one place it fears the most."

CHAPTER TWENTY-FOUR

Trouble

Mayor Arthur Pumpkin sat in his office and glared at his phone. He'd just received another call from the head of the local business consortium, an enterprise called The Devil's Business, headed up by none other than his old pal Mac Newsted. The problem was, Mac wasn't happy. In fact, Mac had sounded just about ready to blow a gasket, which was bad news for him. Mac and the folks from The Devil's Business were the largest single source of funding for his political ambitions. Without Mac, Arthur Pumpkin would still be pounding the asphalt, knocking on doors and begging people for their votes.

Mac, although often foul tempered, a little vulgar, and quite hot-headed, was astute and savvy and had latched onto the gold situation before he had even had a chance to think it over. Like many others in the town, they'd all heard the rumors of what had happened to those miners up at Kiowa Rock, and he'd had no interest in sending a team up to investigate. But Mac Newsted? He'd seen the opportunity immediately. *Who believes all those old fairy tales anyway,* he'd said, *and who did this young upstart from Chicago think he was, thinking he could roll into town on the night train, convince some ex-con Indian to take him on a tour into the mountains, and steal what was rightfully theirs? That gold belonged to the town,* (meaning it belonged to The Devil's Business, with some of the trimmings being left for the mayor's own coffers), *and that meant they had a duty to defend it.*

Sheriff Harris had resisted the suggestion, of course—that guy was so dutiful it was almost pitiful to watch—but Mac had his ways, and he knew Elijah's weakness. Since his wife had left him—which had been a direct result of his dedication to the job, by the way—he'd gradually succumbed to all the things that kept the idle thoughts of a lonely man occupied: alcohol, gambling, and his own carnal desires. Mac had found a woman who could have been his ex-wife's twin sister when she was much younger, of course, and they'd honey-trapped him, tricking him into paying for sex, and videotaping him doing some pretty explicit things, too. They knew the sheriff would never allow his kids to see what they had, so they'd blackmailed him. *Find something to pin on Carter and the Indian*, they'd said, *and make it stick.*

Then the killings in the town had started, much to the mayor's disgust, but the timing in many ways couldn't have been better. Of course, events had conspired against them, particularly when Mac's daughter-in-law had been brutally murdered, giving both Carter and Little Bear a solid alibi, and so Mac had gone to work on another strategy. The mayor had suspected that Mac would bring his son, Travis, into play at some point, driving a wedge between Carter and the schoolteacher—who seemed to have grown quite accustomed to having the out-of-towner around—but now Travis was missing, and Mac was pointing the finger at the mayor.

"This is all because of you!" he yelled into the phone. "You've been as indecisive and ineffective as usual. If you had acted any slower, you would have been moving in reverse. Now Penny's dead and Travis isn't picking up his phone!"

"I understand," he replied. "I do, and I'll get Harris on it straight away."

"Oh no you won't," Mac offered in retort. "That imbecile has caused enough trouble already. Get someone who knows what the hell they're doing onto it, and fast. I've already lost a daughter-in-law!" The mayor could hear all of Mac Newsted's legendary vitriol pouring down the phone line like sulphuric acid. "I will not lose my son!"

The problem was, Deputy Barns had trailed Harris the day prior, and he'd seen the sheriff meeting up with the Indian, Carter and the schoolteacher at The Regal Hotel, before getting into the Indian's truck, armed and loaded, and heading up into the hills toward Monarch's Pass. If the mayor was a betting man, he'd have laid twenty big ones down on them going on a hunting expedition for whoever had killed Chase, Zed, and Penny White. If the Indian was involved, that meant they believed something unnatural was at play, something that may have caused a hundred minors to vanish almost eighty years ago.

Now the mayor sat in his office, glaring at the blank screen of his phone, and wondering what the hell his next play was. He stared at the danish pastry that rested on a napkin on his very expensive walnut desk, and at the screen of his computer, where an image of his wife and two daughters peered back at him, their round faces almost cherubic, and all of a sudden his stomach ulcer flared up, and he reached for the antacids.

As he swallowed two, washing them down with a large glass of Coke, his desk phone rang. He guessed it was

Mac again, this time calling him on the landline so that he would get the full effect of his booming voice.

"Mac, look—"

"It's Audrey, sir." Audrey was his personal assistant. She used to be called his secretary, but that title had seemingly gone the way of the air-stewardess and the waitress.

"Oh, hi, Audrey."

She lowered her voice. "I have a couple of visitors here for you, sir. A Mr Steel and a Mr Hogan. I told them you were busy all morning, but they really were quite insistent."

The mayor rubbed his temples. He really didn't need two more residents bearing down on him, telling him that their neighbor's trees were too tall, or that the dog in the yard opposite had been barking all damn night.

"Tell them I'm just heading out," he said. "Get them to leave me a note or something."

"Okay, sir. I'll tell them that. "

He replaced the phone in the cradle and stood to collect his jacket. He needed some fresh air. He also needed to think of a way out of his current dilemma. Mac Newsted wasn't the kind of man to keep waiting. However, before he'd had a chance to remove his expensive Harris Tweed from the hanger, the door of his office burst open.

"Well, hello there, Mr Mayor!" A man with blond hair and round glasses pushed into his office, Audrey trailing behind, her chipmunk cheeks the color of summer cherries.

"I'm so sorry, sir. They just walked right past me."

Another man followed her inside. He was bald headed, heavily tattooed, and had the look of a man who enjoyed a heated debate, even if it turned ugly.

"No matter, Audrey," he said, reading the room expertly. He'd always had that ability. It had gotten him out of trouble on more than one occasion. "I've found some time in my diary to see these two gentlemen after all. Please," he said, gesturing toward two swivel chairs. "Won't you take a seat."

"Don't mind if I do," the man with the blond hair said before depositing himself on the chair closest to the mayor. "And mine will be a cappuccino with two sugars, Audrey. If you don't mind, that is."

The mayor shot his PA a wink.

"Of course, sir. And you?" she asked, turning to the bald-headed guy.

"I'm fine," he answered, before ushering her out of the room and closing the door behind her. He turned, and the mayor felt his throat start to close with fear. The guy looked like he'd stared death in the face and won.

"What—what can I do for you?" he asked, sipping some more of his Coke.

"First things first," the blond-haired guy said, thrusting out a hand. "Name's Hogan, and this here is my good friend Mr Steel."

He took Hogan's hand, which had the feel of someone who'd worked long hours in the open, and shook it. "Pleased to meet you Mr Hogan. You too, Mr Steel."

Steel offered no hand. He barely offered a smile.

"I'm Mayor Arthur Pumpkin—"

"Like the vegetable?" Hogan asked, laughing.

"Yes, exactly like that. Anyway, I'm the mayor of our little town. I assume you gentlemen are visitors to these parts?"

Hogan nodded.

"And you like what you see?"

"No. Hate it. I feel like I've walked backwards in time for, like, seventy years."

The mayor felt a sudden pang of resentment. How dare they come into his office and insult his town. Who the hell did they think they were?

"Oh, I'm sorry to hear that."

"But," Hogan offered, "it could get a hell of a lot better."

"How so?"

"I hear you've found some yellow stuff up in the hills. Or, more specifically, somebody on my payroll found some yellow stuff in those hills, which de-facto means that I own his share."

Suddenly the mayor felt as if the ground beneath him had fallen away. Not only did he have The Devil's Business on his heels, he now had yet another out-of-towner claiming a stake in the very gold that Mac Newsted was demanding.

"Well now, I don't know where you heard that, but the very idea that—"

"Don't bullshit me, Arthur," Hogan said. "Because I can smell it a mile off."

Steel stepped toward the table and pulled back his jacket, revealing the grip of a meaty looking handgun.

"Wait a minute," the mayor cried, holding out his hands, his voice thin and reedy.

"Don't worry," Hogan said, gesturing for Steel to stand down. "We're not here looking for trouble. You see, my employee ran out on me a couple of weeks ago, leaving me somewhat in the lurch."

"Jason Carter?" the mayor offered, almost apologetically.

Hogan clapped his hands together. "The very same. Anyways, another little bird told me that you all have been having yourselves a little trouble with some sort of homicidal maniac, and J.C. was originally thrown in the slammer for it."

The mayor nodded. If only he'd stayed there. "You heard correctly. But he had an alibi for one of the killings, and we had to release him."

"You don't look too happy about that."

The mayor fought to hide his disappointment, but he knew he'd never had the greatest poker face. "I can't say I am."

"So you still believe he did it?"

"I'm not sure. But I do believe he's been causing me trouble ever since he arrived in this town."

Hogan shot him a grin so wide, the mayor thought it was apt to cut his face in two. "He always was an awkward son of a bitch," he said. "Difficult to like. You see, trouble follows J.C. around like a stray dog. If J.C. shows up at your door, you know his mutt, Trouble, ain't too far behind. Isn't that right, Steel?"

The bald guy nodded. "The guy's a veritable pain in the butt."

"Ain't that the truth. Anyways, given that I own his share of gold in those hills—"

"Well, about that—"

Hogan held up his hand. "Given that I own his share of all that gold, and given that I presume you want J.C. out of the picture for reasons unknown—but that I'm guessing are related to the aforementioned yellow stuff—then I propose to make you an offer."

The mayor glanced at the door, wondering if he could outrun the bald guy and make it out into the street before one or both of them put a bullet in his back. He didn't fancy his chances. "Go on."

"I want J.C. Call me a fool, but he wronged me and I can't let that go. You see, I've always been an eye-for-an-eye kind of guy, ain't that so, Steel?"

Steel nodded once more, his eyes never leaving the mayor. "And there's been a lot of eyes."

"Amen to that," Hogan replied, his expression one of steadfast determination. "And I want J.C.'s eyes more than I want that gold. You tell me where he is and give me a free pass on whatever happens to him when we find him, including what happens to anybody he's colluding with, and guess what?"

The mayor suddenly sensed an opportunity knocking on his door after all. "You'll give up your share in the gold?"

Hogan leapt up, causing the mayor to fly back in his seat, almost sending him tumbling onto his expensive Winchester rug. "You got it, Arthur!" Hogan cried. "You hit the nail right on the goddamn head! I can tell why they made you Mayor! You're as sharp as a tack, Arthur. As sharp as a goddam tack! Now, we got a deal or what?"

As the man with the round glasses and neatly combed blond hair rounded the desk, his hand outstretched—and Steel stood with his arms by his side, his face a mask of barely constrained violence—Mayor Arthur Pumpkin thought that perhaps everything was going to be okay after all. He took Hogan's hand in his.

"You have yourself a deal."

CHAPTER TWENTY-FIVE

Sound the Alarm

We tried to sleep during what was left of the night, but this time we took turns keeping watch. I thought the Wendigo had done what it came to do for now, but there was no guarantee that it wouldn't come back and finish us all off. Little Bear's wound was only shallow and the bleeding stopped after an hour or so, but I also knew that an infection out there in the wilderness could be deadly. We'd had a narrow escape, but our work was far from over. Our hunt had only just begun.

Linda slept fitfully, and I tried to sooth her by wiping a damp cloth on her brow. She spoke in her sleep about demon's in the undergrowth and horned flies buzzing around her head. She'd had a shock, we all had. Nothing could prepare for you coming face to face with hell's own foot soldier. It was as if nothing you were ever taught at school was true, that monsters really did live under your bed, and that the boogeyman spent his nights lurking behind a half opened closet door.

We'd decided to bury Travis's remains in a shallow grave to prevent scavengers from picking at him, which we then marked with a crudely fashioned cross. We planned to head back to the site after we'd completed our mission. His parents would want a proper burial after all. It was only right.

Linda, distraught at his brutal murder, said a few words as we laid him to rest. I could see she was struggling to hold it together, but she did what she could. Travis had been a part of both the happiest and the most stressful times in her life, and for that she would never forget him.

Later, we quickly ate our breakfast and packed our things, ready for a long, elevated hike into the hills. Little Bear told us what he had seen, and it was there that we were headed. It was over a day and a half's hike to the north of our position, and we knew the terrain would be rough and steep.

"You going to be okay with this?" I asked Linda that morning. "You looked really shaken last night, and with all the distress, you really think you're up to it?"

She sipped from her steel cup, the dark shadows of restlessness beneath her eyes. "I'll be fine, honestly. At least now I know exactly what we're dealing with."

"Hell, Linda. I don't think any of us know what we're dealing with. All we know is that it's not human, or at least like no human I've ever seen."

"But it won't stop," she said. "If we don't kill it, it will keep coming back and more people will die. People like Paul Chase, like Penny, like Travis." She paused. "Like my parents."

I nodded sombrely. She was right.

"Then we have to keep going."

What Little Bear had seen was a place deep in a forest known locally as Widow's Hole. To get there, you had to cross part of the Sawatch Range, traverse a vast river of white water rapids, and then drop three thousand feet to the forest floor. It was so remote, very few people had ever visited it, and even fewer had attempted to map the terrain. If we took a wrong turn, or worse still, lost our footing, there was every chance we wouldn't make it back. We all knew the score, but that didn't make it any more easy to stomach. And what made matters worse was there was every chance the Wendigo would be tracking our every step. In fact, it was almost guaranteed. The beast was toying with us. I suspected it was even enjoying the chase.

"If we keep up the pace," Little Bear said, lighting a cigarette. "Then we should be able to make it to Hunter's Point by nightfall, which only has one route in and out."

"If we don't?" Linda asked.

"Then we'll be sleeping out in the open, with no way of knowing which way the Wendigo will come at us."

The gravity of that realization settled in our guts like a heavy meal. We needed to move, and we needed to move fast.

"Well I for one am not about to let that happen," the sheriff said, before marching ahead.

The route through the hills was a lot tougher than I'd thought, but I'd climbed worse. I had gotten used to the slight limp I'd gained during my time in Iraq, and I compensated for it the best I could with my better leg. I wasn't sure about the others, however. I could see Little Bear was still feeling the effects of his wound, and he permanently held a hand to the crudely applied dressing, as if he was attempting to prevent his intestines from spilling out onto the floor. The sheriff was a few years older than me, and a little out of shape, and as the elevation increased, so did his breathing, which sounded like air escaping from a tiny hole in a slowly deflating balloon. Linda was faring much better, and although she'd had no military training, she was clearly an experienced hiker.

"You take me to the nicest places," she said as we clambered across a narrow ledge.

"Oh well, you know," I replied. "I do my best."

We walked a little further, Little Bear and the sheriff someway behind us, before she asked the question I'd been dreading.

"You know, you've never told me anything about your life before you came here. Nothing about your childhood, your parents. I don't know whether you have any family, whether you've been married, or what you did for a living in Chicago."

"There's nothing to tell," I said, feeling the blood rush to my face. "Parents are dead, my brother's dead too. I don't have any surviving family. It's just me."

I sensed Bill's presence but couldn't see him anywhere. He was keeping his distance—for now.

"That's so sad," she said, stopping. "I'm so, so sorry."

"Don't be. It was a long time ago, and I'm over it."

"I don't think it works like that, J.C."

I shrugged. "I don't know what to tell you. I'm fine."

I could see that Linda hadn't expected me to be so cold and that she didn't entirely buy my story, but I wasn't ready to fill her in on the minutiae of my life before Devil's Ridge, and I didn't want to tell most of it. It was my shame to hide, and they were my burdens to carry. They didn't need sharing.

"Okay, well, if you ever want to talk—"

"Don't worry. You'll be the first person I come to see."

We stopped beneath a rocky overhang to eat. We were looking out over the vast expanse of the Sawatch Range, with its many mountainous peaks and wide vistas, formed as the continents divided and shifted, pushing gigantic slabs of limestone and granite toward the heavens. Beneath us, hundreds of miles of lush, green forest carried on endlessly like a thick carpet, interjected by tumbling streams and rolling valleys. The landscape was intoxicating and beautiful, like a painting you couldn't afford, or a photograph that didn't seem real. It was the kind of place you brought your sweetheart to—not the sort of place you came to hunt a demon spirit that was hellbent on bloodshed and carnage.

"How far is Hunter's Point from here?" Linda asked, swallowing a hunk of bread.

Little Bear pointed into the distance. "Maybe a five hour hike. Six if we go slow."

"Uphill or downhill."

"Bit of both."

I could see Linda wince at that. The sheriff too. The elevations were the issue, not the distance.

"We'll take the slower option," I said, trying to boost everyone's spirits. "Nightfall isn't until nineteen hundred hours. It's thirteen hundred now, so that gives us six hours to get there before the sun sets. The slower option will be fine. Let's just take it easy."

"Whatever," the sheriff said before hoisting himself up from the rock he had been perching on. "Five hours or six. Either way is fine with me."

I thought the sheriff would struggle to make it to Hunter's Point in seven, but I wasn't about to tell him that. It wasn't so long ago that I was sitting in his holding cell, wondering if I would ever see the light of day again.

I thought of what lay ahead of us. It wasn't the walk that was worrying me. It was the fear of the unknown. The Wendigo was somewhere out there, watching and waiting for us to make our next move. We were on the back foot, walking into a kill zone with no appreciation of where the enemy was. We had no intel, no drones flying overhead, no eyes on the ground. The creature could strike at any moment, and we were ill-prepared to deal with it. The events of last night had taught us that much. We had played along with the Wendigo's game like compliant little followers without even knowing it.

"We have to get the upper hand here," I whispered into Little Bear's ear as we strode ahead. "We have to do something to change the narrative."

"What are you thinking?"

"I don't know. Maybe we should split into two groups."

He grunted. "Sounds like a dumb idea to me. We cut down our resources by half."

"Maybe, maybe not. I'm thinking we separate our positions by no more than a quarter of a mile. Linda and I can head to the checkpoint from the east, you and the sheriff cut in from the west. As far as we know, this thing is a solitary creature, meaning if it decides to attack, it can only attack one group at a time."

Little Bear pursed his lips. "I'm listening."

"I've got these," I pulled two hyper-whistles from my pocket. They were bright orange with an unusually wide mouthpiece. "The sound from these will carry a quarter of a mile easily in this terrain. If the Wendigo attacks, we sound the alarm and the other pair come, catching the Wendigo off guard."

"That is, if the pair being attacked aren't dead already."

I nodded. I knew he had a good point. "Well, we have to hope that we have enough ammunition to keep the Wendigo at bay long enough for the rescue party to arrive."

We walked in silence for another half a mile. We were around eight thousand feet above sea level and the air temperature was considerably cooler at that elevation. While it made the walking conditions a little more bearable, what wasn't bearable was the deadly predicament ahead of us. We were targets at a duck shoot, just waiting for the buckshot to strike.

"Okay, let's do it," Little Bear said without averting his gaze from the route ahead. "What do we have to lose?"

The sheriff walked beside Little Bear, his body cast in the Native American's enormous shadow. He was thankful for that at least. What he wasn't thankful for were the blisters that were developing on his toes, or Carter's dumb-ass plan to split into two smaller groups. He had always considered safety to be in numbers, but right now their numbers were small and their hopes were even smaller.

"Still don't see why we couldn't have hiked to the checkpoint together," he hissed, checking that he still had plenty of water in his canteen.

"He's trying to give us the edge," Little Bear replied. "Trying something is better than doing nothing."

"Is it?" the sheriff replied. "In my experience, trying something stupid inevitably gets you in trouble."

"It was his plan that caught Caleb."

"His plan killed Caleb, and it almost killed him too. You'd be a fool to forget that."

"And you'd be a fool to forget that he tried to tell you what was going on, but you didn't listen to him."

The sheriff huffed and turned away. There was really no talking to the Indian. He had been allied with Carter since he'd arrived in town. Maybe it was the gold, or maybe it was because they were both outsiders, needing each other for some sort of validation. Either way, he wasn't going to let these men set him up for a fall. He still aimed to follow through with his plan. The creature had to be killed, and Little Bear and Carter needed to be sidelined, preferably permanently. There was no way he was letting those compromising images of him get into the public domain, which meant the mayor and those crooks from Devil's Business had to be placated. He had to meet their demands.

Hunter's Point was now no more than an hour's hike, or so the Indian had told him. That was good, because his feet felt like hell and his back was killing him. He couldn't wait to lay his sleeping mat on the floor and collapse onto it. The years hadn't been kind to his body. He'd put it through the wringer for decades, and at some point in the last five years it had gradually started to crumble around him like stale cake.

The cartilage between his vertebrae was now almost non-existent, meaning that every sharp move, every slight twist, was accompanied by red-hot missiles of pain firing across his body like patriots across the gulf. He'd grown accustomed to it, tuning the pain out, but he hadn't appreciated how badly a long walk up and down steep, rocky slopes would aggravate his deteriorating condition. If he'd have known how taxing it was going to be, perhaps he would have sat this one out, but deep inside he knew that was unlikely. This was his town, and this thing was terrorizing his people. It was only right that he was there.

"Did you hear that?" Little Bear said, turning sharply.

"Hear what?"

The Indian held up a hand. They stood that way, looking out across a darkening horizon, both listening keenly for any sound, any sign that something was nearby.

"I don't hear anything," the sheriff said, glancing behind them.

"It's close," Little Bear said in a hushed voice. "It's watching us."

The sheriff grabbed his rifle and checked it was locked and loaded. They'd nearly caught the murdering creep the night before. This time he was going to make damn sure they finished the job.

Little Bear pointed above them, where the ground sloped upwards and out of sight. "It's up there, looking down on us."

As if to highlight the point, something disturbed the ground overhead, and tiny rocks came pouring down from the ledge above.

The sheriff dropped to one knee and aimed his rifle, waiting for the thing to show itself. His heart was galloping in his chest like a herd of terrified horses.

"I'll climb from the front," Little Bear whispered, pointing to his left. "You go up from the rear."

The sheriff shifted his hat atop his head and nodded. He didn't like it, but that didn't mean it wasn't a good idea. They would pincer the shit out of this thing, and come at it from both sides.

"What about the others," he asked, gesturing toward the whistle hanging around the Indian's neck.

"We'll use it if we get in trouble. Let's not alert it to the fact we know it's here."

The sheriff nodded once more. Again, the Indian was talking good sense, and about time, too.

They moved out, the sheriff watching above him for signs of the Wendigo emerging over the drop. He clung close to the rock face, his rifle gripped tightly in his hands, his finger gently caressing the trigger. He could hear his frantic breathing, could feel his pulse thrumming in his ears.

The sun was really starting to dip as sunset rapidly approached. His shadow stretched out before him like a long, inky patch of wet earth. He made it to the base of a slim path that climbed through the rocks above him, and he spun toward it, turning to his left, half-expecting the Wendigo to be standing there, waiting for him.

The way ahead was clear, but it was strewn with large boulders and bushes—plenty of places for something to be lurking, waiting.

He hoped the Indian was making faster progress than him. Maybe he would encounter the Wendigo first and force it in his direction. Maybe he would even wound it, leaving the sheriff to finish it off as it came crawling toward him, its body broken and bleeding. It had killed four of his citizens and corrupted a fifth. From all the stories handed down by their ancestors, it had also caused those miners to vanish into thin air. It deserved to die. It deserved to suffer.

He scurried from boulder to boulder, peering around the face of each rock before making his next move. His rifle was thrust before him like a mighty spear, his jaw set firm, his eyes narrow and watching for the slightest of movement. He would not be ambushed. He would not be out-thought. His brain might be aging, and his body might be broken, but he still had his wits about him, and he still had the ability to think clearly. If the Wendigo was going to come at him, it was going to do it on the sheriff's terms.

The sky suddenly seemed to get a hell of a lot darker in an instant, and he slowly realized they were not going to make it to Hunter's Point before sunset. Night-time was coming their way, and fast. That one simple fact dampened his optimism. He didn't want to be on that ridge in the darkness, waiting for some hellish beast to confront him. This needed to end, and quickly.

He moved faster through the boulders; checking and moving, checking and moving. He saw nothing, heard nothing. Perhaps the Indian had been wrong. Perhaps the rocks were disturbed by a coyote or mountain lion. Yes, perhaps that was it. Perhaps they were running around pretending to be hunters, when all along they'd been chasing shadows. What fools they'd been. But wait, if they'd been chasing shadows, then they'd have no need to split their group down even further, leaving both he and the Indian out there on their own, with the sun slowly disappearing and the darkness encroaching on them like an ocean of rolling black.

There was a noise from behind him, like the sound of a horse whinnying. He slowly turned, his fingers gripping his rifle tight, like driftwood. He thought of his kids and how much they meant to him, of his wife and how she'd betrayed him. Above all, he thought about how much he wanted to live.

As he came face to face with the grotesque beast, with its flayed skull, dagger-like teeth and eyes that blazed with the eternal fires of hell, he realized he wasn't going to get what he wanted.

"Fuck you," he growled as he took aim and fired.

Little Bear heard the gunshot first, and ran toward it, knowing that the sheriff would have only fired if he believed he had seen something. He ran with his rifle at his side and the slowly setting sun at his back. He ran as everything he feared came crashing down around him. They had been isolated like lone deer, like the weakest of the herd, and like the fool he was, the whole thing had been his idea. The Wendigo had tricked them into thinking they had the upper hand, but of course that was what it wanted. It wanted to pick them off one by one, like meat from a cadaver. They had been out maneuvered again.

The way ahead was covered in the gray film of twilight, and the boulders that littered the way were now like the rolling waves of a turbulent ocean. He moved through them at speed, his eyes keenly trained on the way ahead, but his senses attuned to movement from all sides. There was something darker about the side of the rock just in front of him, and he raced to it, placing his hands on it. It was damp, sticky.

"Sheriff Harris?" he whispered, grimacing as the wound in his side suddenly became a fiery shard of pain across his ribs. "Sheriff?" he said once more once the pain had subsided. "Are you there?"

He slowly moved around the rock, a sickening dread settling in his stomach like bile. There was something lying on the ground, dark and round, resembling a much smaller boulder, except Little Bear knew it wasn't a rock. The spherical object was surrounded by a dark pool of damp earth, as if the heavens had opened and dropped a tiny patch of rain right there. He checked his perimeter, swinging the rifle to his left and right, before dropping to his haunches and reaching out to touch the thing that lay before him.

In the darkness, his hand found something soft, followed by a fur he could run his hands through. There were gelatinous protrusions, but filled with something crisp, like plastic or rubber.

As he rolled the ball shaped object toward him, he noticed the tendrils hanging from its base, and lifted his hand to see what was now coating it. In the darkness, the warm liquid appeared black, but he knew that it wasn't black at all. It was red. A dark, grotesque red. He stared at the misshapen ball and felt a scream rise in his throat.

There, staring back at him with eyes frozen in one horrific moment in time, lips pulled back in a defiant sneer, was the disembodied head of the sheriff.

He frantically grabbed the little orange object that hung from a string around his thick neck and clumsily placed it between his lips, smearing some of the sheriff's blood into his own mouth in the process. He fought the urge to vomit, but he knew what had to be done. He had to call the others.

As he sounded the alarm, the shrill cacophony echoing from the rocky peaks like the piercing cry of a bald eagle in flight, a dark shape moved behind him, towering above him like the grim shadow of death itself.

CHAPTER TWENTY-SIX

The Enigma

Hogan hated mountains. He hated hiking. Shit, he hated the countryside. It was like waking up in the city and finding that all the buildings had disappeared, all the cars had vanished, all the strip clubs were closed, all the bars had evaporated, and all the money no longer had any value. In his mind, the countryside was just a waste of valuable real estate space that ought to be handed over to people with the resources and the good sense to turn it into habitable land for the masses—like a lemon ready to be squeezed and manipulated by people with the skills necessary to get as much juice as humanly possible from its dappled husk. People like him.

What good were forests, mountains, valleys, canyons and wide open plains to people like him. He needed bustle, crowds, dialogue, confrontation, discrimination and good old fashioned sweat, to survive.

He watched as Steel led the way, the three of them following behind like tourists. Hogan didn't like letting one of his henchmen take point, but Steel knew how to navigate across such terrain. Hogan, on the other hand, knew his limits. The only thing he knew how to navigate was a nubile female body, and even then he often lost his way.

Hogan was a fit man. He took care of himself. He went to the gym daily and ran five miles every morning. In his business, you had to look after yourself. It seemed that every street kid these days wanted the run of the city, and he couldn't give them even an inch. He had to be as strong as them, as smart as them, and as energetic as them. Nothing other than perfection would do, and for fifteen years, Frank Hogan had been at the very pinnacle of his game. No-one could touch him. Nobody else even came close. If a footsoldier did good, they were rewarded, often handsomely. If one of his men was lazy or was coasting, they were dragged before him and made to see the error of their ways. And if any one of them stepped out of line, then they were put out to pasture in the most painful, visible way possible. Examples had to be made, lessons had to be learned, and the flock had to be culled. That was the way of it, and Hogan didn't shy away from making tough decisions.

To him, a hike through the mountains was just another thing that had to be done. Carter could not be allowed to get away with disobeying him. There were too many predators watching Hogan's every move, seeing how he dealt with such impudence. If he had to walk all the way to Vancouver, Carter would suffer, and everybody would know about it.

They hiked for most of the day through dense forest and over ground that was uneven and treacherous. Campbell was the slowest of their pack. The kid had only been with them a short time. He was the nephew of one of Hogan's most experienced enforcers, but he had a quarter of the aptitude and almost none of the intelligence. However, he was a good driver and he was obedient, so Hogan had kept him on. The problem was, out there in the wilderness, Campbell was slowing them all down.

"You want to head back, kid?" he asked. "Go wait in the car?"

"Nah, I'm okay, boss."

"You don't look like you're enjoying the walk," Hogan replied, watching the kid grimace as he slipped on a patch of wet earth.

"I think it's kinda fun. It reminds me of when I used to go camping with my uncle."

Hogan scowled. The kid wasn't going to take the bait. "Well, pick up your pace, wontcha. I don't want to be stuck out here all week."

They walked that way for a few hours, just about keeping up with Steel who was plowing ahead like a steam train. Eventually, they found something. It was Ethan Crane who spied the campsite first. It was nestled in a small clearing, overlooking a stream. Steel approached it, dropped to his knees and plunged his hand into the ashes of an abandoned camp-fire.

"Still warm," he said. "They've definitely been here."

"So we're on the right track?" Hogan asked, watching as Crane mounted a slope to their rear.

"Yeah, we're maybe half a day's hike behind them based on how warm these ashes still are."

Hogan smiled. Half a day. That was better than he'd expected. Carter was almost in touching distance—or, more appropriately, close enough that Hogan could reach out with his bare hands and squeeze the backstabbing life out of him.

"That's good," he said. "Real good."

"Hey boss!" Crane yelled from the other side of the slope. "You might want to see this."

Hogan followed the sound of his concierge's voice, scrambling clumsily up the incline.

Crane stood on the other side of the drop, next to what looked like a crudely made cross, plunged into a freshly disturbed mound of soil—a mound that looked suspiciously like a hastily dug grave.

"Maybe one of them died," Campbell said, sliding haphazardly down the hill.

"Or maybe they killed someone," Crane added.

Hogan felt his pulse racing. He didn't like it. Whatever had happened here, it was something that Hogan hadn't anticipated, and that bothered him. He was usually three steps ahead of his staff, but Carter was something of an enigma to him. J.C. had been a closed book since the get-go, with an expression that barely gave away even the slightest hint of emotion; and not only had he deliberately failed to carry out Hogan's instructions, but he'd also caught him off guard by pulling this little disappearing stunt. And now there was this. This wasn't good.

"I suggest we stay alert," Hogan said. "Carter's up to something here, which means he's dangerous. If you see him, and especially if he makes any kind of move, you shoot to kill, you get me?"

Steel's expression cracked. "Boss," he said, his lips curling up at the corners, "now you're talking my kinda language."

CHAPTER TWENTY-SEVEN

Something in the Trees

L inda and I arrived at the checkpoint just as the sun started to fade into a long red and orange line that resembled a raging inferno, blazing across the broad horizon. Hunter's Point was a large plateau that overlooked a stunning landscape of lush green forest and gargantuan peaks. If it had been a different time, different circumstances, it would have been idyllic; except we were both acutely aware that we were being pursued by a demonic creature that could kill us in an instant if we let our guards down. We couldn't let ourselves become distracted. Nothing mattered at that exact moment other than protecting each other, and finding and killing the beast.

We'd just started to set up camp when we heard the gunshot in the distance, followed shortly afterwards by the piercing, shrieking sound of one of the hyper whistles. It caused us both to stop dead in our tracks and look back toward the trail.

"The others," Linda said. "Something's happened."

"Yeah," I nodded, stepping away from the tent and toward the tightly packed copse of bushes that led the way toward the rock strewn path. I fingered my gun and ran options over through my mind. Little Bear and the sheriff should have been walking neck and neck with us, keeping pace half a mile west of our position. Instead the gunshot sounded like it was some way back. "I'll go check it out," I said.

"You're not leaving me here alone!" Linda cried. "Not with that thing out there."

"What do you want me to do?" I replied. "I can't leave them. This was our plan, remember?"

Linda tossed the firewood on the ground and strode toward me. "That's right, it was. So if we go, we go together."

We pushed through the bushes and emerged onto the trail. We ignored the route that we had come in on, and descended the slope to the lower path, heading back the way Little Bear and the sheriff should have come up from. The sunlight had almost entirely dissipated, giving everything an eerie gray and orange glow, as if we were walking through some tacky theme-park landscape. In every shadow, every dark crevice and murky corner, I could see the Wendigo lurking, crouched low to the ground like a sleeping tiger, it's long, spindly fingers gripping the edge of the rock like ivy, it's claws leaving deep indentations in the limestone. Every firefly was one of the beast's malevolent eyes, every sharp splinter of rock one of its gore-soaked teeth.

Linda gripped my elbow, so close to me that we almost moved as one. The air was cold and damp, and I could feel the plummeting temperature seeping through my clothes and onto my skin, chilling my bones. There was no sound. It was as if someone had turned the volume down on nature, as if all the nocturnal creatures had been given the evening off. Below us, the rock face fell away sharply, leaving nothing but an ebony blanket of nothingness.

"They're not here," Linda whispered from behind me. "Where are they?"

I shook my head. I didn't know but the silence was deafening. I felt a sickening dread descend on me. I pictured the Wendigo ambushing them both, slicing through them with its razor sharp claws as easily as a steak knife through a short-rib. The thought made me want to throw up. It had been my plan, my idea. Had I inadvertently led them to their deaths?

My brother was up ahead in the gloom, standing back from the path in the undergrowth, watching as we approached. He was shaking his head slowly, as if he was disappointed in me. What did he know? He'd sent me down to this hellish place, after all, knowing, but not revealing, the stories of the terrible, unnatural thing that lived in that mine. If this was anyone's fault, it was his. He'd been driven by greed and the lust for wealth, and I'd fallen for everything he'd said. He didn't look well, now. His skin had a deathly pallor, like spoiled milk, and there was blood in his hair and on his neck, and when he grinned I could see that it was on his teeth, too. I passed him without speaking, and he slowly faded into the darkness, as if he had never been there at all.

There was a noise up ahead, like something being dragged across the earth, and I reached for my handgun, thrusting it out in front of me like a wand. I didn't know whether to shoot or use it to ward off evil spirits, but I could feel the fear growing within me like a tumor. Linda held out her bowie knife, but I knew that if the Wendigo got close enough for a knife to be effective, it would already be too late. We stood in the blackness, waiting for the thing that was dragging itself through the earth to creep toward us. My gun was trained on the ground, waiting for the blood-soaked creature to emerge. With every scraping, scuffling sound, my heart beat a little bit quicker, and the sound of my pounding pulse resonated in my head like a kick-drum. I imagined the zombified remains of Little Bear pulling himself along the path, his skin peeled away as it revealed bloodied tendons and arteries, his face a red mask of tissue and bone. Louder and louder the noises came, and faster and faster my heart raced.

I glanced at Linda and she peered up at me, her brilliant blue eyes now seemingly black like coal. She was terrified. Her hands were shaking and her lips were trembling. I knew then that I'd made a terrible mistake in bringing her with me. Once more I'd led her to danger, and once more she was in fear of her life.

Suddenly the noise stopped. We waited to see if it resumed, but after a few minutes watching and waiting, I realized that whatever it was had gone.

I stepped forward and shuffled down the slope. A silhouette of a barren tree was visible just up ahead, like the crooked arms of a wizened old man, waiting to be embraced. I walked toward it, sensing that something wasn't right about its angular shape. There was a darkness to it that appeared out of place, as if it had grown limbs that were out of proportion to its thin, twisted frame. Linda stood close to me, but I needed her anywhere but there. I didn't want her to see the very thing I feared was about to present itself to us. It was hanging among the gnarly branches of what I now knew to be a dead tree.

The bark hung from its flesh like peeling scabs, and the trunk was split down the middle, as if it had been cleaved in two by a mighty ax. Its hands hung limply, its arms fanned out as if on a crucifix. Its legs dropped limply from a distended waist, its feet no more than three feet from the ground, but there was something wrong with its head. It wasn't connected. It sat among the branches, as if it was some sort of strange fruit. I approached it, unable to avert my gaze.

"J.C." Linda cried, her voice a hissing, urgent rasp. "Don't."

I knew she was right, but I couldn't help myself. If this was the Wendigo, I wanted to see. I wanted to know what had been pursuing us, I wanted to know what had been trailing me ever since I'd convinced the residents to re-open the mine. I wanted to destroy every tissue of its undead being.

I reached out toward the disembodied skull, wanting so badly to turn it to face me. Nothing mattered in that exact moment except looking the Wendigo in the eyes and confronting it. My hand was mere inches from it now. I could almost feel its cold flesh, and its rotting, festering skin.

I stepped forward to grab it in both hands, to crush it between my fingers if necessary, but that was when someone stepped out of the darkness and clutched my shoulders. I whirled round, almost firing off a couple of shots, but then I saw Little Bear's face and everything came rushing back into focus.

He looked like he'd seen a ghost, or more accurately, like he'd been attacked by one. His voice was a frantic whisper, his muscles tensed as if he was readying himself for a fight to the death.

"We need to go," he said. "We need to go now!"

"But the Wendigo?" I cried, turning back toward the tree. That was when I saw it: the sheriff's boots; his handgun loose in his belt; his hat hanging from the farthest branch. The sheriff's head fell from its place among the branches then, and it rolled toward Linda. She screamed as I stepped back, walking into the sheriff's dangling legs. He'd been dragged toward us by the Wendigo, and then thrown into the tree, creating some sort of grotesque display.

"He's gone," Little Bear said, "but we're still alive."

I couldn't find any words. I simply nodded. Linda was simpering on the ground, her shoulders shuddering, her head between her knees.

"If we don't move," he continued, his voice frantic. "We'll be next."

We headed back to Hunter's Point, Little Bear setting a frenetic pace. We didn't speak. All I could hear was my own heavy breathing and Linda's occasional sobs. The sheriff was dead. We hadn't been friends, but we'd respected each other. He was a good man. I knew that. He'd only ever been trying to do his job, even if he had been guided by corrupt leaders. That didn't matter. We'd headed out into the wilderness to kill the Wendigo, and so far our mission was failing. We'd lost one of our own, and we had no idea how to trap the beast. We weren't hunting—we were the hunted.

We emerged onto the plateau and Little Bear pointed toward the tents that we'd pitched.

"Grab your things," he said, whirling on us. "We need to keep moving."

Linda rushed to the tent and folded it down. "Where...where are we going."

"To the end point," Little Bear replied. "There's no time to waste. We have to finish this tonight before any more of us are killed."

"What happened back there?" I asked, packing my own things. I cast an anxious glance toward the bushes, expecting that at any moment the giant form of the undead beast would emerge from their thorny embrace.

"We split up," he said. "I thought we could trap it on the path above us, but it's far smarter than I gave it credit for. It tricked us."

Linda went to him. "And it attacked the sheriff?"

"I found him the way you saw him," he said. "But on the ground. Not in the tree."

I nodded. I knew that particular set up was just for Linda and I.

"It came at me from behind and I thought I was a goner, but it just placed a hand on my face. It smelled like death, like the end of the world. It's hard to explain. I just knew that whatever it is, it died many thousands of years ago."

"But it didn't harm you?" I asked, glancing at him. Aside from his dressed wound from the night before, he looked unscathed.

"No, but it showed me."

"Showed you what?" Linda asked. "Little Bear, tell us! What did it show you?"

His eyes fell to the ground as he spoke in a low, guttural tone. "You and I, Linda. It plans to kill us one by one, just like the sheriff. Pick us off when we're least expecting it."

Linda gasped, holding her trembling hands to her lips.

"But you J.C.," he said, turning to me.

I approached him. "What?"

"It has plans for you. I couldn't see what exactly, but I saw a throne made of a thousand bones situated on a rocky ledge, somewhere deep. Somewhere below."

I shuddered as my blood turned cold, and the hairs on my arms stood on end.

"But why me?"

He exhaled. "Because you were the one who brought them to its home, and because you have darkness in you. It is drawn to it like a moth to a flame."

I turned from him and faced the shadows. The darkness swirled like eddies in the ocean. My brother stood within its soft embrace, looking at me the way he used to when I was a kid—when he knew I'd done something stupid but didn't know how to make amends. I needed his help, now more than ever. I was in dee* trouble and there was only one way out. We had to find the Wendigo's lair, and put an end to its reign of terror, once and for all.

CHAPTER TWENTY-EIGHT

White Water

The river ahead of us was a dark, simmering mass of angry water and jagged rocks. I had no idea how Little Bear planned to get across, but it appeared to me that we'd headed toward a dead end, effectively backing ourselves into a corner.

We had hurried down the trail that descended a thousand feet through rocky terrain, all the while keeping one eye on the path behind us. I couldn't forget what Little Bear had said. The Wendigo had a plan, and it sounded like I was going to live to see the finale.

"How are we getting across that?" I yelled at him. "We don't have a raft."

"Don't need one," he cried, sliding down the bank and approaching the water. He bent down, plunged his hands into the rampaging river, and after a while he extracted the ends of two ropes. He dragged the lengths toward us and tied one of the ropes to the base of a rock, and the other higher up around the thick branch of a tall spruce. When I looked back toward the river I saw the other ends of both ropes were tied in a similar fashion on the other bank.

"What are we supposed to do with those?" Linda asked, glancing anxiously at me.

"It's easy," Little Bear said, planting one foot on the lower rope. "You walk along this one," he reached up and held the higher rope with both hands, "and you pull yourself across with this one."

"You have got to be kidding me!" she cried.

"Do you have a better idea?" he asked, placing both his huge feet on the rope, and walking sideways along it, his arms taking his weight overhead. Linda and I both watched as he started to move above the water, the violent waves thrashing angrily just below his feet.

"I can't do this," she said. "I'm afraid of the water."

I turned back toward the trail we'd followed to get there. It was approaching eleven pm, but there were no stars tonight. The sky was blanketed in thick clouds that suffocated the landscape of any light. At the top of the slope there was the shadow of something ominous, something filled with hatred and loathing. I knew the Wendigo was close. We had no choice. We had to cross the river. Any other decision would lead to our death. I was sure of it.

"You go first," I said, turning back to her, my jaw set firm. "I'll be right behind you. Just don't let go of the rope and you'll be fine."

Little Bear was now approaching the halfway point, and the rope jerked and moved as he shuffled across. Linda flinched every time she tried to place her feet on it.

"Take it steady," I said, glancing at the silhouette on the hill. "Don't rush. You can do this."

"I don't know if I can."

I kissed her then, pulling her toward me. I could feel the beating of her heart, and her frantic breathing. I cared for her—I really did. I hadn't felt that way in such a long time, I'd almost forgotten what it was like. I wasn't going to let anything happen to her, even if it meant putting myself between her and that creature.

"You can," I said. "I know it."

I could see something shift in her then. A determination. She looked at the rope, grabbed it, and hoisted herself up.

"Just do what Little Bear's doing," I said, "and I'll be right here beside you."

We shuffled above the river, the water kissing our heels as we gradually edged further and further across its wide expanse. I glanced back toward the top of the bank, but the silhouette was gone. If it had been the Wendigo, I silently wondered where it had gone. Had it moved closer to our position, lurking in the undergrowth? Or was it circum-navigating the river, crossing further upstream where it planned to wait for us after we'd made it to the opposite bank? I didn't know, but neither option sounded good.

"I'm here!" Little Bear called as he dropped to the ground. His voice was barely audible above the roaring cacophony of the pounding waves beneath our feet. I knew that if we slipped, we'd be swept away in the current in an instant. "Just take it easy and you'll be fine."

I could see Linda was focussing all her strength in her arms and chest. Her mouth moved from side to side as she kept her eyes fixed solely on the rope overhead, not daring to look at the spitting, swirling white foam.

There was the sound of something shrieking behind us, like a horrifying, blood-curdling battlecry, and suddenly the undergrowth began to open up as something unseen approached the river bank.

"It's coming," I said, turning to Linda. "We need to hurry."

She glared back at me, her eyes wide and her mouth drawn down in a silent scream. "I can't," she said.

"You have to," I replied, pulling myself toward her. We were barely past the halfway point. The river bank was over forty feet away, but the creature was less than sixty feet behind us. We had no time to think, no time to delay. We were literally hanging out to dry, like halal meat in a marketplace.

Linda started to pump her arms and widen her stride, and I followed suit. The deep welt in the undergrowth was moving faster and faster toward the bank, and I knew in a few moments the Wendigo would be dragging itself along the rope toward us.

I could hear Linda grunting and gasping beside me as she half shuffled, half swung across the water, but we were still twenty feet away and not moving quickly enough.

"Little Bear!" I yelled. "You need to slow it down. Shoot into the reeds. Now!"

He looked beyond us and saw what I was looking at. His mouth fell open as he swung his rifle from his shoulder, pulled back the bolt, and let off a shot that zipped past the two of us and buried itself in the tall grass. The Wendigo stopped moving, but I knew the reprieve would only be temporary.

"Keep going!" I cried. "We have to keep moving!"

Linda swung her legs wider and wider apart as she dragged herself along the rope. I did the same, but I could already see the silhouette of the Wendigo emerging from the tall reeds and approaching the river. It was over seven feet tall, its long arms like giant scythes, its horns twisted and angular like pitchforks. Its eyes burned red with a malevolent evil. There was blood in its glare, and terrible pain.

Linda was less than fifteen feet away from the river bank now, but I knew it was still too far. I had to do something. I turned and faced the creature, pulling myself toward it.

"You want me?" I cried. "Well come on! Take me! If that's what you want, I'm here!"

The Wendigo stood still on the bank, silently watching me as if I were an animal in a cage.

"You leave them be, and you take me! You hear me, you bastard! You take me!"

It looked at the rope and grabbed it, clutching it in its gnarled hands and hoisting itself toward me, arm over arm. I stood above the raging waters, their icy cold fingers kissing my ankles, and knew that death was fast approaching.

I heard Linda cry out as she surely made it to dry land, and I made a snap decision. There was only one way to stop the Wendigo killing us all right there on the riverbank, and it involved a sacrifice. I gripped the rope above my head with both hands, and yelled with all my might.

"Little Bear! Cut the ropes!"

"You gotta be kidding me!"

I could see the evil lurking within the monster as it dragged itself toward me, foregoing the rope beneath its feet for the one overhead. The power in its arms was immense, and its eyes never left my face. I could see the hunger lurking within it, the intense, unabated hatred that it felt for mankind. It had been sent here to hurt and to kill, and it had some catching up to do. I couldn't let it butcher anyone else. If it wasn't for me, it would still be in that mine, hibernating for another thousand years or more.

"Cut the goddamn ropes!"

Suddenly the rope beneath us disappeared, and I found myself hanging above the water, my feet dangling in the rampaging waves. I gripped the rope with all my strength, waiting for the inevitable. The wendigo was now ten feet away and closing, and it reached for me with one long arm, its claws slashing at the air in front of my face.

"Come on!" I hissed, spitting every word with spite and malice. "Come on!"

There was a jerk on the rope, and in an instant it was gone. I was underwater, the waves barrelling over my head and dragging me down. I felt something big and solid crash into me, and fingers like branches reached for my ankles. I kicked out, knocking the thing away, and then it was gone. Water poured into my mouth and in my eyes, and I felt the current drag at my clothes, trying to pull me away and suck me into its cold, damp embrace. I knew the rope was my savior, and so I held it tight, pulling and pulling, using every ounce of strength I had left to stop myself from being tossed like a ragdoll onto the hard rocks.

I knew Linda was safe. She'd made it. That gave me some comfort. Little Bear, too. They'd both made it.

I started to black out then, oxygen deprived and exhausted. I tried to hold the rope but my energy reserves were drained. I felt like I was floating in the clouds, high above our heads, and looking down on the earth from somewhere among the stars. I remembered Bill and how he used to make me laugh. I thought of my mother, and how she had loved us both, how our father had taught us survival skills and shown us how to shoot. I thought of Linda and her gentle touch, and the deep waters of her forever blue eyes. I wondered if this was what death felt like, because it wasn't so bad

As I lost consciousness, I looked up and saw the sheriff. He peered down at me through the murky water. He was smiling, which made me happy, but then the shadow of the Wendigo painted him in a sickly gray hue, and he exploded into a million pieces, floating into the water like burnt ash.

CHAPTER TWENTY-NINE

A Wolf in the Mountains

H ogan knew they were close. He had a feeling in his head, as if his brain had somehow been turned into ferrous metal, and a giant magnet was dragging him forwards, sucking on his melon so hard that it was almost pulling the gelatinous, blood filled lump out through his eyeballs like spoiled meatloaf. His fingers were itching and his jaw ached, as though he had a bad toothache. Teaching J.C. a lesson was going to be almost as good as having dirty sex with a woman of god; hell, two women of god.

He'd found through years of experience that the virtuous ones were always the most difficult to get in the sack, but when you did, all their inhibitions seemed to fly out the window like the new testament in a hurricane. It was mind-blowingly good. So much so that he always made a bee-line for the local church whenever he visited a new town, except in this new town, squeezing the life out of the one guy who'd had the audacity—the downright brass cajones—to turn his back on him? Well, that was going to feel much better than a meaningless one-night stand. Carter was going to get what was coming to him and then some. He couldn't wait to see the look on the turncoat's face when Hogan walked out of the shadows to confront him. It was going to be like a Picasso in a pawn shop window: priceless.

"Something bad happened here boss," Steel said, walking back along the lower path that snaked through the mountains, leading to a shelf-like plateau the locals called Hunter's Point. He was holding something in his hands, which were encased in latex gloves.

"Sure did," Campbell said, pinching his nose. "Smells like someone took a shit up here."

Hogan shot his young driver a sideways glance. The kid was starting to get on his nerves, and that was putting it mildly. "Go ahead," he said. "What did he find?"

"Nothing good," Steel replied, tossing the object he was carrying onto the ground where it rolled toward Hogan.

It spun three times before coming to rest at his feet, two blackened eyeballs staring up at him, the skin puffy and beginning to turn purple.

"Shit!" Hogan cried, checking the images on his phone. He'd searched for photographs of Carter's traveling companions on the internet before they'd headed out on their expedition, wanting to know exactly who it was he was dealing with. Straight away, Sheriff Elijah Harris's image came into view. "They killed the sheriff."

"Mutilated him, more like," Steel replied. "Hung him up in the tree back there like they were letting a deer bleed out. Gutted him, too."

"Carter's turned into a sick bastard since he's been away," Crane said, standing over the decapitated head and sneering. "Maybe you're better off without him, boss."

"This wasn't Carter," Steel said, interjecting. "This was something else entirely."

"What do you mean?"

"You forget, I've known Carter since Fallujah. The guy might not care about beating your rivals to a bloody mess—or even people who've tried to steal from you—but he's not a cop killer."

Hogan glared down at the sheriff's bloated face; at the black blood oozing from his lips, and the festering flesh and shredded veins that were hanging from his torn neck.

"Well, looks like he turned over a new leaf, because this cop is about as dead as they come."

"Maybe it was the Indian!" Campbell blurted out. Hogan thought the kid looked like he was just about ready to throw up. "I mean, they scalp people, right? Cut the skin right off their skull, like...like—" He held a hand to his stomach and turned away.

"This isn't the eighteenth century, son," Crane hissed, glaring at his inexperienced colleague as if he were looking at something particularly disgusting in the dirt. "Have you really got to use such outdated racial stereotypes?"

"Then what?" Hogan asked. "What are you saying, Steel?"

"I don't know. I just don't like it. Either Carter's turned into a first class psychopath, or something else is going on. Either way, I reckon this little fishing expedition isn't going to be the cake walk we expected."

Hogan looked up at the night sky just as a shooting star raced across the dappled black carpet that hung overhead. He took it as a sign. It didn't matter whether Carter had an army of undead soldiers walking alongside him. He was getting what was coming to him. And just for this little scare tactic he was pulling, he was going to make sure he got it real good.

Once I'd thrown up what felt like six lungfuls of ice-cold freshwater, I started to feel like I was almost human again. The images were still with me, however. I thought of the Wendigo, how it had almost caught up with me, and how its powerful, unearthly fingers had reached for my ankles as it tried to drag me into the swirling depths of the raging waters with it.

My plan had worked, but only just. I'd had a lucky escape, but I wasn't an idiot. I knew that the Wendigo hadn't been vanquished entirely. It was already dead, so drowning it just wasn't going to work. I'd bought us nothing but time, but no more than that. We still had to see our plan through if we were going to survive the night, and while our odds of success may have improved, they were still slim at best.

At first I hadn't known how the hell I was going to get across the deep, pummeling waters of the angry river—which suddenly looked and sounded a little angrier, a little more vengeful—but Little Bear had had the good sense to cut the ropes with plenty of slack, so all I had to do was tie two reasonably large rocks to each of the cut ends and toss them back over to the other side. It took me six or seven attempts, but eventually I hit the opposite river bank, and Linda and Little Bear tied them around a wide pine, making sure the crossing was tight and secure.

Making my back across the river was no easy feat—not made any easier by me constantly fearing the Wendigo lurking just behind me, its finger gently caressing the skin at the nape of my neck—but eventually I got there, exhausted and depleted of most of my reserves. Linda was the first to get to me, throwing her arms around my neck and kissing my face as if I'd just crawled back from the dead.

Little Bear patted my arm and grinned. "That was a close call," he said. "Too close. Maybe next time we'll do things the easy way."

"You let me know what it is," I said, still tasting the silty water on my tongue, "and I'll do it in a heartbeat."

The three of us laughed, but everything sounded false. So much about the world had changed in that one fleeting instant. We'd almost been set upon by a creature none of us could even begin to understand, and we all knew that it was still out there, blood hungry and hellbent on wiping us off the face of God's green earth.

"We need to keep moving," I said, dreading the journey ahead. I didn't even know if my legs would obey my exhausted brain, but I knew I had to try.

Little Bear turned to the darkest part of the forest, and pointed the way. "Follow me," he said as the darkness enveloped him. "We have maybe four hours before sunrise."

I turned to Linda who was still visibly shaken. "Don't worry," I said, trying to sound optimistic. "This will work."

She grabbed my hand and attempted a wry smile. "Thanks for the lie," she said, "but you don't need to. I'm a big girl, and I know a long shot when I hear one."

I nodded before pulling her toward me. "If it's the only shot we have, I say we take it."

Hogan and the others followed the trail left by Carter and his two conspirators, along the scrambling slope that led down the side of the mountain, oftentimes steep and treacherous. When Scott Campbell went over, almost rolling his ankle, Hogan fought the urge to grab him by the shirt and knock some sense into him. The kid was turning out to be a real liability.

They made it to the river bank, its white waters leaping from its rocky depths like angry trolls, and eyed the crushed reeds at the water's edge. After a few anxious minutes walking along the water's edge, Steel spotted the two lengths of rope that traversed the breadth of the river.

"Looks like they crossed here," he said, testing how taut the rope was. "Maybe Carter knows what he's doing after all."

"Or he has help," Crane replied, peering across to the opposite bank. "There's a trail that leads through those trees. I reckon that's where they're headed."

"We gotta cross that?" Campbell cried, his voice nasally and shrill. "You gotta be kidding me?"

Hogan was on him then, knocking the kid to the floor, his knife held at his throat. "You know, son? You're really starting to piss me off? If it wasn't for your uncle, I swear I'd—"

"Sorry boss," Campbell replied, his face suddenly a mask of terror. "I'm sorry."

Hogan felt the hot steel cowpokes of anger prodding at his temples. Carter was doing everything in his power to lead them on a merry dance, dragging them halfway across Colorado into God knows what and who knows where, and his two-bit cartoon henchman was making it a thousand times more difficult. He thought about slitting his throat right there in the mud.

"I suggest you keep your mouth shut for the duration of this journey, you half-assed piece of good-for-nothing crap. I've had about three times more of you than my stomach can take."

He hauled himself to his feet and turned to the river, casting an anxious glance at the two lengths of rope that signaled the next phase of their trek. He didn't like the look of them or the water that was moving at a hell of a velocity just a few feet beneath, but he also knew that if they were going to catch up with Carter, it was the quickest way across an impassable object. He suddenly had an idea.

"You first," he said to Campbell, dragging him to his feet. "I think it's about time you started adding some value to our little expedition."

The young driver initially looked like he was going to explode with anxiety, but he turned to the water, watching as the heaving waves crashed into the impenetrable rocks, before swallowing hard. He reached up, grabbed the rope that stretched above his head to a tree on the opposite bank, and pulled himself up. He swayed violently, the rope above pitching forwards as the rope he was standing on pitched backwards. He let go with one hand, gasping in surprise as he plummeted face first onto the dirt.

The other three burst into laughter, Hogan doubling over as he let out a belly laugh, holding a hand to his side.

"Fucking imbecile," he said, before composing himself. "Again. Get up there and do it again."

Campbell's next attempt was a little better, and he slowly shuffled sideways until he was at the water's edge. He looked back toward the others, his eyes revealing the level of unabated terror that he was being forced to endure."

"Well go on then," Hogan said, wagging his fingers. "Show us how it's done, big man."

As Campbell reluctantly reached one leg out and inched himself over the first vestiges of tumbling water, they heard a sound like the battle cry of a banshee echoing across the valley.

"What the hell?" Hogan said, glancing at Steel. "Did you hear that?"

His head of security had already drawn his weapon, and was heading toward the foot of the mountain. "I did."

"What is it?"

"Wolf, maybe. Coyote."

"Sounded like a crazy person," Hogan replied. "Doesn't sound like any wolf I've ever heard."

Crane approached the water's edge. "You sure it came from the mountains, Britt? It sounded like it came from the other bank."

Hogan reached for his gun and pointed it at Campbell. "Keep moving, boy," he said. "If there's a wolf pack in them there hills, we'll be a hell of a lot safer on the other side of this river."

Campbell peered down at the barrel of Hogan's gun, glanced anxiously at the water at his feet, and appeared to decide that he stood a better chance of making it through the night by traversing the river and getting as far away from his boss's vitriol as humanly possible.

"Thataboy," Hogan growled, wanting to take back control of the situation, no matter how hard his heart was pounding.

Just as Campbell reached the halfway point, there was another piercing, agonized howl— this time much closer to them. Hogan jerked toward it, not knowing exactly where it had come from. The mountains were so close, every sound resonated off their rocky facade as if they were standing in the middle of a giant echo chamber.

Steel let off two rounds, firing at something ahead of him on the trail which snaked into the darkness overheard.

Hogan dropped to the floor and Crane ducked behind a boulder, while Campbell hung like a sacrificial lamb above the river. He glanced at his boss, and then the river bank, and started to shuffle at pace toward the other side.

"Steel!" Hogan cried, as his head of security disappeared along the track. "What do you see?"

"Stay there, boss," he called back. "Whatever it is, it's up here."

Hogan eyed Crane who had pulled his handgun and was now training it at a spot just above Hogan's head. "Stay low, boss," he said. "I have you covered."

Hogan felt like a useless imbecile, lying there in the dirt like a low-life waster, watching while two of his men covered his ass, and another was doing his best to get as far away from danger as possible. He thought of the sheriff's disembodied head and the shallow grave they'd discovered early on. Carter was toying with them, he was sure of it. He was probably out there in the darkness, laughing with the others while they watched him lying face down in the mud and trembling with fear. He wasn't going to let them mock him like that. No way. If Carter wanted to play games, he had a game of his own.

"Fuck you Carter!" he cried, before leaping to his feet, raising his gun, and letting off a barrage of shots into the swirling black.

Across the water and stepping off the rope onto dry land, Campbell let out a huge sigh of relief. Not only had he made it across the river—which he was totally terrified of because he had never actually learned to swim—he'd also put some distance between himself and both his crazed boss and whatever the hell was lurking out there in the darkness. Whatever it was, it sounded like it was hungry, and he reasoned, with some degree of certainty, that it was most probably the thing that had made dog chow out of the sheriff dude. None of that mattered now, though. He'd crossed the river, he'd put raging waters between himself and mortal danger, and now all he had to do was follow the trail and pray to God that it led to civilization. He'd had enough of risking his life for a lunatic who didn't appreciate him. Uncle of no uncle, he was out.

He smirked and turned toward the forest, just as the seven feet tall creature emerged from the shadows, its horned skull illuminated by the faintest of light cast by the stars overhead, its eyes seemingly burning with a boiling inferno of hatred. As it gripped his throat with one enormous, powerful hand and plunged its saber-like claws into his abdomen, he felt an agonizing surge of pain that rippled through his body like a searing jolt of high-voltage electricity. He tried to cry out, but his vocal cords had been severed, and his neck was now hanging from his shoulders on the thinnest slithers of tendon.

Then, there was nothing.

CHAPTER THIRTY

Shot in the Dark

The descent toward Widow's Hole was difficult and treacherous in the darkness. Each of us were feeling the effects of the night's frantic exertions, and the shadow of the Wendigo hung over our every step. The valley ahead was dark and rolling, like black water, but I was eager to get out of the mountains. We'd lost the sheriff and had been pursued like game through the rocky landscape by a creature that would not give up, and seemingly could not be killed by conventional means. As much as our plan to destroy the Wendigo at the very place it feared the most sounded like a ridiculous notion—one saved for only the most outlandish fantasy novels—it was the only plan we had, and one that Little Bear seemed convinced would succeed. The only problem was, it meant we had to face the creature head on—a thought that I pushed to the back of my mind where it lay restless and anxious.

My brother walked alongside me as we scrambled down the increasingly steep descent. He didn't look himself; his skin was a little gray and his eyes were bloodshot and swollen, as if he'd not had enough sleep, which of course was ridiculous, because Bill couldn't sleep. Bill was dead.

"You don't look so good," I whispered so as not to be heard by the others.

"You try looking good when you've been blown to pieces by Iraqi insurgents."

"No, I mean, you looked okay before, but now you look a little faded, like an old picture."

"Don't worry about me little brother," he said, scrambling through the bracken and over a large rock. "Just focus on the gold back there in that mine. Once this little distraction is over, you're still going to have to clear your debts."

I'd been thinking about that. While the gold was tempting, it had brought me nothing but bad luck. I wanted no part of it. I'd decided that if I made it out of my little situation alive—a possibility that was looking less and less likely with every passing second—then I would walk away from the money and suffer whatever consequences were coming my way. If that meant I had to give up on the thing I had with Linda, then so be it. All that mattered was that she was safe. Hogan could go to hell as far as I was concerned.

"Hogan can bite me," I said, my hand caressing the gun tucked in my belt.

"Oh, he will," Bill replied, shaking his head. "Of that there's no doubt."

"Did you say something?" Linda said, turning to me as she lowered herself onto a ledge below us.

"No. I was probably just talking to myself," I replied, watching as Bill disappeared into the shadows. "I do that sometimes."

She forced a laugh, strained and cold, as though the weight of what we were about to face was weighing down on her like a heavy bag. "You can be pretty weird at times, you know that, J.C?"

"Yeah. I get that a lot."

We were approaching the bottom of the slope, and ahead of us lay a dense forest full of ancient pine and spruce. Gnarled roots leapt from the earth like a giant's wart covered fingers, and thick branches reached across the trail, black and twisted like the limbs of the long dead.

"Through there," Little Bear said.

"How far?" I replied, shooting a sideways glance at Linda, who looked like she was almost out on her feet. I felt the same way. My calves were burning and my back was aching from the climb.

"Three miles or so, maybe a little more."

I shook my head in resignation. That was another hour's walk at any sort of pace, longer if we encountered any difficulties on the trail. Sunrise was around two hours away, which meant we were cutting it fine, and that was lowballing it. I knew we wouldn't survive another day out there in the wilderness, hungry and exhausted, waiting for the Wendigo to come at us one last time. It had to end tonight, one way or another.

"We can do this," Linda said, touching my hand. "We've come this far."

I faked a smile in an attempt to give her some reassurance, but I knew it was unconvincing. I suddenly felt like it had all been for nothing. Who were we kidding, thinking that we were able to kill the unkillable, defeat the undefeatable? We were walking into a blind alley with the devil himself on our heels, and a faint, flaccid hope that God would intervene and save us from one of Satan's unholy minions. In Iraq, I knew what I was facing—human beings with the same fragilities and vulnerabilities that I had. They bled the same blood, felt the same pain, suffered the same anxieties and uncertainties. This thing, however—this monstrous, unyielding creature—it was something I could never even begin to understand. We had no idea how to hurt it, let alone kill it, which meant we were at a disadvantage that was impossible to overcome, like hunting a tiger with no gun.

"Okay," I said, letting out a long sigh of resignation. "Okay. Let's go."

The forest was not welcoming. It didn't want us there. It became obvious as soon we stepped into the writhing, sickening shadows. At once the trees around us were static, unmoving, and then a branch would stretch across the path like an extending tentacle and block our way. Of course, I never actually saw the trees move, but as soon as a way ahead became clear to us, it would become irreparably blocked. There were so many impassable avenues that I no longer knew which way we were facing or how far we had traveled.

"How much further?" I asked Little Bear once more, feeling like a kid in the back of his parents' Station Wagon.

"Not far."

His answer told me all I needed to know. Little Bear was as confused as I was, which both comforted and terrified me. We were in it together, which meant that the hands of both success and failure were hanging above us all like the Sword of Damocles.

A branch cracked someway behind us, followed by the sounds of footsteps through the undergrowth. I turned to see what it was, but once again the forest fought to block my way.

"You hear that?" Linda said. "I think there's someone out there."

"Keep moving," Little Bear replied, trying hard to push us on. "We can't face it out here."

The thought of facing the Wendigo anywhere filled me with a noxious, suffocating dread, but I knew Little Bear was right. We had a plan and we needed to execute it, no matter the odds. We'd tried to fight the creature in the open before, and it had only led to bad things happening.

I grabbed Linda's arm and pulled her alongside me as I followed the trail that Little Bear forged.

There was the sound of more twigs snapping behind us, followed by frantic footsteps through leaves, and then the sound of an urgent, hissing voice. Was the Wendigo speaking to us, I wondered? If so, did that mean we could try to communicate with it somehow? The noises were closer now, as if whoever or whatever it was, was moving at a pace that far outstripped our own. Perhaps, I thought, the Wendigo was able to manipulate the forest so that it allowed it free, unfettered passage, or maybe—and perhaps more realistically—we were just so exhausted that our pursuer was finding it easier to move quicker than its much slower prey. We were like a wounded animal, dragging itself along the ground, bloodied and battered, hampered by our depleted energy and numbers.

"I don't like this," Linda said from beside me. I felt the weight of her in my hand, as if she was pulling against me.

I didn't like it either, but what choice did we have? "Just keep moving," I replied. "It's not far now, I'm sure of it. We have to face this thing on neutral ground if we're to stand any chance of sending it back to wherever it came from."

There was a screeching cry from somewhere behind us, as if whatever was chasing us had caught the scent of us in its nostrils. It sounded hungry, unable to resist the tempting delicacies weaving through the forest, slow and cumbersome.

"That sound came from a different direction," Little Bear said, glancing over his shoulder. "There's somebody else in this forest with us."

Suddenly there was a loud crack and the branch above Little Bear's head splintered in two, as if an invisible hand had cut through the air and cleaved the wood in half.

"Shots fired!" I yelled, as I pulled my handgun and dragged Linda to the ground alongside me. "Stay here," I said to her, her expression etched with fresh confusion and fear.

"J.C." I heard her say, but I was already moving. I didn't know what was going down, but I did know that the only way to deal with whatever was happening to us was to fight back. "New plan," I said to Little Bear who was coming up behind me. "We fight whatever this is, here and now. We can't risk getting outflanked."

"The Wendigo doesn't use a gun," he said, grabbing my shoulder. "It doesn't need to. There's other people out there. Hunters maybe."

A thought struck me then. One of our number was down, hanging from a tree at the apex of the mountain and no doubt being picked at by carrion, but if we could coerce whoever was shooting at us into helping us, then maybe we stood a chance.

"Hey!" I cried out. "Hey! You out there! We're not your enemy! We just want to talk."

The silence was deafening as Little Bear and I crouched beside a large tree trunk and waited. I thought I could reason with these people. Perhaps they'd mistaken us for poachers, but if they knew who we were and what we were doing—particularly if I filled them in on the gold at Kiowa Rock—then I thought there was a good chance I could reason with them. Everybody had a price, right?

"Is that you J.C.?" the voice came back. "Is that you, old friend?"

I knew the smooth, crisp tone instantly, as if the words were coming from the mouth of my own brother. They crept into my ears and wormed their way through my veins, where they jabbed like tiny pins into my flesh. I didn't know how he'd found me all the way out there, but he had.

"Hogan?" I replied.

"As I live and breathe. Glad to know that you recognise your boss's voice, even if we are thousands of miles from home and walking around in the woods like a couple of hobos."

"You're not my boss," I said. "Haven't been for a little while."

"Not since you walked out on me," came the reply. "You know, that wasn't very nice of you. And after all I've done for you, too."

"You didn't do anything for me, Hogan. You just assist-ed in my slow decline."

"That hurts, J.C. That really hurts."

I wasn't an idiot. I knew that Hogan was stalling for time. I also knew that he'd have never tracked me down on his own. He usually traveled with two others; his adviser and confidante, Ethan Crane—who I trusted about as much as I'd trust a senator's Twitter feed—and his head of security, Britt Steel. If Hogan was talking, that meant that Steel was out there somewhere, moving stealthily toward the sound of my voice like a cobra preparing to strike.

I turned to Little Bear and gestured for him to circle to my left. We needed to split up if we were to stand any chance of defending our position.

"What are you doing all the way out here?" I called. "I never took you for a country boy."

That caused Hogan to laugh, long and loud as if I'd just told him the world's funniest joke. "Hell, you know me too well. I hate the country. Give me the smog and smoke of the big city, please. All this fresh air is killing me."

"So, why are you here?"

Hogan seemed to pause, as if he was considering his next move. "I thought I'd come find you; see if we can't make things right between us."

"You wanted me to kill an innocent woman," I said. "Threatened me if I didn't. Ain't much gonna make that right, unless you can convince me you've turned over a new leaf."

"You didn't think like that when you were taking my money."

"I was a different person then. I was in a bad place. Ain't in that place no more."

"Huh, that's not how it seems to me. Something's coming after you, J.C. Seems like it's not just me that has a beef with you. We left Campbell lying in the mud back there. Someone had seen fit to relieve him of his intestines, his liver too. Looks like you've pissed off the wrong people this time."

I hadn't known Campbell well, but I knew enough to know that the kid didn't deserve that kind of ending. If he'd been killed by the Wendigo, that meant that the creature had made it across the river. That thought alone made me shudder.

I crept along the tree line, which gave me a hindered view of Ethan Crane. He was standing, legs spread, arms outstretched and aiming his gun into the shadows to my right. Hogan's voice was coming from just ahead of him, but a large pine was blocking my way.

"Maybe so," I said. "But that doesn't change anything between us." I could see Little Bear someway off and slowly circling Hogan's position, but I still didn't know where

Steel was. The guy was ex Special Forces, which meant he was a formidable adversary. He could be standing right behind me that very second, and the first I would know that I had been outmaneuvered was when the bullet entered my skull from close range.

"You're right," Hogan replied. "We're probably past that point anyways."

"Who don't you just turn around and go home, Hogan," I said, knowing there was no way the crime boss would even consider giving up. "We have nothing to talk about any more. I left your organization. That's it. I'm not coming back, and there are a million more young wannabe thugs out there that could do an equally despicable job."

There was an eerie silence again, and for a moment I thought that something had happened. I took stock of my position. I knew Linda was someway back there in the darkness, and I hoped with all my being that she was staying hidden. This beef was between me and Hogan. She didn't need to get involved in this. I couldn't see Steel, but that didn't mean he wasn't nearby and taking aim.

"You don't get it," Hogan said at last, his tone now more authoritarian and all-business. All the fake camaraderie had evaporated. It was the kind of tone I recognised from him. "You fucked me over! You don't get to do that! You worked for me, still do. You don't get a notice period, you don't get to retire early, you don't get no goddamn pension. You join my organization, you join for life. Life! You get me!"

"Well, maybe I'm the exception."

"There are no exceptions!" he yelled. "None! I let you go, then what does that mean for my other guys? Suddenly, anyone who's been thinking about leaving but can't, they see a way out and they try to do the same thing. Then, someone else sees what happens there, and they decide to walk out, too. Before you know it, I've got everyone thinking they can just come and go as they please, like a bunch of schoolkids or fast food workers. This ain't no big city bank, J.C. This is a criminal operation worth hundreds of millions of dollars, and all that success depends on one thing. You know what that is?"

I grunted. I knew exactly what he was talking about.

"Control!" he yelled. "Control is the key to everything. If I lose that, I have nothing."

I edged closer to the clearing and watched as Crane stepped away from me, walking slowly to the other side of the small space. Then Hogan came into view. His back was to me but his gait was unmistakable. The guy exuded confidence like sociopaths exude a lack of empathy. He was a force of nature, but in all the wrong ways.

"You see," he continued, narrating into the nothingness. "That's why I can't let you walk away, J.C. It just wouldn't be the right thing to do. No offense."

"Hey, none taken."

I raised my gun and aimed it at Hogan's head. Not since Fallujah had I ever wanted to hurt someone so badly. Hogan was everything I hadn't wanted to be when I left the military, but somehow I'd become just like him without ever noticing the transition.

"So you have to be dealt with, like I might deal with a rodent problem, or a nasty zit."

"Thanks for the analogy."

I rested my hand on the trigger. My finger was millimeters away from solving the very problem I'd been running from. I took a deep breath and trained my eyes. It was now or never.

"I wouldn't do that if I were you," Britt Steel said, the muzzle of his gun pressing into my temple. I cursed under my breath. I'd been outmaneuvered after all.

"Hey Britt. Nice to see you again."

"Drop the gun."

I let it fall to the floor. I let out a long sigh, thinking about my next move, which at that exact moment eluded me.

"Now hands behind your head and turn to me. Slowly, you asshole."

I clasped my hands at the back of my head and gradually swiveled toward Steel's voice. He was standing between two trees, mud smeared on his face and hands. I hadn't seen him coming, hadn't even heard him. I had to give it to him; the guy knew what he was doing. My thoughts went to Linda and whether she was safe.

"Where are the others?" he asked, the gun aimed squarely at the spot between my eyes.

"There aren't any."

He smiled and nodded. "Same old J.C. Always trying to be the hero."

I shrugged. "Same old Britt Steel. Always trying to be *the* asshole."

He cracked me across the cheek with the butt of the pistol, and I went down hard. I laughed and spat out warm blood. "I see you still can't take a joke," I said.

"I have him, boss!" he yelled. "He's over here with me. What do you want me to do with him?"

There was a silence again, and I could almost hear the gears in Hogan's head whirring as he considered the best move.

"Do you know what?" he said. "I've had enough of this shit-stain. Just shoot him, Steel. Finish that sonofabitch."

I peered up at Steel's black gaze and readied myself for the inevitable. It wasn't the way I thought I was going to go, but what the hell? I just hoped that Linda and Little Bear would make it out okay. I could see my brother looking down at me from just behind my executioner, smiling as if he thought the whole thing was a joke. I shook my head, confused.

"See you, J.C."

A shot rang out, but not from the direction I was expecting. Steel glanced to his right, and it was just long enough for me to react, kicking out with my legs and sending him tumbling. As I leapt to my feet, I glanced to my left and saw Crane slumped against a tree. The side of his head was no longer there, and brain matter was spilling down the side of his neck. Little Bear had come through.

"Holy shit!" Hogan yelled, racing toward his stricken adviser. "Crane. Crane!"

I was up now and barrelling toward Steel, but the guy was quick, and he was on his feet before I was able to pin him to the ground. He swung the side of his hand into my throat, and I felt my windpipe crumple under the force of the blow. I stumbled backwards, coughing and wheezing, trying to catch my breath. He came at me, head down, shoulder low. I whirled to the side, just in time to lessen the impact of the blow, but I was still knocked backwards as his arm swung into my chest. I managed to stay on my feet, but Steel kicked out a leg, striking me in my abdomen. I went down hard, winded and struggling to breathe.

"I thought you'd put up more of a fight!" he yelled, laughing as I tried to pull myself to my knees. "You had such a good reputation in the army. Maybe it was all bullshit."

I saw my gun, half buried in a pile of leaves and dirt, and I reached for it, but he was on it before I'd had a chance to move. He raised it to my face and grinned as I lay helpless in the dirt. He laughed at the fear that was clearly evident on my face, but it wasn't him I was afraid of. It was the thing that rose up behind him like an obelisk erupting from the soil, a spirit created by the darkness itself. Its horns appeared to grow from Steel's own skull, but it was no more than a terrifying optical illusion. Its skull face became visible through the gloom, its eyes unyielding, its body grotesque, yet powerful.

"Time to die, J.C." Steel said as he held his finger to the trigger. "Say hello to your brother for me."

It happened so fast, I still don't know what I saw. In one moment, Steel was about to blow my brains out; in the next moment his head was flying through the air like a blood soaked bowling ball and his body was slumping to the ground as if all the air had escaped from his body.

My body responded instinctively as I leapt up, grabbing my gun and running toward Linda, who I hoped was still hiding in the same spot I'd left her in only minutes before.

There was a screech behind me as the Wendigo let out a blood-curdling cry, and I hoped with everything I had that it was going after Hogan rather than pursuing me through the forest. If it chose the latter, I knew I would be dead before I got to Linda, and I would have inadvertently led it straight to her.

I almost yelped in joy as she stood and came toward me.

"It's coming!" I yelled. "It's coming for us. We have to go—now!"

Her eyes opened wide as she realized what I was telling her, and we ran together then, racing blindly into the darkness like two wild animals fleeing a forest fire.

A gunshot rang out behind me and I heard Little Bear yell something in his mother tongue. There was another shot, and then the sound of a man screaming in horrible pain, but I had no time to think, no time to feel. All I knew was that we needed to get away from that hellish thing. We needed to keep moving until our lungs burst and our bodies gave way. We couldn't pause, we couldn't breathe. Our legs were all we had, and they needed to carry us somewhere, anywhere.

Branches slapped at our faces, raised roots tried to send us sprawling into the dirt, and uneven earth threatened to trip us at every turn. We ran in a haphazard, random pattern, trying to find a path through the moving, swirling maze that was the forest.

There was another shrill, piercing howl from behind us, and I thought I could feel the Wendigo's hot breath on my neck. I imagined it no more than two steps behind me, preparing to slice me open like a cooked turkey. I urged Linda on. Her legs were a blur but her eyes said that she knew what was at stake. We had to make it out of the forest. We had to make it to daybreak.

The Wendigo shrieked as another gunshot resounded, and I knew then that we were moments from death. We had no way out, no route through the impenetrable landscape. Nature had conspired against us, bringing the creature toward us like a vulture to a carcass. We would die out there in the wilderness, rotting in the leaves and mulch like so many other dead and decaying creatures before us. We would become part of the godawful forest, just like the Wendigo was a part of the landscape, a part of everything that had gone before. We would become nutrients in the soil, fractured bones among the rocks.

All of a sudden the ground gave way, and Linda and I were sent tumbling down a steep drop, soil and rocks falling around us as we crashed through vines and bracken, the stone scraping our skin and the branches tearing at our clothes.

We came to a stop in a circular basin, surrounded on all sides by tall pines, black like obsidian, their bark cracked and splintered like old skin. In the middle of the bowl was the remains of a timber hut, thirty-five feet long, its roof semi-collapsed and its walls rotten and crooked. Above us, a tattered long length of rope hung from a thick, scorched branch, the noose now vacated. I knew instantly what had once hung there between its rough, vice-like grip.

I turned to Linda who was wiping blood from a split lip.

"Welcome to Widow's Hole."

CHAPTER THIRTY-ONE

Widow's Hole

B efore my trip to Devil's Ridge, I had scoffed at anybody that suggested they'd had dalliances with witchcraft, palm readers, fortune tellers or the occult. If a movie that contained anything but hard, in your face realism came on the TV, I would switch to another channel immediately. Fantasy wasn't my thing, and neither was horror. I'd seen enough of it in Iraq and on the streets of Chicago. Science fiction turned me off, fuzzy, out of focus UFO videos just made me laugh, and if anyone dared mention Area 51, I was out of the room and walking. If I couldn't see it, touch it, or taste it, I didn't believe in it.

Standing in Widow's Hole and staring at what Little Bear had described as *bruja* Whispering Wind's lair, I knew that my transformation into a true believer was complete. I was aware that somewhere above me, at the top of the basin, the Wendigo was prowling, hungry and full of rage, and no doubt figuring out what its next move would be. However, down here in the epicenter, in the heart of ground zero, a thousand spirits were swirling.

The miner's were all dead. I knew that now because they were there with us. Not visible as such, but not invisible either. It was as though the air was thick with energy, the dust particles floating down from the canopy, at once converging into distinguishable shapes—a hand clutching a hammer, a body dressed in dirt stained coveralls, a man's face, with small eyes, thick beard, scrawny neck, a sadness etched into his features like graffiti. I glanced at Linda who was standing motionless, her face a mask of wonder and fear.

"What's happening?" she asked. "Are these—"

I nodded slowly. "I think so."

There was a sickening green and dark red mist that floated above us, like a grotesque version of the aurora borealis spectacle I'd once witnessed during an ill-fated trip to Alaska. It shifted and distorted, compressing into a shape no bigger than a small car, and then stretching and pulling into a wide sheet that covered the whole basin, its texture seemingly like a semi-transparent dough. There was a blackness at its center, and dark veins that mottled its skin. I couldn't tear my eyes from it, as if there was something lurking within that I just had to see. It seemed to whisper to me, mouthless and soundless but penetrating my skull with a startling clarity nevertheless.

You have brought it back, the voice said, hoarse and thin, like tissue paper. *You set it free.*

I shook my head, as if trying to dislodge something from my ear.

"Are you getting this?" I asked Linda, but she frowned and shook her head.

"Getting what?"

"I don't know. It's just—"

It will come for you, but not directly. It will not enter this sacred soil.

I reached for my handgun, but where it had once had been tucked into my belt, there was simply sullied denim and thin air. I glanced at the flattened soil and bracken where Linda and I had tumbled from a spot some forty feet above us, and I realized I'd dropped my weapon during the chase. I was unarmed, and I noted, with a growing despair, that so was Linda.

"What do we do now?" Linda mouthed, her cheeks trembling. "Where's Little Bear?"

I shook my head. I had no idea, but what I'd heard hadn't sounded good. The problem was, this plan was my friend's idea, and I did not know the next move. After a moment of indecision, I pointed to the wooden shack. "I think we have to go inside."

"In there? Are you serious?"

"I wished I wasn't, believe me."

The dust formed in front of me as the pained features of an elderly miner floated before me. His eyes were as large as my hand, his mouth open and sneering. I felt my pulse quicken, but I grabbed Linda's arm and pulled her through him with me. I instantly felt the dead miner's pain, only fleetingly, but it was like something was trying to peel the skin from my flesh. Linda cried out momentarily, but then we were through and the open darkness of Whispering Wind's home lay before us. The hut breathed out, as it were expelling centuries of lost souls.

I shot Linda a reassuring glance. "You ready?"

She gave a curt nod, but I knew it was a reluctant one.

I reached out a hand and brushed thick webs from the open doorway. Above us, the noose swayed back and forth, and for a moment I thought I could see the festering body of the dead bruja, her black eyes glaring down at me, her face puffed and split, her mouth like a scar, open in some sort of maniacal grin. As quickly as the image appeared, it was gone.

I placed a foot on the timber floor and entered. As we stepped into the hallway, the fallen roof above us allowed some starlight to enter. I could see where the skin of a goat once lay, like a welcoming rug. Now it was simply black and torn like old paper. A smell hit me like nothing I had ever experienced before. It was like spoiled meat mixed with the sweetness of sage and elderberries. Beside me, Linda pinched her nose and groaned.

A door lay ahead of us. It too was open, but the roof above it was solid and undisturbed, meaning that the darkness was able to flourish, reaching from wall to wall, floor to ceiling. Try as I might, my eyes could not penetrate the gloom.

Linda gripped my hand, and the firmness of her grip comforted me. I had cleared whole buildings in Fallujah, moving from room to room—the skills I had learned during my training were the only thing standing between me and certain death—but I had never felt the kind of fear that was ravaging my body in that very instant. I didn't understand my enemy, and that made it all the more unreal, all the more deadly.

We entered the room slowly, pushing into the darkness as if we were peeling away layers. The floor was thick with dust, and spider webs hung from the ceilings and kissed our skin, as if whatever lurked in the darkest corners was caressing us with the softest of touches. My eyes started to adjust and I could see that we were in a sitting room. A wooden stool lay on the floor to my right, upturned in the dust, one of its legs split down the middle. Ahead lay what would have once been a bench, pots spilled over on its thick surface, their contents lost to the passage of time.

I stooped down to look at what first appeared to be a pile of sticks on the ground, but I jerked away when I realized it was a collection of rotting bones. When I'd re-gathered my composure, I reached out and took one, holding it up in the darkness and narrowing my eyes as I tried to focus on its features. The first bone was the skull of a bird, the second the femur of a deer or a goat, the third a talon or claw. I rummaged around some more and found something more substantial, solid and dimpled. I held it more closely and dropped it as soon as I realized what it was. I had been holding the spinal vertebrae of what was once a human being.

Behind me, Linda screamed and I spun round, kicking the graveyard of bones away as I leapt to my feet. She was in the farthest corner of the room, something hanging over her shoulder, as if some creature was attempting to pull her into the very walls of the shack.

"I'm coming!" I cried, and pushed the thing away, recoiling at its damp, stiff texture. The thing stood some six feet tall and hung from a nail in the wall. It was dark and fur-covered, but its life had evaporated long ago. The bear skin was now coarse and stiff, but some of its lush pelt remained, bugs now making a home among what had once been fine hair.

"I thought it was that thing," she said as we moved toward a further door. She was trembling, so we held each other for a moment, waiting for our beating hearts to calm to a slower tempo. My skin itched with heat and my bones ached. Every muscle in my body was tense and taught, ready to react as soon as something flitted across the darkness or grew from the very walls that surrounded us.

When our pulses had ceased their endless racing, we moved toward the next room. It too was dark, although a small amount of light crept through from a hole in the roof. The timber beneath was damp and rotting. I placed my feet carefully as I traversed what I guessed had been a sleeping area of sorts. There were the remains of a rug made from hide on the floor, and something hung from the center of the room. It looked like a rudimentary dream catcher, but instead of circles woven with thread, there were animal skulls, tied together in something black and tissue like.

My foot struck something on the ground and I bent down to collect it. I held it to my face and recalled Little Bear's story about Chief Cunning Wolf and the necklace he made from the rattlesnake that killed his wife. What I had in my hand bore an uncanny resemblance to a snake's head, a leather strap looped through the base of its skull. The object was blackened and fragile, but I decided it might be important, so I slid it into the pocket of my jeans.

Linda was ahead of me now and looking at something beneath her feet. She was in the center of the room, and above her, the hole in the roof cast a sickly white sheen on her. For one moment she looked like all the life had been sucked from her once limber body, and she was standing there, now no more than a corpse in the starlight.

"What is this?" she said, her mouth moving, but her eyes unblinking.

"What?"

I stood beside her in the milky light and looked down. There at her feet was a hole, four feet in diameter and deeper than the light could penetrate.

I didn't know what to think. The wood around the hole had not rotted like other areas of the floor, but the edges were burned, as if the hole had been created by something so hot that it had instantly disintegrated the hard timber and densely packed earth. I leaned over and peered inside. Where the light could not reach, the darkness was blacker than tar.

For a moment I saw something move in there and I got to my knees, gazing down into the hole as if I'd found more buried treasure. However, what I actually saw made me cry out. Bill was down there, his face gray and pale, blood vessels visible around his mouth and nose, and his eyes black and marble-like. He peered up at me and tried to speak, but dark gray hands covered his mouth and dragged him downwards. Over his shoulder and beneath him I could see the shadowy form of the bruja. She was grinning once more, her blackened teeth and slug-like tongue visible between her dark, thin lips.

I tried to reach into the hole to save my brother, but he was dragged into the soil as the bruja pulled and tugged at him. She laughed at me as I screamed, but there was nothing I could do.

The door behind us burst open then. Linda leapt backwards and cried out, and I rolled to the side, just in time to Frank Hogan toss Little Bear's lifeless body to the ground. The Indian's face was a mess of blood and bone, his chest pierced with a dozen knife wounds.

"You looking for him, J.C?" Hogan cried out. "Don't worry, he put up a fight, like the good little Indian soldier that he was."

"You bastard!" I yelled, rising to my feet as he raced into the room, a knife held in one blood soaked hand.

"I've been looking forward to this," he said, lunging forward with his arm extended. The blade missed my neck by a whisker as I whirled to my right. "I guess Steel must have gotten a little slower, allowing you to take him down like that, but I aint't Steel, and I ain't slow."

I dodged to my left this time as Hogan came at me once more. In the corner of my vision I watched as Linda edged toward the far wall and scoured the ground for some form of weapon. She stooped and pulled a sharp length of timber from the floor and raised it up.

"I wouldn't, little girl," Hogan yelled. "This is between me and him. You don't want no part of this."

I danced across the thin beam of starlight that shone through the hole in the roof, placing the deep hole between the two of us. If Hogan was going to come at me, he was either going to have to circumnavigate the shaft in the earth, or leap over it. Either way, I thought it would give me an edge, which was something I desperately needed.

"You know there's something out there, right?" I said as Hogan tried to come round the hole to my right. "Something that killed Steel, probably killed Campbell too."

Hogan brought his arm down as I almost let him catch up to me, and the knife whistled past my cheek, slicing a shallow groove.

"I think you've been dragging too hard on the Indian's pipe," he said, his eyes full of vengeance and spite. "You're seeing things."

"It's out there, Frank. It killed the sheriff, four others in the town, too. While we're in here fighting, it could be out there. Anywhere."

Hogan stepped over the hole, slipping and almost falling in. As he tried to regain his balance, I clocked him in the jaw, knocking him backwards and spilling his knife onto the floor.

"You'll pay for that," he said, spitting blood on the ground. "I'll add it to the list."

"I'm serious," I continued, buoyed by the fact that my assailant had been disarmed. Part of me hoped that he would see sense, but the realistic part of me knew that seeing sense was the furthest thing from my old boss's mind. All he wanted was my head on a stick, and he wasn't going to stop until he had it.

I was close to Linda now, and she tossed me the length of split timber. I held it out like a sword and parried Hogan's advances, jabbing the end of the stick into his nose for good measure. Blood streamed from his nostrils and water poured from his eyes.

"Enough of this!" he yelled, feinting to his right and coming around to my left. He'd sold me on the dummy and I was caught backfooted. He swept a foot across my legs and suddenly I was on my back as Hogan came toward me. I began to rise to my feet, fancying my chances of being able to take him in a fist fight, but he grinned at me, depressing a switch beneath his shirt, and a spring loaded knife erupted from his cuff. He held the long blade out, a look of grim determination on his bloodied lips.

Linda cried out from somewhere in the darkness as he approached me.

"You don't need to do this," I said. "Just let it go."

He loomed over me as I lay beneath him, blood pouring from his nose and mouth, his voice hoarse and ragged.

"Oh, but I've come all this way," he said, raising the knife. "I can't stop now."

I peered over his shoulder and saw Linda trying to squeeze herself into the corner as something crawled from the hole, its claws digging into the wooden floor, its jagged antlers rising from the depths like the saplings of a blackened, ancient tree. Its eyes were red and smoldering, and its faceless, expressionless skull peered down on us in a terrifying, unyielding silence.

Hogan caught my expression and he half turned, catching sight of the giant, shadow filled form that was now standing behind him.

"What are you?" he asked, diverting his attention.

I kicked backwards across the ground, pushing myself toward the rear wall as the Wendigo let out a scream that made every ounce of my being shudder and shake. Linda was hunched over in the corner, her hands over her ears, her shoulders trembling.

"What the hell's going on here?" Hogan cried, getting to his feet and thrusting the knife toward the creature before him.

The Wendigo moved with a swiftness that belied its enormous size, and in an instant a serrated object emerged from Hogan's spine as the creature pushed its claws into his abdomen. He let out a pained shriek as blood erupted from his mouth. The Wendigo lifted him from the ground, his feet rising two feet above the wooden floor. The knife clattered to the ground as Hogan peered down at the festering skull beneath him. He spat blood from his sneering lips.

"Well, ain't you a handsome boy," he said, forcing a grin, as crimson saliva fell in long slimy strands from his open mouth.

The Wendigo pulled him in close and opened its mouth, its teeth like razors. It breathed out, and I watched as a silver-gray mist emerged from its lips and wafted across Hogan's face.

"Looks...like...you win, Carter," Hogan said, his voice now barely audible. I watched as his life seemed to leave him, his eyes slowly closing as his head sagged.

The Wendigo turned to me and tossed Hogan's body against the wall with such force that I heard his bones splinter against the timber.

I stood up and backed as far away as possible, but the Wendigo strode toward me, its arms outstretched. I felt a fear like no other, as if everything I was, everything I had ever been, meant nothing. The battles in Iraq, my brother's death, everything that had gone down in Chicago. None of that meant anything. This thing was inhuman, ungodly, but it was real all the same. There was no escape, no way out. All I wanted was for Linda to be safe.

"Take me," I said. "If that's what you want. Take me, but leave her."

The Wendigo was before me now, its tall body covered in the ancient roots of trees long dead, hair hanging from its head and down its back, its skull face expressionless and pale, the red fire of hell burning in its stare. I stared at something hanging limply at its waist, and realized with some disgust that I was looking down at Travis Newsted's lifeless eyeballs hanging from their sinewy tendrils. It seemed that the Wendigo had indeed taken them from the wealthy landowner as some sort of sick prize—a realization that made me feel sick to my stomach as I began to imagine my own eyes hanging there beside them, black and bloodied, staring unseeing for all eternity.

I looked at the creature's face and knew I was staring at what remained of Chief Cunning Wolf, but the chief was no longer there. This was the spirit of Chenoo, full of hatred for everything that had been taken from him. He wanted blood, he wanted lust, and right now he wanted my soul.

I fingered the object in the pocket of my jeans and remembered what I'd found. I knew then what the hole in the ground was. It was from inside that deep cleft in the soil that Whispering Wind had summoned the spirit Chenoo before he had betrayed and slaughtered her, eventually tricking the chief into providing him with his own body within which to forever roam the earth.

I knew then that if the charm had been used to perform the possession, the very act of destroying it would be the only way it could be reversed. Perhaps that was Little Bear's plan all along—I just hadn't been paying enough attention to my learned friend to work it out for myself.

The Wendigo wrapped its fingers around my throat and lifted me from the ground. I could feel the tendons in my neck stretching like rubber bands, and my windpipe compressing to little more than a tiny tube. I couldn't breathe, I couldn't see, but I knew I had to do something. I grabbed the rattlesnake's head, and attempted to pull it free. At first it caught in my pocket and I thought I wouldn't have the strength to unhook it, and then it almost slipped from my grasp as I pulled with all my might.

The Wendigo leaned forward and I could smell the foul stench of death on its breath. It opened its mouth once more, but I spat, yelling into its face with every ounce of energy I had. I was so angry, so full of rage.

"Fuck you!" I cried. "Fuck you to hell!"

I tossed the rattlesnake charm across the floor and screamed with a voice that was barely there.

"Toss it in the hole!" I yelled. "Linda! Grab that thing and toss it in the hole!"

She moved, uncertain at first, but then quickening her pace, just as the Wendigo realized what we were doing. It dropped me to the ground and turned. I fell in a heap at its feet as it started to cross the room, but Linda was quick, and she had a hand on the charm before the creature had taken two gigantic steps.

My vision was swimming but I watched through bleary eyes as she stood, evading the Wendigo's arm as it swung a clawed fist at her, diving onto the ground and tossing the charm into the air. Before it came down to earth, I realized I was slowly losing consciousness. As darkness descended upon me like a dense fog, I just hoped that she'd made the shot.

She had to make that shot.

CHAPTER THIRTY-TWO

Revival

I came to on the forest floor with the bruja's noose hanging over my head, swinging back and forth, creaking and groaning like an old chair. It was the sunlight that woke me. It was streaming through the canopy and kissing what remained of the wooden shack with tiny strips of yellow and gold. The structure had finally given way and succumbed to the passage of time, sucked back into the earth as if the ground itself had tried to swallow it whole.

I sat up as shards of hot lightning fizzed across my eyes. I felt like I'd been hit by a truck, which I guess I kind of had. I swung my head, searching for the Wendigo. The last thing I had seen was it bearing down on Linda as she tossed the charm into the air. I had no way of knowing which way the chips had fallen, but I prepared myself for the worse.

I pulled up by the overhead branch and steadied myself as the world swam around me. I felt as though I was standing on a spinning carousel which was tilting and swaying like the cars on a waltzer. I leaned over and threw up, but all that spilled out of my lips was yellow bile and gross breath.

I shook off my nausea and searched for Linda. I couldn't see her anywhere. I started to wonder whether the Wendigo had stolen her away as revenge for tossing the charm into that god awful hole. I thought of my brother, about the bruja dragging him down into the earth with her. I thought of Hogan, his body battered and broken. He was nowhere to be seen either. Perhaps, I mused, I was dead or dying, and everything around me was some kind of weird, surreal purgatory.

"You're awake," a voice said from behind me. I whirled around and there was Linda, using broken bits of timber to create steps on the steep hill. "I figured you'd need some help getting out of here. That thing almost killed you, you know?"

"You made the shot," I said, barely able to make a sound.

"It was never in any doubt, soldier."

It took us a while, but we eventually made it out of Widow's Hole in one piece. We never found Hogan's body, or any sign of the Wendigo. Linda said that as soon as she tossed the charm into the well, everything turned into a bright inferno of black and silver streaks, and the earth literally opened up, long scarlet vines reaching up from some subterranean chamber and coiling around the Wendigo's body, pulling him down through the mud and clay and then closing in around him like a heavy blanket. I guessed that Hogan was down there with him, his decaying body now home to the worms and termites. Little Bear's body had gone too. It was as if the forest had reclaimed what rightfully belonged to it. I was okay with that and I knew Little Bear would have been too. He always saw himself as part of the landscape.

There was only one way back, and that was the way we came in. We both knew it was a long hike, but it didn't matter. We were walking without fear, without having to look over our shoulders or worry about the night time creeping toward us like an ominous shadow.

We talked a little, but I don't think either of us knew how to explain what we'd experienced. It all just seemed like some drug addict's hallucinogenic induced dream. I was a soldier, taught to deal with the unexpected, to react to dynamic situations, but nobody could have ever taught me how to defend myself against that undead abomination.

I think Linda was in shock, too. She had been drained of all her usual color and joy. I knew it would take a long time to recover, and I thought that I owed her some space to let her come to terms with everything. Maybe, I thought, I'd return to Chicago alone until the dust had settled.

As the sun began to set on the first leg of our return journey, we passed the spot where the sheriff had been murdered, his body still hanging from the blackened limbs of the long-dead tree. Linda and I worked in silence as we retrieved his remains. We dug a hole in the soil and buried him. I couldn't bear to leave him up there any longer where the carrion had already begun to feast on the festering meat.

A day and a half later and we were walking along Governor's Boulevard, exhausted, covered in grime, and shuffling as if our bodies had also been possessed by an undead spirit. I felt like I needed to sleep for a week, and Linda looked about as tired as tired could get.

We stood outside her house, the police cordon now thankfully removed, and held each other. I looked into her eyes and knew that something had been lost between us.

"I'll head back to the hotel," I said, not wanting to intrude on what would be a long recovery. "If it's still open, that is." I recalled the bodies of Penny and Travis, their innards ripped from their mutilated bodies.

"You can stay here," she replied, but her eyes belied her true feelings. She wanted to shower and clean herself of everything that had happened up in those mountains, and that included washing me away too, for a while at least.

I shook my head. "It's better this way," I said, and kissed her tenderly on the cheek. My feelings were as strong as ever, but I knew only too well that time and space were the greatest healers. They were also free.

I headed back to the Regal Hotel, my head held low and my body sagging. I thought of my brother Bill in that hole, the bruja's hands around his shoulders, and wondered if it was truly his spirit being dragged into the eternal, smoldering pit of hell, or whether the Wendigo was playing games with my head. The only thing I knew for certain was that I hadn't seen Bill since that moment. Guilt tainted the relief I felt at not being faced with the reminder of my brother's death every single day, but I felt it just the same.

The hotel foyer was empty, save for Sylvia sitting behind the counter, her glasses perched on the end of her nose. She dropped her pen when I entered.

"Well, there you are!" she exclaimed, eyeing me with a look that was both accusatory and sympathetic. "Hell, you look like you've been dragged through the mountains by your pants."

I smiled. At least some things hadn't changed in Devil's Ridge. "It sure feels that way."

"Your room's still the way you left it," she said. "Although don't get too comfortable. Rumor has it that Mac Newsted is thinking of knocking the place down and replacing it with some fancy apartments. Thirty years I've worked here and for what? I know the man's lost his boy, but, shit."

I felt for Sylvia, but I wasn't surprised. The hotel was just a painful reminder of what had happened to Penny, although there was worse news to come for the wealthy landowner. I looked around. The Regal Hotel was a piece of Devil's Ridge history, but history was just that, wasn't it? Something in the past, faded and tainted.

"That reminds me," she said, remembering herself. "The mayor came by here looking for you. He looked none too pleased, too. You want me to let him know you're back?"

I shook my head. I needed time to prepare myself for a meeting like that.

"In the morning," I said. "It can wait 'til the morning."

Even though I was as exhausted as hell, sleep didn't come easy to me. Every time I closed my eyes I saw Bill in the hole and Hogan's body being tossed aside like an old rag. The Wendigo was always in my thoughts, its fearsome skull head, its blazing eyes and festering breath.

When sleep did come, it was fitful. I woke at midnight, searching the room for water, something cool. My throat was as dry as dust and my tongue as heavy as an old sack. I headed for the faucet and thrust my head beneath it, taking in huge mouthfuls of barely cold liquid. It would have to do. I wiped my chin with the back of my hand and turned back to the bed. The Wendigo stood there in the darkness, mere inches from me, its mouth open and its crimson eyes burning. I hit the light switch and it disappeared. I sat in an upright chair with the overhead light still burning for the rest of that night. I thought about calling Linda, but I hoped with everything I had that all thoughts of the Wendigo had escaped her.

When daylight came it was a blessed relief. I made two coffees, drank them both in quick succession, and then took a long, steaming hot shower. I shaved, too, trying to return myself to something close to normality. I wanted Devil's Ridge out of my life as fast as possible, but I knew I had things to do first.

Like explaining what the hell had happened to the sheriff.

I sat outside the mayor's office, feeling like a schoolkid waiting to see the principal. The seat was uncomfortable and the room was small, and the mayor's personal assistant—an elderly, petite woman with sharp eyes—kept glaring at him as if I were a nasty stain on the furniture.

"Send him in, Audrey," the intercom boomed.

The PA removed her glasses, her eyes narrow and focussed. "The mayor is ready for you now, Mr Carter," she said, spitting out my name as if it were a foul taste in her mouth.

"Yeah, I'm sure he is," I said, pushing through the door where I was immediately assaulted by the stink of cheap aftershave and cigars.

"Mr Carter," Mayor Arthur Pumpkin declared as he rose from his chair. "Well, we've been looking all over for you."

I didn't know how to begin, so I just came out and said it. "The sheriff's dead. Little Bear, too. Only Linda Thornton and I made it back in one piece."

All the color seemed to drain from the mayor's cheeks, as if somebody had boiled his skin. He eyed me furtively, and I could see he was wondering who was standing before him in his office. A murderer? A deceiver?

"Well...well," he stammered. "I'll wager you have a story to tell."

"That I do."

"Then please," he said, gesturing toward a chair. "Please, tell it."

I decided not to sit. I didn't plan on staying long. I wanted to get everything off my chest, say goodbye to Linda, and get as far away from Devil's Ridge as possible. I hadn't thought about the gold in days, and as far as I was concerned it was a fool's prize. The people of the town were welcome to it.

I started from the time I'd found Zed's body, the trap we'd set for Caleb, what Linda had told me about the thing that had broken into her home. When I told him about how we'd found Travis's body in the forest, his body torn open and soaked in gore, he visibly shook.

"Well, now, that is a tragedy, right there." He looked as though somebody had told him his wife had died. "Shit, that really is going to upset a lot of people."

His reaction disgusted me. Zed, Caleb, Paul Chase. They were all dead too, but their demise had barely registered on Mayor Pumpkin's dial. The son of the richest, most powerful guy in town, though? The guy that pulled the mayor's thin strings of deception? I knew that was what was bothering him. It had all happened on his watch, after all.

I continued, describing how the Wendigo had attacked us before following us into the mountains, killing the sheriff and attempting to drag me into the white water rapids. I left out the part about Hogan and his cronies, not wanting to complicate the tale or give the mayor information about my past that he could use against me. I was in no doubt—Arthur Pumpkin was listening intently, but he was considering his options, too. Somebody would have to pay for the murders—particularly the slayings of the sheriff, Penny White and Travis Newsted. They were high profile killings, and the sort of headlines that could force a man out of office if they weren't dealt with swiftly. At that moment, I knew I was the prime and only suspect.

I paused before I told the mayor about what had gone down at Widow's Hole. I was still trying to comprehend it myself. Had we really seen the ghosts of all those miners who had been lost at Kiowa Rock? Had the rope that had been used to hang the bruja, Whispering Wind, really still been there, swinging from the decaying bark of the scorched pine as if what had happened had been mere days ago? Had Linda and I really entered the remains of her home? Had we really seen that perfectly circular hole in the ground, its edges burned as if it had been created by an intense heat? Had the Wendigo risen from that hole and confronted us in all its malevolent glory? These things now seemed ridiculous notions to me, a fantasy landscape on my painted memory.

I told them nonetheless, and the mayor peered at me curiously, his eyes flitting, his mouth twitching with my every unbelievable word.

When I finished, I sat down and breathed out a long sigh, as if tossing the words from my body was cathartic in some irrational, illogical way.

"A complicated tale," he said after a moment of consideration. "And one that will take some explaining to the people of this town. Some believing, too."

I nodded, but I was in no mood for hanging around.

"Well, that's how it happened," I said, feeling like I needed to get out of there. "Linda will corroborate. She can even show you on a map where the bodies are. Travis, the sheriff too. They're both in shallow graves, so they can have proper burials back here in town."

"That's very thoughtful of you," he said, thrumming his fingers on the desk. "Very thoughtful."

"Whatever," I replied. "Anyways, I have a train to catch."

"You're leaving?"

"No reason for me to stay around any longer than I have to." There was—Linda was as good a reason as any—but I had been a bad luck charm hanging around her neck ever since I arrived. I'd come to realize, with a lot of sadness and much regret, that I was the sort of friend she could do without.

"But this whole thing will need to be dealt with appropriately. We're talking about several murders here, including the slaying of a town official, and at the moment, we only have your version of what went down. And, might I say, your version is hardly believable."

"Believe it or not," I said, heading for the door. "It's up to you."

As I reached for the handle, the mayor pressed the intercom and the door burst inwards, almost smashing me in the face. Deputy Barns strode in alongside Deputy Mckinley. They both had their guns drawn and were pointing them straight at me.

"You arresting me?" I asked, backing away.

"Why, you done something wrong, boy?" Mckinley yelled, pushing me backwards.

"No. I've done nothing wrong."

"Well, from what I heard," Deputy Barns said, pointing toward the intercom, which I now realized had been an open line ever since I started talking, "you pretty much confessed to the murders of Travis Newsted, Sheriff Elijah Harris, and your pal, the Indian."

I shook my head. This was going the way I'd feared. No-one was about to believe the story of an evil, malevolent spirit that was wreaking its revenge on the town of Devil's Ridge.

"Hands behind your back, son," Deputy Mckinley said, turning me around. "This don't have to hurt if you make it easy for us."

The two deputies pushed me against the office wall, my face pressed against the teak paneling, and cuffed me. I pictured myself back in that tiny cell once more, except this time I wouldn't have my brother with me. I would be truly alone.

There was a commotion in the outside office, and I heard Audrey's raised voice, a hint of panic in her tone. I turned in time to see a disheveled looking man walk into the room, blood in his hair and over his shirt. He had chiseled features and a distinctive gait. My mouth fell open as the intruder turned to face me. I thought he'd been killed in the mountains, but somehow he'd escaped and followed us all the way back to Devil's Ridge.

"Hogan," I said. "How the hell—"

There was something behind Hogan's fiery glare that made me shudder. It was as if I was looking into the eyes of a feral animal, its singular thought one of hunger and need.

"You two know each other?" the mayor said, rounding the desk, his jowls juddering beneath his plump cheeks.

Hogan turned to him then, and within an instant he was upon him, tearing at his clothes and clawing at his skin. The mayor fell to the floor as Hogan pounced, saliva running from his blackened lips, his teeth gnashing and biting.

The two deputies let me go and reached for their guns, but it was too late. Before either of them had a chance to react, Hogan had taken a bite from the mayor's throat, and the spray of fresh blood that ejected from his writhing body reached almost to the ceiling. He tried to cry out, but his mouth and lungs were flooded and all he could muster was a bubbling, spitting gurgle. Hogan took another bite and then another, and within seconds the mayor's face and torso were covered in sticky, crimson gore.

Deputy Barns fired first and the bullet struck Hogan in the shoulder. He spun round and faced us, howling like a banshee. This wasn't the Hogan I knew, that much was clear. This was the Wendigo. It had escaped the hole by possessing its last victim. The rattlesnake charm hung from Hogan's neck, blood staining the ancient bone.

Hogan leapt up and charged toward the two officers. He was so quick that the two rounds Mckinley managed to get off missed him by a mile. I watched as Barns succumbed first, Hogan pummeling him with his fists, before clawing out his eyeballs with fingers like pokers, digging and probing. Mckinley dropped his gun and headed for the door, screaming and crying out as Barns's throat was torn open by Hogan's snarling, ravenous teeth. I spied something on the floor and grabbed it while Barn's thrashed between his attacker's powerful mass.

I sat back on a chair and looked down at the blood-soaked remains of Mayor Arthur Pumpkin, and the slowly expiring life-force of the deputy. It had all come down to this. So many deaths, so much pain, and all of it because my brother had convinced me that there was money to be made in Devil's Ridge—a whole bunch of it. None of it was worth it. Nothing would ever be worth this.

Hogan continued to grunt and slurp as he feasted on the deputy's mutilated remains. I sat in the chair and waited for the inevitable. It was me who Hogan wanted, the Wendigo too. I knew that none of this would stop until I allowed them to have what they came here for.

After a few moments passed, Hogan lifted his head and turned to face me. His was a death mask of blood and torn flesh, but his eyes were unyielding. I saw the wendigo's eternal hatred and disgust within them, the fires that raged within that undead skull now burning brightly behind my old boss's undead stare.

He stood and walked toward me, and I leaned backwards, attempting to move my face away from the deathly stench that emanated from his soiled torso. He leaned toward me, his hands on the arms of the chair, and he grinned.

"You tried to kill me," he said, with a voice that creaked and scratched like old metal.

"You don't belong here," I replied, trying to steady my voice. "You should never have been released."

"But it was you who released me."

"I made a mistake."

"Some mistakes cannot be undone."

The grin never left Hogan's face, but it never reached his eyes. His glare never left my face, and his eyes never blinked, never moved. They were the eyes of the murderer, the eyes of the hungry, the eyes of the eternal.

"Your brother is with us," he said—five little, seemingly innocuous, words that turned my blood cold.

"You leave my brother alone."

"Too late," he said. "She brought him to us."

I suddenly couldn't breathe, couldn't think. Was it true? Was Bill really down there in that hellish pit? If he was, that was my fault. I'd led us to it. I'd walked into a trap set by the Wendigo, and now my brother's soul would suffer for all eternity.

A rage coursed through my veins like no emotion I'd ever experienced before. I wanted to rip Hogan's possessed body limb from limb. I wanted to gouge at his eyes, rip at his insides, tear at his throat.

I fingered the object I'd found on the floor when the deputy had fallen—the keys to my cuffs. I jabbed the key home, turned it, and all of a sudden my hands were free and reaching for Hogan's face. Shocked, he staggered backwards but I was on him, slamming my fist into his bloodied jaw, over and over and over again.

As my rage poured out of my body, providing me with a strength far beyond that which I normally possessed, Hogan laughed, his wheezing, shrieking cackle spilling from his split lips and shattered teeth. His laughter spurred me on, and I doubled down on my assault, slamming the palms of my hands into his eye sockets and clawing at his cheeks.

"You can't kill us," he said, his words bubbling up through saliva and blood. "You can never kill us. We have lived on this earth for millions of years, since before man. We will be here for a million more."

I thought of Bill down there in the burning inferno of hell, and of Linda, alone and without protection from this foul beast, and I let out a roar that shook every fiber of my being. I spied the rattlesnake charm around Hogan's neck. It seemed that everything that had happened had happened because of that one, simple object. I lowered my head, grabbed it in my mouth and tore it from the leather strap.

"You're wrong," I said, the skull clamped between my teeth.

"You can't touch that," the Wendigo cried through Hogan's destroyed mouth. "That is mine."

"Not any longer," I said, biting down with all my anger, all my fear, and crushing the skull between my incisors, turning it into tiny, sharp fragments of rotted bone.

"No!" the wendigo screamed as if a portal had opened to eternal suffering. The walls shook and the ground beneath us trembled. Paintings fell from the walls and glass tumblers dropped from the cabinet, smashing on the rug. Something oozed from Hogan's lip, like dark gray smoke. It drifted into the air and circled us, as if it were undulating and shaping, like a gross, amorphous blob. I watched as it passed over me, smothering me in its undefined mass.

I turned and reached for the letter opener that lay on the mayor's desk, raising it above my head and slamming it down into Hogan's exposed throat. Immediately a black jet of oil-like gloop burst from within him, smothering me. Some of it fell into my mouth and I spat it out. It tasted like old meat.

"Die you bastard!" I yelled, bringing the sharp object down into his throat.

There was a loud blast, like an explosion going off, and suddenly I felt like I was back in Iraq and cradling my brother's broken body in my arms. I saw him then—he stood before me in the mayor's office, no longer gray and washed out as he had been in the mountains, or when the bruja was holding his terrified face in her blackened hands. He was his old self once more, smiling and assured, peering down at me through eyes that only a brother could possess.

I knew I had to end it, right there, right then. For Bill, for Linda, for everyone that had been affected by what had happened.

I glared at the letter opener, the black blood running down its long, steely length, and knew what I had to do.

I raised it high above my head, roared above the cacophony, and slammed it into Hogan's heart.

Immediately the room was engulfed in a bright orange flame and I was thrown ten feet into the air. As I lost consciousness, I saw something floating above me, dark and silent like the approaching night sky, and then it was gone.

Epilogue

The days after passed by in a fog. With both the mayor and the sheriff deceased, Mac Newsted stepped in as acting mayor, and he appointed Deputy Mckinley as acting sheriff. Of course, Mckinley had witnessed what had gone down in the mayor's office—most of it anyway—and he also knew that I'd watched him run from there like the coward that I knew he was. I was off the hook, and people started to come to terms with the fact that their town had been terrorized by something from another realm. It was a hard pill to swallow, but eventually people got on with their lives. What else was there to do?

The new mayor ordered the mine to be closed up for good, sending a team up there to make sure nobody could ever find their way into that haunted graveyard ever again.

The people whose relatives had disappeared long ago while digging down there found some relief in that. It was a closure of sorts, if not the kind of closure they had expected or even hoped for.

Old Boomer passed that fall. The guy was old and had led a good life, but I knew that being a party to what had happened gnawed away at him at the end. He'd sent the team down there after all, and while he wasn't to blame, he'd ordered the detonation. I felt for the guy, but those were the facts, plain and simple.

Linda met with Little Bear's father and informed him of her son's death. She said that he'd fought until the end, which was really a lie. Little Bear had let himself get overrun by Hogan, which really wasn't a fact to be proud of. His ancestors wouldn't have been proud of that. They were brave warriors that succeeded against insurmountable odds. Cunning Wolf would not have succumbed like that. Linda agreed to take on Little Bear's dog, Axle, which had been cared for by Old Boomer while we were on our adventure in the mountains. The old dog deserved a caring home, even if it didn't seem to care for me any more.

I decided to stay with Linda, after all. We had something good, and I couldn't bear to let that go. She told me she loved me, and I told her the same, even though I wasn't sure what love was really. By the time the winter came, we were engaged to be married. It seemed like people could be happy in Devil's Ridge. They just had to find the right path.

Bill sometimes tries to visit me, but I push him away. He's dead, after all. What good can he be to me now? I have everything I want. A beautiful fiancee, a house that we now share, and a baby on the way. Oh yeah, that's right. I got her pregnant. Cool, right? Little Jason Carter from Chicago, Illinois, ex-soldier, ex-enforcer, now part time mechanic and husband-and-dad-to-be. This boy did good, even if it did take a dalliance with the devil to get there.

We were sitting out one night on the front porch, drinking iced tea and watching the sun set.

"Do you ever wonder whether it's still out there?" Linda asked, idly rubbing a hand across her slowly expanding abdomen.

"What? The Wendigo?" I asked, sipping on my sweet drink.

"Uh-huh. It came back once. What's to stop it from doing that again?"

I fingered the object in my pocket, and it felt deliciously cool to the touch.

"No," I replied. "That thing's long gone."

"Good. I don't think I could stand to raise a baby in a town where the streets are haunted by the ghosts of our past."

I smiled. If only she knew the truth.

Linda stood and grabbed my glass. "Another?" she asked.

"Baby, I thought you'd never ask."

As she walked into the house, the screen door closing gently behind her, I lifted the object I had been hiding from her and peered down at it. It was just as I remembered it, beautiful and sleek, like porcelain.

When I'd come to, after I'd been thrown across the room by that terrible, mind- scrambling explosion, I found that everything felt different to me—as if my whole body was pulsing with some sort of invisible, powerful energy. I saw things I'd never seen before—a time long ago when the land was new, when the ancients roamed the hills, and when giant, all-conquering gods carved the mountains from the rock with their bare hands, and filled the deep valleys with water shed from their unyielding tears. I saw the flames down below and the stars up above, and I stepped through the portal that separated our two very different planes.

I had collected the pieces of bone from the rug, and later on, when I was alone and unwatched, I carefully glued them together, Linda lay sleeping, unaware of everything that was going on inside me. I was transforming. I was becoming.

I stared at it now. The head of the rattlesnake, its slit-like eyes peering at me with a thousand years of all-seeing wisdom. Cunning Wolf had chosen wisely when he had given it to me. It had protected me all these years, even when I lay dormant in that damp, festering hole in the ground.

I felt an anger and a hunger burning inside me, like the roaring flames from an erupting volcano. I would have my revenge. The people of Devil's Ridge would be made to pay for their treachery and their greed. I was not ready to return home just yet. Not until my son was born and every soul in this god-forsaken town was made to yield before the Wendigo.

Also By Joseph Sackett

Dark Skies: A Kerrigan Survival Saga

Book 1: *Echoes of the Dark Sun: A Kerrigan's Quest*

Book 2: *Dark Horizons: A Kerrigan's Journey*

Book 3: *Veiled Shadows: Kerrigan's Redemption*

Book 4: *Fading Light: Kerrigan's Legacy* **(Coming Soon!)**

Echoes of the Fallen: Matt Groover's Tale **(Out on 31 October 2023) *Ties into the second book of the series.**

Link to Books

About the Author

 Nurtured by the vibrant heart of Minnesota and the animated streets of Chicago, Joseph A. Sackett's formative years were steeped in the rich tapestry of America's diverse landscapes. Yet, it was his twenty-year expedition within the military's special operations that left an indelible imprint on his psyche. It was here that he encountered the harsh realities of human nature, witnessing society's vulnerability and understanding the precarious balance upon which it teeters.

In the face of these stark truths, Joseph found refuge in literature. The captivating tales spun by C.S. Lewis were the spark that ignited his passion for written word—a passion that, like a well-tended flame, only grew brighter over time. His literary appetite led him to the spine-chilling narratives of Max Brooks, a virtuoso of the modern zombie genre, and the grim tale of survival showcased in "The Road" by Cormac McCarthy.

Joseph found profound resonance in these books. He was enthralled by stories of everyday individuals morphing into extraordinary heroes in the face of unimaginable adversity—an echo of the harsh realities he'd observed in his own experiences.

Now, as a writer, Joseph wields his words as a conduit for this fascination. His writing is a mural depicting mankind's raw vulnerability yet fierce resilience. He infuses his tales with his life lessons, sculpting narratives that expose societal frailties and the indomitable spirit that rises in opposition.

As an author, Joseph extends an invitation into his universe. He beckons you to set sail on an expedition of revelation, where every page unravels a fresh insight, each tale bears witness to the resilience of the human spirit. Embrace this journey of discovery. Welcome to the literary realm of Joseph A. Sackett.

Milton Keynes UK
Ingram Content Group UK Ltd.
UKHW020616071223
433828UK00014B/609